UNDER THE
TUSCAN GUN

Tess Rafferty

ISBN-13: 9798687314510

Cover design by: Tony Puryear
Cover photo by: Chris McGuire
Author photo by: Justine Ungaro
Library of Congress Control Number: 2018675309
Printed in the United States of America

*For Julie N., who taught me that
life is short,
take the trip,
travel in style.*

CONTENTS

CHAPTER 1

"I've killed Elin and put her body in the trunk of my car."

That's how Sunny greeted me when I arrived at the villa.

"That's exactly what it feels like, Kat," she clarified. "I have the run of this amazing house and she's not even here."

At exactly five feet tall, I doubt that Sunny could murder anyone, let alone stick the body in a trunk, although her husband may beg to differ. As it is, she has to stand on tiptoes just to hug my husband Mike and I "Ciao!" and we are no giants, being half Irish with mothers who smoked during pregnancy. We slowly took in the view from the "house," which is situated on an old hillside olive grove. Overlooked by the medieval hill town of Capalbio, whose crenellated walls and stone castle loom above, Elin Corini's villa sits above the vineyards of the Maremma, which undulate below. The green and gold slopes of clay and grapes and earth eventually dissolve right into the sea a few kilometers away. It was every stunning photo you've ever seen of the hills and valleys of Tuscany, plus a beach, in case you were wondering how Tuscany could get any more amazing.

Oh, and the house had a pool.

A few weeks earlier when she had called us with an amazing offer—one that had words in it like "Tuscan apartment" and "free"—we'd hoped for the best but also tried to manage our expectations. Accommodations in Italy, even in the best of circumstances, are not without their quirks—whether it's a vineyard with a view of all of Campania that has a toilet that bellows like a sea otter giving birth, every time you flush; a Roman suite overlooking the Pantheon with a mattress that has two sagging depressions exactly where the people should lie; or a suite on Venice's Grand Canal that includes a tub that comes to a 'V' in the middle so that when you stand in the shower you have to place one foot in front of the other, like you're on a balance beam.

We accepted the offer immediately for two reasons: Number one, I have never not loved every moment in Italy, no matter how rustic and quirky the accommodations were; and number two, it was free.

I lied. There was also a third reason: The Husband and I were running away.

We called it vacation. And according to our tickets, we would be returning. But we had packed our bags and headed to LAX feeling like fugitives escaping a pack of police dogs—if fugitives absconded in Town Cars. A little over halfway through the calendar year, and we had had enough. We were jobless, childless, and, after some recent dinner party drama, damn near friendless, too. It was fight or flight. The entertainment business was all about the fight and I decided that I had had enough of that, which left me one option that I gladly took—along with a quarter Xanax and three-quarters of a bottle of Aglianico consumed in the business-class cabin of Alitalia. (I recommend putting all purchases on a credit card with a decent miles program. If you're going to run away from your problems, you should do it in comfort. What are we: Hobos riding the rails?) I was going to do a face plant into every vat of wine, bucket of gelato, and trough of pasta I came across, and if I was unfortunate enough to live through it, then I'd figure out the rest of my life after that.

Sunny took us on a truncated tour of the place she was calling home for the summer, because we were smacking right into the lunch hour and the lunch hour is sacrosanct. The Husband hates to miss lunch. If you do not arrive where you are going in Italy in time to order lunch, you are shit out of luck, as they say in America. The restaurants are then closed until the dinner hour, and you have to find a less formal bar or café at which to order something small: A panino or a slice of pizza. To be fair, Italy being what it is, you can often be blown away by something as mediocre as the panini you get at the Autogrill along the Autostrada. I'm sure real Italians wouldn't agree, but take my word for it: Compared to the GMO roadkill we're used to at rest stops across America, it's ambrosia.

She quickly showed us the main house. A formal dining room opened onto a living room, behind which was the kitchen. It was beautifully appointed; appliances, furnishings, décor— everything was elegant and modern. Nevertheless, the home had a warmth, as if real people lived there. A row of jackets hung above a pile of sneakers and boots near the front door. The shelves were overflowing with books along with a few pictures of Elin, her supermodel looks in very un-supermodel settings: Camping, painting, cooking with friends. The most glamorous photo was from her wedding a few years before, and even that had a casual beauty to it. Elin was in a simple white silk slip dress standing in what looked to be the Capalbio town square, next to what I assumed was her husband and our "landlord" for the next week, Silvio Corini. He was shorter than his wife (who was, after all, a model, and wearing heels) with thick, wavy, dark hair. But when I looked closer, I saw that his face, while handsome, was scarred on the lower half. The flesh across his jaw and neck was puckered and dimpled, a raw pink in contrast to his olive skin. I guessed that the scars were from burns, but Sunny had never mentioned any incidents or fires in all the times she had talked about the couple. I was dying to know; a dramatic backstory is something I have an insatiable curiosity for. If someone mentions a rock bottom, I need to know how hard was the rock and how far was the bottom. Nevertheless, the first four minutes I was a guest in his home didn't seem like the right time to start prying into my host's secrets. I told myself I could ask Sunny later as I admired the picture one last time. Silvio's confidence, I observed, was not at all marred by the scarred flesh. He smiled broadly. They looked happy.

Sunny took us to the kitchen, which was very important because that's the place where we chill our wine. When it finally cooled off at night we would switch to red, but it was July and currently ninety-eight degrees during the day, with near ninety -percent humidity. White wine would be required, and lots of it. We had brought a few bottles of Gavi that we had picked up at an enoteca in Rome before driving up that morning, and they were quickly taken out of our hands by a friendly older woman, who introduced herself to us as Tina before efficiently depositing the bottles into a state-of-the-art wine fridge.

Sunny explained to us on the way out, "Tina does the cooking and cleaning. Her husband, Renato, takes care of the grounds, the pool, the olives."

We walked across the driveway and slightly down the hill to where it had been terraced to accommodate an infinity pool on the edge of the hillside. To the right of the pool was a large guest house, with two doors opening up onto the poolside, and two more around the back.

"So we're staying at a villa for free—with two full-time staff members?" I asked.

"Three. The butler arrives from Rome later this week. He always travels with Silvio."

"They have a butler?!" I couldn't believe it. "Does he ring the dressing gong?"

Sunny laughed and explained, "It's not all *Downton Abbey* and *Remains of the Day*, Kat. He's in charge of everything that happens in the house: Overseeing the staff, scheduling repairs and maintenance, keeping Silvio's schedule and making sure he has everything he needs, picking up the dry cleaning and having the car serviced. He's like a personal assistant except he doesn't really want to be an actor."

My ever-frugal husband raised a salient point. "Why are they paying people to be here if they're not even here?"

"There's a circus in town," Sunny replied, as if that should explain everything.

I meant to ask her to elaborate, but we had just arrived at our apartment in the guest house: An airy bedroom with an en-suite bath and private balcony overlooking the vineyards and hillside below. Our excitement took precedence over investigating Sunny's cryptic answer. Besides, it was after noon in Italy, perhaps she'd already been drinking. And speaking of drinking, I was feeling parched. Sunny handed us the key to the room and instructed us to put on our bathing suits and get ready to leave. We were having lunch at the beach.

Mike immediately started sorting through his cash and gadgets, trying to figure out which of the highly steal-able possessions he should take with him to someplace they could get stolen. The Husband was a technophile and quite the amateur photographer, as well. On this trip alone, we were traveling with a laptop, a removable hard drive, an iPad, two iPhones, an Apple watch, one Canon 5D camera, numerous lenses, and a GoPro on a selfie stick. He considered it traveling light that he had left the tripod at home, although he had managed to pack something called a "monopod," and made sure he could turn his phone into a wireless hotspot "just in case." Next to all that, my second-generation Kindle looked like a rotary phone—or an actual book. He looked at his gear and furrowed his brow like a kid who just realized he can't take all his stuffed animals to the sleepover with him and had to make some hard choices. He looked at Sunny. "What should I do with my camera and wallet? Leave them here?"

"They'll be safe there," she nonchalantly assured us. "We're going to the beach club. Elin has a cabana rented for the summer."

Mike and I looked at each other and smiled. This was exceeding even our "hope for the best" scenarios. I grabbed a wide-brimmed hat, threw on a fake Pucci caftan, and walked to the car feeling like a vintage Italian movie star, or at least non-vintage Euro trash.

The feeling didn't lessen when, an hour later, we were sitting on the beach under a large canopy, eating linguini with bottarga and clams and ordering our second bottle of Vermentino.

"Marco! Put your penis away!" Sunny yelled in English to her youngest son.

It should be explained here why Sunny was called Sunny. As a child, or so the story goes, Claire Sullivan had a bossy and often abrasive disposition and a string of swear words to go along with it, picked up no doubt at the construction sites her contractor father would have to take her around to after she got kicked out of one kindergarten or pre-school or another, and he had to check in on his crews. When reporting on their youngest daughter to each other at the end of the night, one of her parents would always refer to her sarcastically as "Sunny." "Sunny" told Sister Mary Alice that if she was going to Heaven, then she'd rather go to Hell to get away from her bad breath. "Sunny" asked her grandmother if she was going to leave her any money when she died, and if not, then why did she have to be nice to her.

"Sunny," it should surprise no one, became a stand-up comic.

That's what she was doing when we met her in Los Angeles over a decade ago, in a laundromat that a mutual friend was running an open mic in. (They can't all be Carnegie Hall.) Thirty-five people had shown up to put their names in a hat, hoping to get picked for one of the twenty-some four-minute spots.

And if you've ever done your laundry in a laundromat (as most of us have at one point or another) then you know how the only thing that could make it worse would be having to listen to twenty-plus comics try out their new material while dryers buzz, clothes tumble, and homeless people come in looking for spare quarters, displaying far more dignity than those of us who came to LA to be somebody and ended up begging for laughs at a fluff and fold.

Fortunately, Sunny had the same dark sense of humor about the business that I did and lived within walking distance. This proved to be very convenient, whether we were drowning our sorrows over the latest career disappointment late into the night at one of our apartments, or splitting a cab we couldn't afford to a party on the Sunset Strip that Sunny had gotten us on the guest list for. Even then she was good at making friends who could invite her to desirable places, and we drank through a large portion of our twenties on the expense account of one agent or another who Sunny had befriended.

Together we survived the Cosmo, the Bellini, and the Appletini crazes. We wore strappy heels, which Sunny always painted my toes for, the both of us being too poor to afford pedicures and me being a disaster with a nail-polish brush. We did ridiculous things, like the time we flirted with the guys cleaning the closed bakery at two in the morning because we were drunk and wanted a cookie, and somewhere in England there's footage of interviews of us at the Standard hotel, shot by a guy claiming to be making a documentary. Growing up one of seven kids, Sunny already had three sisters, but I had none. Sunny was the closest thing I had. We worked in stand-up comedy, a male-dominated industry where you had to act like a guy or it was seen as a sign of being "other," and no one wanted that. It was nice to have another woman you could be a woman around and who understood what you were going through, whether it was existential angst about your life's goals or just a need for gravy fries at three

7

a.m.

Eventually Mike and I became television writers. But Sunny got an even bigger break: She got out. She met a sommelier from Rome, fell in love, moved to Italy and had two kids, one of whom never had on pants. To be fair, he was only five, but I don't know at what point these things become inappropriate. I mean, I know that at fifteen you can't pull down your pants in public. But I don't know what the exact cut off for the penis is, so to speak. (And scusa me, for putting that image in your head.) This was the same country where young girls only wore bathing suit bottoms, and some not-so-very-young girls, as well. I once saw three women, approximately eighteen years old, get off a yacht only in bikini bottoms, and then all have a drink in the hotel bar before getting back on the yacht. Surely some penis in certain social situations was no big deal.

With penises put back in pants and lunch being cleared away, talk turned to dinner. Sunny's husband, Nino, was driving up from Rome and would be joining us. The waitress brought the check and, handing it to Sunny, said, "Ecco lo, Signora Corini."

"No," Sunny corrected her. "Siamo gli ospiti di Signora Corini."

The waitress apologized and took away our cash. It appeared the money of Signora Corini's guests was just as good. Only on her way back to the main building I saw a man stop her and point to us. He was a thin man, early forties, with black hair that was pulled back into a ponytail. He was attractive, I suppose, but I immediately got a bad feeling from him—and not because it was the new millennium and he was still wearing a ponytail in his forties. Maybe it was because he caught me looking at him and for the brief, accidental moment when we locked eyes, his weren't friendly. The waitress looked back at us, then said something to him and continued on to the kitchen.

"Sunny? Are you sure it's OK if we're here?"

"Yeah, why wouldn't it be?"

"I just thought I saw a man pointing at us…"

"We're Americans. Everyone's pointing at us," she said, dismissing my concern. "It's totally cool. Elin has guests all the time."

"Where is Elin?" The Husband asked.

For the last few years Sunny had been talking about the elusive Elin but we had yet to see her in person. As I said, Sunny had a wonderful gift for meeting people. In LA it was because she was always outgoing and forthright, saying whatever was on her mind in such a way that people immediately felt like they knew her. Honesty in Los Angeles is as rare as atheism in Oklahoma, and people were both amused by her and relieved to not have to decipher a lot of bullshit. In Italy, however, her openness was an even bigger gift among the many ex-pats from a variety of countries who all spoke English and were all having one issue or another adjusting to life in Rome. Sunny stubbornly insisted on celebrating the Fourth of July and asking for milk in her coffee after lunch, two things that just weren't done.

She and Elin met in a yoga class for English speakers. (Sunny required a lot of Namaste to balance out all of that opinionated behavior.) Elin had just moved to Rome and knew no one. She'd been a model from a very young age, and it wasn't the type of business that was conducive to making a lot of quality, lifelong, female friends. I mean, sure, she knew who to call if she needed speed, but certainly no one who would go out and eat carbs and gelato with her.

"Elin is with some friends up north, in the Lakes region. It is so much more civilized up there." I looked at our cabana with table service, the sparkling blue sea, and the white shoreline dotted by matching beach umbrellas, and wondered how it could get more civilized than this. "She originally told me she'd be here, but I guess her plans changed at the last minute. She's supposed to be back by the end of the week, but I've been texting her to confirm and I haven't heard anything back, which isn't like her."

Sunny's concern was only betrayed by the two grooves that formed between her eyebrows as she said this. The Husband, being a husband and therefore totally oblivious to any subtlety expressed by a woman, paid no attention and instead raised his glass. "To Elin. Who was thoughtful enough to invite us, and then thoughtful enough to not be here." Sunny's concerned look immediately vanished, and we all laughed and drained our glasses.

"Scusa mi, Signora."

Suddenly Ponytail was standing right next to us as if he had just transported himself there or we were too buzzed to notice him coming. He addressed Sunny in Italian. "I am looking for my friend, Elin."

I heard Sunny explain to him in Italian that Elin was away, or at least that's what I think she said. To be honest, I can speak Italian, but understanding what gets spit back at me is another matter. And that's before two bottles of wine.

Ponytail's outfit was impressive, especially given the humidity. He had on a pair of deep-green, flat-front pants that would look ridiculous on anyone who wasn't Italian. They were slightly cuffed above a pair of light-brown driving moccasins. His white linen shirt looked like it had just been pressed—not like he'd been pitting out in it all morning like the rest of us.

God, I love this country! No cargo shorts and Adidas shower shoes for these guys.

He made his goodbyes to Sunny in Italian and took off, but my gaze followed him, as if I wanted to make sure he was leaving. And I saw him look back at us more than once, as if he wanted to get a look at us one last time without our noticing.

Of course, all of this suspicion may have just been the wine talking.

Mike had already taken his camera out and started fiddling with it while Sunny was talking to the man, but I was still curious. "Who was that?"

"He says he's a photographer friend of Elin's and that he needs to speak to her. He even went so far as to say it was urgent. Said his name was Pietro Romano."

Despite the heat, I shuddered in my chair. "He creeped me out."

"That's just the ponytail," Sunny said.

Having now had a large pasta lunch and my share of two bottles of wine, I was ready to swim, and I stripped off the caftan and headed to the sea. The water was surprisingly warm. Having grown accustomed to the brisker temps of the Italian seaside over the last couple of years, I had actually grown to prefer the refreshing quality of the cooler water, especially in this heat. But this water was practically air temperature. Even The Husband, who notoriously wouldn't get in a pool until it had reached eighty-two degrees, couldn't complain about this.

Despite its warmth, or maybe because of it, the water had a soothing quality, and I was soon out past where my feet could touch the bottom, looking at the dramatic silhouette of the peninsula and the surrounding islands just to the north. I flipped over onto my back and just stared up, my body rising and falling as the waves came in.

"There are worse things than to drown in Tuscany," I thought as I allowed the current to take me further out into the Tyrrhenian Sea. I hadn't been this happy in nearly a year, and if it all ended right now with my belly full of linguini with clams and bottarga it was a much nicer end than sitting in Los Angeles traffic.

Because there _are_ worse things than to drown in Tuscany; you could be murdered there.

CHAPTER 2

If the owners of the villa weren't actually there, they were the only two people in all of Central Italy who weren't.

When we returned around five to nap and get dressed before having an aperitivo and heading out to dinner, we were greeted by Elin's sister-in-law, Paola, a former Miss Albania who was married to Silvio's younger brother, Antonio. Tall, with a long mane of sable hair pulled back by what appeared to be an Hermès scarf, she was having a cigarette and a glass of wine on the patio and asked if we wanted to join her. It would have been rude not to.

Mike went back to our room to change out of his trunks and grab a few hundred pounds of camera equipment that he couldn't take to the beach, while I followed Sunny to the patio and sat down underneath the large umbrella—not that it provided any relief from the humidity. That's what the wine was for. Paola poured us each a glass. She and Sunny had become close over the summer, as they had children the same age and similar tastes in wine: They both liked it. She had brought over her two sons, who she said wanted to play with Marco and Sunny's other son, Luca, who was slightly better about keeping his penis in his pants.

"They love your sons," Paola explained, the evidence of which was loudly being shouted from every corner of the yard and pool as the four boys chased each other with water guns and super soakers. Every few minutes, their screams of delight were punctuated with actual screams of anger as Italian insults mixed with calls for their mom to intervene in English. The noise was grating, and I found myself wondering why the annoying presence of the children did nothing to alleviate the pain of my own recent troubles. It really should have, I thought in a detached way, as if I was standing outside of myself looking at someone else, but it didn't. There was probably a good chance it was the wine. There was also probably a good chance that it had nothing to do with the wine, but instead was just because pain is terrible and if it could have been alleviated that easily, I wouldn't be in the situation I was currently in.

Paola continued, "It is always so boring at our house. No other children. Just those old women."

Sunny had already told me that the old women she was referring to were Antonio and Silvio's great aunts, Assunta and Immacolata, neither of whom had ever married, although they'd dressed the part of the widow every day for the last forty years. They religiously napped daily between two and four, and therefore got mad at the children if they were outside playing during this time. The children were also forbidden from having bare feet in the house—no matter what the weather—because they would get sick, or having ice in their drinks because "it could cause a blockage in the stomach and they might die." Also, the "house" Paola was referring to was actually three houses on the family's vineyard.

Sunny nodded in sympathy. "They bless themselves every time they see Marco, because he's left-handed. They say it's the mark of the devil. And I'm like, 'If that kid is holding an actual pencil and not just his penis, I don't care which hand he's using.'"

"Didn't you say that was hereditary?" I asked.

"Holding their penis? Yes, their fathers do it all the time, too."

Paola and I laughed before I went on. "No, being left-handed. I thought there was a story of the nuns beating it out of your father."

"Kat remembers my life better than I do," Sunny told Paola. "Probably because I drink too much," she smiled, topping off all of our glasses.

"Anyway, they love coming here so I hope I'm not imposing," Paola added. "I didn't realize you had company." Despite her five-hundred-dollar Chanel sunglasses, I could tell she was rolling her eyes, and I worried that Mike and I were the object of her irritation. But I soon realized that she was motioning her head towards the pool, where, spread out on a lounge chair, was a woman we hadn't met.

She had olive skin, black glossy hair, and no top. I quickly guessed that she was either an average twenty-eight, or a well-preserved thirty-nine.

"I didn't either," said a shocked Sunny. "Tina," she called in something of a stage whisper.

Tina came out onto the patio and asked in very good English, "Did you need something?"

"Yeah. I need to know who the hell that is."

"Oh," Tina began. If rolling your eyes had a tone, then this was it. "She's a friend of Silvio's. He invited her, apparently."

"But he's not even here!" Sunny protested.

"Like that should matter around here," Tina muttered, giving her a pointed look.

"I know!" agreed Sunny. "That's my job!"

The two women laughed, and Tina continued, "She wouldn't be the first one and she won't be the last. Elin runs this place like a refugee camp for la Croce Rossa," before disappearing again inside the house. Sunny, once again, looked over at the pool.

"I guess we should say hi...?" she began.

Paola shrugged and lit another cigarette. "It's not my house."

Mike had returned in dry clothes, and Sunny looked to him and me for back up. He finished his glass in one gulp, grabbed his camera and announced, "I'm going to take pictures of the olive grove."

I explained when he was barely out of earshot, "He's useless if you're looking for back up. I could be getting sodomized over a pinball machine all *Accused*-style and he'd wave at me from across the room and say, 'Looks like you're having fun.'"

Sunny shrugged and decided to drop the topic of the stranger, at least for a while.

"How was the beach?" Paola asked. "We were going to meet you there, but Assunta spent the morning convinced Silvio Sr.'s ghost was trying to tell her something. Plus, Fabrizio thought there was something wrong with the car. He said it wasn't driving right, and what do I know?"

Paola, Sunny had also told me, hated to drive, in fact flat-out refused to, so they hired a driver, Fabrizio. She said the Italians were crazy and they were going to kill her and her children, a fear that disappeared as long they were in the back of an Audi sedan, even if it was being driven by one of these same crazy Italians.

"It was great, even with my nightmare children there."

"It was perfect," I agreed.

Sunny suddenly remembered. "Oh, but one of Elin's friends was there and came around asking for her. Some photographer. Pietro something."

"He creeped me out," I interjected. "He had a ponytail."

"Ugh, Pietro Romano?" Paola asked with disdain.

"Yeah, you know him, too?"

Paola lamented, "Unfortunately, every young model in Italy meets him on her way up or her way down. I think Elin used to actually date him, years and years ago. He likes to tell people he's a photographer, but he's never been very successful so he's always living off whoever he's dating."

"How's he still in the business after all this time, if he's not very successful?" I asked Paola.

"In Albania we have a saying. It means, like, 'Cunning like a whore.' Pietro is supposedly into some things..." she trailed off, looking to Sunny for help with the words she was looking for. "Come in nero..."

"That means under the table," Sunny explained to me, even though I was more than familiar with Italians' love for being paid for things in cash and not having to pay taxes on the money. Because of the practice, it was illegal for them not to give you a receipt, which was why most proprietors still painstakingly wrote out one for you by hand, as well as the one from the register. They might as well have been doing it in calligraphy with a quill, too. In this digital age, the handwritten receipt was practically an artifact everywhere else.

"Sì," the former model agreed with her. "But also forse illegale maybe."

She seemed to be beating around the bush, so I just asked, "You mean like supplying the models with drugs?"

"Among other things..." Paola began, somewhat unsure what to say next, although whether it was the language barrier or some other call for reticence, I couldn't say. "There's always rumors that he's into other things, some much worse. Let's not waste time with talk of Pietro. I only hope that he's looking for Elin because he's in town taking advantage of someone else, and not to ask her for money."

It was certainly a possibility. Capalbio and its surroundings were known as a vacation destination for film people and other moneyed Italians. The Bulgaris owned a vineyard not too far away and were often seen in the area. It was highly conceivable that Pietro had a sugar momma who was spending the summer nearby. Or maybe a sugar daddy, although I couldn't imagine any gay man I knew tolerating that ponytail.

Sunny nodded absently, her mind clearly turning to other things. "Speaking of strange people, I really think I should go over and at least say 'Hi' to whoever that is."

I offered to go with her, and we made our way across the drive-way to the pool. I should say that I wasn't looking forward to meeting new friends, that's not really why I was here. If it was easy, like with Paola, great. But I didn't have it in me at the moment for small talk, as most of my energies these days had been taken up with trying to get through the day without bursting into tears in the middle of Starbucks. But since Sunny did hook me up with a totally free week in Tuscany, I figured I owed it to her.

Fortunately, our good-will mission was interrupted by the sound of tires on loose gravel. We looked to the driveway where Nino's red Fiat was pulling in, and changed course to greet him. Nino unfolded himself out of the compact car and quickly bent down to give me a hug that lifted me partially off of my feet.

"Where is my best American friend Michele?" he asked, in beautifully accented English.

"Where else? Taking photos."

Sunny chimed in. "He's in the olive grove now, so you can get your camera and meet your lover." Sunny always teased her husband that he was in love with mine, a joke that I wish was true as we'd probably come to Italy more often.

Either in an effort to prove his loyalty to her, or just because he's Italian and that's how they do it, Nino kissed his wife deeply before telling her, "Your sister called right before I left the house."

"Which one?"

"Jen."

This information aggravated his wife. "What? Why'd she call the house and not my cell?"

Nino looked to the sky as if to ask the gods why Sunny's sister did anything. "She said things have changed and she's arriving tomorrow."

"What?! And you told her this was OK?"

Again Nino looked towards the heavens. "What can I say, Sunny? No?" he finally asked. And without skipping a beat, the two began arguing in rapid Italian, the passionate kiss a memory— or perhaps a coming attraction. Some couples were like that. My husband was Irish, so getting angry didn't lead to sex, just drinking. Drinking and video games.

Having settled something in Italian, Sunny reverted to English. "All right. I'll have to call her before dinner. She wasn't supposed to arrive until next week! I don't even know if there's enough rooms here!" Sunny complained, although looking out at the large guest house and even larger villa, it was hard to believe that would ever be a problem. Sunny, however, did not care about the logistics and just continued her litany against her sister. "I swear, since Jen had that kid, she thinks she's the only one with a schedule. It's like that kid is a "Get Out of Jail Free" card to just change plans whenever she wants. I have two kids. And they're animals. But you don't see me disrupting everyone's life," Sunny finished.

I stepped away for a moment to allow them to fight, and also to check our car door, which The Husband insists on never locking even though he's been ripped off twice. When I walked back, Paola was approaching cautiously, seeing that Sunny was getting wound up about something. "Sunny, I have to go and make sure dinner is ready. It is all right if I send Fabrizio to get the boys later?"

"Do you want to come to dinner with us tonight? Tina said she'd watch the kids."

"I would love to, but I have to eat with the old women. They don't like being alone since Antonio's father died." Paola exhaled puff of smoke in annoyance and a note of bitterness crept into her voice. "Elin is lucky not to have to take care of them. But they hate coming here."

Sunny wanted to help her friend so she began hesitantly, "Do you want to bring them to dinner..." letting it hang there, the image of two old, angry women in black at a restaurant appealing to no one.

Paola smiled as she ground her cigarette into the driveway. "Thank you, Dear, but I wouldn't do that to you. Besides, the circus is in town, so they won't leave the house."

As Paola drove away, Sunny said, "Now that she's gone, I can go yell at my sister."

I meant to ask her more about that. I mean to ask her about this whole circus thing everyone kept talking about. But just then we looked across the driveway to the pool. And as we did, we simultaneously remembered our earlier mission of introducing ourselves to Silvio's guest. However, when we looked over to the lounge chair she was gone. So I went to go find Mike to see if he wanted to get a nap in before dinner. And if we still had time, maybe we'd actually sleep.

CHAPTER 3

Almost three hours later we were rested and making our way up the winding hill road towards town. It was only a ten-minute walk, but the road was steep, with half a dozen switchbacks and no shoulder, lined instead with trees and brambles and then steeply dropping off. After the pasta and three bottles of wine, I welcomed the exercise, but not so much the chance to cheat death—Italians aren't known for their caution when driving. Despite being almost nine o'clock it was still light out; the walk home would be more treacherous.

We cleaned up well. We'd scrubbed the sand off our bodies and the salt out of our hair, which Sunny and I had then pulled back into very chic, vacation-friendly knots. Mike and Nino wore crisp linen shirts over jeans, while Sunny had on a simple green cotton asymmetrical shift dress. It was sleeveless on one side, while on the other side was a billowing bat-wing sleeve that ended just above the elbow. I had decided on my paisley Nanette Lepore with a halter neckline, because it screams "1960's Roman girl getting off the ferry at Capri," to me. When I travel, I like to look the part and I urge you to do the same. You'll thank me when you look at your vacation photos.

According to the travel guide The Husband insisted on reading out loud to me in the airport bar, Capalbio as a town dates back to the early 800s when it was gifted from Charlemagne to the Abbey of the Tre Fontane. But it wasn't until the twelfth century that the castle and the surrounding fortress walls were built. The air was still close but cooling ever so slightly as we walked through the entrance of these walls. It was like a medieval Escher drawing: Once inside the stone wall that encircled the apex of the hill, you walked up a maze of narrow cobblestone streets that sometimes took steep turns upwards, sometimes dead-ended, and sometimes led you lower until you were back where you started. Sunny and Nino expertly navigated them until we were at what seemed to be the center, off of which was four or five stone steps that led upwards to a walkway. We climbed up and found ourselves on top of the wall that went around the perimeter of the fortified paese, offering us stunning, 360-degree vistas of the surrounding country. Mike and Nino immediately went for their cameras; Sunny and I immediately rolled our eyes but smiled.

We walked ahead of them, along what must have been the former battlement, the crenellated wall on the hillside protecting us from falling.

"Paola seems nice," I remarked.

"You would have to be, married to Antonio."

"You don't like him?"

"Paola doesn't even like him. And Elin really doesn't like him. He's terrible with money... was always asking Silvio Sr. to invest in one doomed business or another. A few years ago, he bought a yacht as an 'investment' and then almost killed himself and his father on it. And since his father died late last year, he's been after Silvio to sell off the land, and blaming Elin because he won't. I think that's why the aunts don't ever want to come over. I think Antonio poisoned them against her. Although jokes on him because now they're going to live with him until they die, and those two are going to live forever. It must be all the never having sex."

"If he needs money, why doesn't he sell his house then?" Not that it was any of my business, but I just can't help but troubleshoot sometimes, even when I'm watching TV and it's not even a real situation. I'm always two steps ahead of the TV cop, asking for a tox screen for the deceased, or wondering about the alibi of a minor character. Unfortunately, I've never been nearly as good at solving my own problems, unless running away to Italy was a solution.

"Ahhh, but see, Silvio Sr. left everything to the both of them. Everything is in Silvio and Antonio's names. He wasn't stupid. He knew his younger son was a fucking idiot."

"Why'd she marry him?"

"Same reason we all get married. We don't know they're fucking idiots yet," she laughed, and we looked back at where our husbands were studying the photos they had just taken and comparing shutter speeds or penis sizes or whatever. Despite just calling him a fucking idiot, Sunny's face softened when she looked at Nino. I understood it well. There's something to catching the person you love when they don't know they're being watched. They're so caught up in their own private moment, no matter how simple and ordinary a task it might be. There was one night a few years before when Mike and I had been staying not too far away from here in the town of San Gimignano. Our hotel room overlooked the main square that centered around a well, and late one night after the crowds had dispersed, Mike went out with his tripod to get some shots of the ancient cisterna. I watched from our windowsill as he walked around the square, set up his tripod, looked through the lens. He was so focused on what he was doing, and just doing it for the uncomplicated enjoyment of it. I could have watched him all night.

Sunny looked back at me and returned to her gossip about Paola and Antonio. "But you know how it is, she's a model, he's a football player... Then someone breaks his leg whether accidentally or on purpose and he squanders their money buying boats and cars and grappa distilleries."

"Antonio used to be a professional soccer player?" I asked, so impressed I slipped into the American vernacular.

Sunny discouraged my excitement. "It's not that big of deal. Every guy in Italy used to be a soccer player if you listen to them."

We went down some steps to the square below, and as we walked along the narrow alleys towards dinner, I noticed a small church, white but weathered, with a dark wooden door and a circular stained-glass window above that. It looked to be the same church Elin and Silvio were standing in front of in their wedding photo.

I asked Sunny about it as we went into the restaurant and were led to a covered outdoor patio.

"Yeah, that's the same one. Chiesa di San Nicola. Isn't it charming? They could have gotten married anywhere: On the Gucci's yacht; at the Ferragamo's vineyard. Instead they went to that church with thirty or forty people. It was very sweet."

"It was," Nino agreed. "And at their reception they served a magnificent twenty-five-year-old Barolo."

"Yes, speaking of wine, maybe our sommelier should order us some?" Sunny nudged her husband.

"How can I do that? I don't know what everyone's eating yet."

This was the drawback of eating with a sommelier: A rigid, almost evangelical interpretation of what wine goes with which food. Look, I get it. I mean it's not like I'm going to pair oysters with a red wine. I'm not a savage. But I don't want to hear that I shouldn't drink red wine with my chicken, and I never want to hear that I should drink a chardonnay with anything.

Luckily, Mike intervened. "I have no idea what I'm eating, but I know I'm drinking red, so order away." We were in Tuscany after all; the land of the Sangiovese grape and Brunello and Vino Nobile wine. We weren't not going to take advantage of that.

Nino obliged, no doubt rolling his eyes Christ-like to the Heavens yet again, begging us to be forgiven for we know not what we do. He ordered a local wine, and when the waiter brought the bottle back for him to taste, they had an exchange in rapid Italian, most of which I didn't catch. But Sunny did, and she looked concerned. I started struggling harder to understand.

While Nino took a sniff of the glass, Sunny explained. "There was a break-in last night at the owner's house."

Nino nodded his head in understanding before asking the waiter, "C'é un circo a Capalbio?"

That I understood. I slapped my palm on the table, and blurted out, "What is it about the fucking circus here? Scusa mi."

"Oh, everyone always gets ripped off when there's a circus in town. The people who travel with the circus are thieves," Sunny explained very matter-of-factly. The waiter and her husband nodded in support of her story.

"Do they wait until everyone is at the circus and then sneak out and rob the empty houses?" Mike asked.

Nino shook his head. "No. They just rob them during the day."

My Husband, suddenly a master criminal, was incensed. "Well, that doesn't make sense. Why go during the day? That's when everyone's home. They should go at night when they're all at the circus. That's what I would do."

"At night they have to work in the circus," Nino answered very plainly.

"That's just stupid. That's a wasted opportunity. They're leaving money on the table," The Husband continued like he was a systems analyst for circus thieves, trying to increase productivity.

"Well, when you're in charge of your crime syndicate, you can run things your way," I said.

"I may need to if we don't get hired when we get home," he grumbled.

"*If* we get home," I added, somewhat under my breath. I still wasn't sold on that as an option. I mean, I knew it was unrealistic to think I was just going to stay in Italy forever. Who would feed my cats? But at the same time, staying in Italy also seemed like the best solution. For the last six months, every major aspect of my life had been a spectacular failure. Living it was a constant reminder of this. Starting over in a picturesque locale felt like the opposite of failure. It would feel like I had won something. And I needed to feel something other than loss.

It was then that I noticed Sunny trying to surreptitiously check her phone, a less-than-carefree look on her face.

"Any word from Elin?"

"No…" Sunny began before The Husband interrupted her.

"What's wrong with Elin?" Since I've been known to faint and lose consciousness and my husband referred to it as just a panic attack, I found his concern for the supermodel he'd never met slightly irritating.

"What? Are you afraid that we're going to lose our hook up at this amazing place or something?" I asked him.

"Can't I be concerned for the nice lady who's letting us stay in her house and never met us? *And* also afraid we're going to lose our hookup to this amazing place?"

Sunny laughed. "Please, she's been dying to meet you both for years. She's actually thrilled you're here. That's why it was weird that she decided to take off and even weirder that she hasn't returned my text."

Nino began in a soothing voice to his wife, "Sunny, you don't need to worry. She's at the Lakes. She probably is having too good a time to think of you."

Sunny gave him a look like she wanted to call him a fucking idiot again. "Thanks."

Nino looked to Mike. "This is not what I meant."

"You don't have to tell me. I understood what you meant, Man." Mike then turned to Sunny. "Cut him some slack. English isn't even his first language."

But to me it looked like something other than her husband's poor syntax was bothering Sunny. "It's just not like her." The crease crept back between her eyes. "She texted me from her honeymoon."

Nino tentatively tried to hold his wife's hand before saying, "All the way up on the lake, with the mountains and trees... She may have no telefonino service."

"He's got a point," Mike agreed. "I don't think I've had two whole bars since the plane landed."

"Call Silvio if you're worried," I suggested.

"No, I'm just being paranoid," Sunny relented. "And Silvio has enough of his own problems, between Antonio's bullshit and stress at work."

"What's he do?" The Husband asked, no doubt wanting to know what kind of problems at work this soft-looking millionaire had compared to the nightmare talent and vindictive executives he had to constantly battle between.

"He's un avvocato, a lawyer," Nino answered very nonchalantly. "He takes on big corporations and sometimes they threaten his life."

"So it's a little more serious than the network censors not letting your host say 'blow job,'" I teased Mike, hoping he was in a teasing mood. You can never be too sure with husbands.

Thinking about husbands made me think about their wedding photo, which reminded me of the question I had been dying to ask. "Is that how he got those burns? Did someone make good on a threat?"

"Oh," for once Sunny's voice turned low and serious, "that was the kidnapping."

"The kidnapping?!" I exclaimed incredulously, and probably too loudly. This vacation, which was already the stuff of movies, was taking an even more dramatic turn.

Nino nodded gravely as Sunny continued. "Yes, he was kidnapped when he was very young, only three or four years old."

"No shit," my husband whispered next to me. Even the criminal mastermind didn't expect this.

I had only known one other person who had been kidnapped, a classmate in the second grade who was "kidnapped" by her father in a custody dispute. They found her two days later in a hotel on Cape Cod watching Pay-Per-View and eating gummy worms. Something told me this was different.

"Who kidnapped him? Why?"

"Oh, everyone got kidnapped in the '70s," Sunny shrugged, back to her usual tone.

"Sunny, it is not true. Well, yes, it's true many, many people did get kidnapped in the '70s in Italy," Nino began. "It was a terrible economic time here, especially in the South..."

I am always impressed and embarrassed by how much people in other countries know about their own country's history. In America, we know four facts and three of them are inaccurate.

If you know anything beyond that people think you're a history major. But when we walk around Rome with Nino, he can tell us the history of monuments going back to the Etruscans, and he's a sommelier.

"They called the '70s 'Anni di Piombo,'" Nino began.

"Years of lead?" I asked. "Why?"

"Because of all the violence and crime." He took a sip of his wine before continuing, "Italy had all this growth after World War II, but it slowed down by the end of the '60s."

"At one point in the early '70s, six million workers were on strike," interjected The Husband who <u>was</u> a history major.

Nino nodded. "Many people became communists, socialists. They fought with the Neo-fascists and Christian Democrats. Everyone was desperate and angry. There were bombings, assassinations. And kidnappings. Hundreds of kidnappings."

I felt my eyes go wide. I had heard of how the Getty heir had been kidnapped but I thought it was because he was an American and it was an isolated event. I didn't realize they had targeted their own many, many times.

"Sometimes they were done for political reasons, like with our Prime Minister, Aldo Moro..."

Mike nodded. He had read about this, too. I smiled. I liked having a smart husband.

"Other times," Nino continued, "it was done for money. They would kidnap children of the very wealthy and keep them someplace remote—in a cave or in a hole—until the ransom was paid. Not everyone made it home again."

"Moro didn't," Mike added. Nino shook his head as if to confirm the tragic end.

Sunny picked up the story. "Silvio's family had a lot of money: A yacht, a jet, even an island. Who owns an island?! And Silvio and Antonio were the only two heirs. Their father was an only child. He'd had one sister, but she died of polio, and his mother died of cholera right after the war, so there were no more children."

"What about the aunts?"

"They're Silvio Sr.'s aunts. That's how fucking old they are. And of course they never married, so Silvio and Antonio were desirable targets. Silvio was snatched right from the beach. They think the kidnappers had help, someone on the inside, and every single staff member was fired as a result. Everyone except Enzo, the butler, only he wasn't the butler then. He was just a teenager, but his family had been with the Corini's for decades.

The kidnappers held Silvio for almost a year. The family finally got word of where to find him, some remote mountainous region in Calabria, I think, only when they arrived, a nearby cabin had been on fire. Presumably that's where they had hidden him, and they wanted to get rid of all evidence or something. Silvio, being so young, must have wandered in before the fire got out of control and then gotten trapped. He was badly burned. If they hadn't gotten there when they did, he would have died."

"It was Enzo, who rescued him. That's another reason he was never fired," Nino concluded.

Sunny shook her head and took a sip of wine, as if to stifle the thoughts of this ever happening to her. "It was such a tragedy. The mother went insane with grief. She was never the same, even after he came home. She took a lot of pills and drank, just to deal with all the fear that someone would take one of her kids again. She drowned in a bathtub just a year after Silvio was rescued."

"Holy shit! Has anyone optioned this as a movie?" Mike wanted to know.

"Trust me, that's the first thing I asked," Sunny answered.

"Oh my god, we're all dead inside," I lamented, and finished my wine.

After a truly transcendent meal of smoked cinghiale, baked pecorino with truffles, and rabbit braised in the local wine, we made our way back down the hill, drunk enough to no longer be so concerned with our safety, which was exactly why we probably should have been. But it was a quiet town, and not many cars were coming or going at that time of night. There was no light coming from anywhere: No cars, no streetlights, not even the occasional lit window in a house from the valley below. It was pitch black except for the thousands of stars speckling the sky like so many pointillist dots in a Seurat painting. You never saw this many stars in the city. But then as soon as you looked off to either side and the valley below, you saw nothing but a vast absence of light.

That's probably why the corpse scared the shit out of me.

We were using our phones as flashlights; there was no shoulder and neither Sunny nor I wanted to twist an ankle by over-stepping the edge of the road, a distinct possibility in our chosen footwear. (What? Were we supposed to ruin our outfits with sneakers, like we're businesswomen who walk the mall at lunch? I was in Italy, not a Zumba class.) Suddenly the quiet of the valley was interrupted by the sorrowful moan of half a dozen or so dogs, howling into the night. After all these stories of kidnappings and death, I have to say it was more than a little unnerving and I may have screamed.

"It's OK," Sunny explained. "Those are just the hunting dogs. They do that all night, unfortunately. They hunt the cinghiale, the wild boar, in season and are kenneled the rest of the year over there."

And with her phone's flashlight she pointed out through the trees, the beam of light illuminating both the location of the kennel, and a human body ten or twenty feet away.

CHAPTER 4

"Oh my god!"

"Is that...?"

"No, you're just drunk."

"Shut up. You drank more than me."

"That's not true."

"I wasn't the one who decided to have a scotch after three bottles of wine."

"You guys, it can't be!"

Finally it was Nino who spoke, in the blunt and plaintive way he had. "Sì, it is a dead person, yes."

"We should call nine-one-one!"

"Unfortunately, 'nine-one-one' won't help you here," Sunny pointed out. "Nino, call the cops."

Nino tried for a moment, but then gave up. "Sunny, I have no signal here."

We all checked our phones. Not one of us had a signal on this rural road.

"We'll have to walk back to the villa and call," he suggested.

"Well, first we should make sure the body is actually a body and it's actually dead," Sunny offered. "I don't need to get the polizia out here for a prosciutto wrapped in a carpet."

"Good point," I agreed, although I didn't know anyone in Italy who would throw out a perfectly good prosciutto. Still, I didn't need to get flagged by the local authorities, especially as my current plans were to never go home and just live here illegally. I turned to The Husband. "Hold my purse."

"What? Why do I have to be the one to hold the purse?"

"I'd hold yours, but you don't have one."

"I'm going with you."

"Let's all go together," Sunny suggested.

I slowly made my way down the embankment, taking care not to misstep, hoping I wasn't ruining my heels in the process. The Husband reached out his hand to help. "Why'd you wear those shoes for?"

"Because when I dressed for dinner, I didn't know dessert would be looking at corpses! Speaking of, whatever we do we shouldn't touch the body. They always say that's a mistake on *Law & Order*."

"What should we do then?" Mike asked. "I mean what are we doing this for?"

"You know I was in an episode of *Law & Order*, maybe I should run point?" Sunny suggested. "In fact, it was a lot like this. I was walking down the street after dinner with friends and we saw a body. And then it was all, "Bum Bum..." She nervously started singing the theme to *Law & Order* and Mike and I chimed in under our breath. Nino stood silent. Clearly, *Law & Order* hadn't made it to Italy.

It was definitely a body. The back was to us, as if the person were merely resting on their side. The corpse was long; tall enough to be a man, but much too narrow, and the two shapely and delicate calves on one end confirmed it was a woman. The feet were bare, kicked free of their shoes during the fall, no doubt. One could only assume it was a fall, given the grade of the ridge and the peril of the road. Any hope the person might be alive felt weak at that moment. The hair was dirty and matted, the legs covered in dirt; it had been there for a few days at least. This was suddenly very real and scary for all of us and no one wanted to be first to cross in front of the body, to see the lifeless face that was staring out into the valley, at the howling dogs.

We left a wide perimeter around her as we slowly inched a few feet lower on the hillside. Four phones turned their flashlights onto the victim's face. And there was the face from all the pictures, in her final pose, Elin.

CHAPTER 5

"Oh, my god, no," Sunny said as softly as I've ever heard her talk. Her husband pulled her into an embrace, and she started sobbing.

He said quietly, "Do not look, Sunny."

"But I thought she was up north." It was the only thought in my head. Not a very helpful thing to say, I will admit, but then what is in that moment?

"Sunny, let Nino take you back and you guys call the cops," Mike advised. "You shouldn't be here."

"Maybe none of us should be here," I threw out there. "I'm not sure we should be sitting in the dark in the middle of the night with a corpse, armed only with iPhones that have no signal."

Sunny's sobs got louder.

"We'll be fine. What are you afraid of?" my husband who loved to minimize my feelings asked.

"What if the killer comes back?"

"What killer? She was probably hit by a car and knocked into the ravine," Mike argued.

"A., Hit by a car still means there's a killer," I pointed out, not because it was at all pertinent, but just because I like to be right. "And B., Since when do cars shoot bullets?"

Mike and Nino just looked at me. Even Sunny stopped sobbing and looked up. I once again took my flashlight across poor Elin's face and let it rest on the side closest to the ground. Because of her angle and the dark, it was hard to see, but you could make out a small entry wound and a trickle of blood running down. With all the dirt and matted hair and leaves, it was easy to miss.

"Oh, Jesus," Sunny said, turning suddenly and vomiting.

"I think we definitely need to call the police now," Mike suggested again. Nino, who was rubbing his wife's back, nodded.

"Oh my God, Silvio. We have to tell Silvio," Sunny whispered as the awful reality set in.

No one spoke for a moment, but I have no doubt that we were all coming to the same realization: Everything was going to be different from this moment forward. Every moment after this could not be anticipated or planned for. Nothing was going to unfold as we had hoped it would on the beach that afternoon. Something irrevocable had happened. It was a feeling I had far too much experience with recently.

Nino walked Sunny back up the hill towards the road. I could hear her asking him, "The kids? What are we going to tell them?" The last thing I heard her add before they disappeared around the bend was, "You know those little monsters are going to ask to see the body, right?" I knew then that she would be OK. She was Irish. She got her strength from gallows humor.

I looked back to where The Husband was futilely trying to get his internet to work.

"You're not tweeting this are you?"

"Of course not."

"Instagram?"

"No!"

We sat there for a moment, before I had an idea. "Maybe we should be..."

"Are you crazy?!"

"I don't mean actually posting on social media, but you have a very expensive camera with you. Maybe you should take photos now, so the police have them when they get here. That way in case anything gets disturbed... this is the most pristine the crime scene is going to get."

He fiddled with the settings a little bit and tried taking a few shots before admitting, "I don't know if I can."

"Not enough light?"

"No, Kat, it's a body. The fucking body of the nice lady who let us stay in her house even though she'd never met us. I don't know if I can take photos of her."

He sat down on the edge of the road and I joined him

"I just don't understand," I said after a beat. "She was supposed to be up north with friends."

"You said that. Clearly she didn't make it."

"Exactly. Why didn't anyone call? If I was expecting a friend from out of town, and they didn't show up, I would be worried that something had happened, and I would call."

"That's because you're Italian and you worry too much."

"Well, duh, these people are Italian, too."

I had him there. "Maybe she did call," he ventured. "Maybe she decided not to go at the last minute, and she hadn't told Sunny yet."

"Or her staff? Or her husband?"

"Maybe she told him and he forgot. You always tell me I never listen. Maybe he doesn't either."

I put my head on my husband's shoulder, suddenly overcome

with how lucky I was to have him. "I love you," I told him earnestly.

"What? Why?"

"You listened when I told you that you never listened."

CHAPTER 6

It was almost two hours before the polizia arrived. Nino explained to us later that they had to come all the way from Grosseto, which was an hour away, and that was after they probably had to wake the investigator and his team up. At one point I had offered to go back to the villa to grab a bottle of wine while we sat there, but Mike and I agreed it was unwise to split up. We also agreed it was probably unwise to be shitfaced when the police got here and we were standing in front of the body of the woman whose house we were squatting in.

It also occurred to us at that point that we would probably need to book a hotel for the rest of our trip.

Fortunately, once the polizia got there, they wanted us gone pretty quickly. They wanted us nowhere near the crime scene, which was fine with me; I had had enough sitting vigil by a corpse to last me whatever might be left of my own lifetime. A number of uniformed polizie swept in and immediately taped off the area, followed by a forensics team in white suits and booties who took photos as they slowly searched the ground around Elin for evidence. Finally, a medico legale arrived who appeared to actually pronounce her dead.

A man in plain clothes who introduced himself as Vice Questore Patti walked us back up to the road and wanted to ask us a few questions immediately, which was smart; between the late hour and the amount of Morellino we consumed, our memories (unlike the Morellino) wouldn't improve with age.

But there wasn't much we could tell him.

"Did you know the deceased?"

"No."

"How is it you had come to be guests in her home then?"

"Just lucky—for once," I added without thinking. The Husband shot me a look.

"And how is it you found the body?"

"Just unlucky. As usual." I couldn't resist. The Husband then took over and explained the story of our walk home. It was over quickly.

Still, the Vice Questore seemed good natured. He smiled when The Husband finished. "Yes, it is very unlucky for you, Signora. Sfortunatamente, it is more unlucky for l'altra signora."

I nodded and smiled back, trying to curry favor in Italian even though his English was flawless. "Grazie, Vice Questore. Potremmo tornare a casa?"

"Sì, signora." He turned to my husband. "Your wife, her Italian is molto brava."

"Yes," Mike agreed. "She speaks very well, but she understands nothing."

The Vice Questore laughed. "Who among us does?" posed our philosopher polizia. "Yes, please, go back to where you are staying. But I will walk with you. I want to ask your friends a few questions before they go to bed."

I wanted to tell him he had all night because I didn't suppose Sunny and Nino would be sleeping anytime soon. And despite how exhausted I felt, I didn't suppose I would be able to either once I actually got into bed.

We walked along in an awkward silence for a few minutes, but considering we had just left a murder scene, were accompanied by a cop, and the victim was no less than our host, small talk seemed in poor form. It didn't seem like the moment to ask, "So, how do you like Lazio's players this year?"

As I had suspected, when we reached the villa we found Sunny and Nino sitting near the pool, drinking a bottle of wine, despite the late hour. Sunny's face was streaked with eye makeup and a pile of tissues had accumulated in front of her.

"We didn't want to wake the kids," she explained. "Or Tina and Renato, either. Although, I'll have to tell her soon. Silvio's on his way up and I know she'd want to be awake in case he needed anything."

Vice Questore Patti nodded as she talked and at the mention of Silvio's name asked, "So her husband knows? And he's on his way?"

Sunny and Nino nodded their heads gravely, the memory of telling Silvio of Elin's death all over their faces.

"And he is OK to drive here in the middle of the night, knowing his wife has just been murdered?" The Vice Questore sounded concerned but I could see where he was going with this.

"He has a butler, Enzo; he will drive him," Nino explained.

"Signore e Signora, I understand you have had a tragedy tonight," the Vice Questore began in English to Sunny and Nino, I assume for Sunny's comfort. She wasn't thrilled to speak only in Italian on days when her best friend *hadn't* been killed. Sure, there are days when it all seems to come to you so easily and you marvel at your ability to communicate in a whole other language. And then there are other days when your tongue won't work in conjunction with your mind and your brain seems to glitch as you can't find the word that you know you should know, and it's everything you can do to not dissolve into a puddle of flop sweat and frustration tears. If nothing else, it's made me a lot more patient with people in my own country for whom

English isn't their first language. And it's filled me with a lot more admiration for them, too.

Patti continued, "You have lost a very good friend and it is very late. If I could ask you a few questions, it is better for the investigation, and then I can return when you have rested."

Our friends agreed and he took them aside one at a time. Sunny wanted to go first so she could go wake Tina after. Patti agreed this was wise, since he'd probably want to ask Tina and Renato questions, as well, before Silvio arrived.

Mike and I sat down and Nino poured us both a glass of wine. We didn't tell him not to.

"This is so strange," Mike began. "Who do you think could have done this?"

Nino shrugged, not out of indifference, but out of weariness for how the world worked. "She was a wealthy woman. And she was very well known in town. She was probably walking back from town and she got mugged. Perhaps they did not even mean to kill her."

"And the circus is in town," Mike finished.

Nino smiled at Mike's reference, but I could see from the seriousness of his eyes that he had already considered it.

"I just wonder when it could have happened. Sunny said the last she saw her, she was leaving for the Lakes. And why would no one call here if she didn't show?" I still wanted to know.

"I'm sure the polizie will answer all those questions, because that's their job," Mike said in an effort to get me to drop it.

Sunny came back just then and told Nino it was his turn. "I have to go tell Tina now," she announced before draining what was left in her glass and going about her awful task.

I looked over to where Mike had taken out his iPad.

"You're playing sudoku?!" I asked, in probably a more accusatory tone than I normally would have. But a man's wife had just been murdered. You'd think he'd want to spend a little more time comforting his own wife.

"I'm looking for a distraction, and I suggest you do the same; otherwise, you're never going to get to sleep tonight."

I had to admit he had a point, and I hate admitting that. I planned to head back to the room to get my Kindle, when all of a sudden, a loud, wrenching sob broke out from Tina's room on the backside of the guest house. Her anguish echoed through the otherwise quiet valley, waking the hunting dogs who began to join her with their own cries.

And that's when the guest house door nearest the pool swung open, revealing the stranger from that afternoon in a too-small kimono robe, who screamed in a less than elegant British accent, "What the fek is going awwwwn?"

Nino was just walking back with the Vice Questore, who looked at the woman and then back to us.

"Who is this?"

The three of us looked from each other to the Vice Questore.

"No idea," I told him.

He turned to the woman. "And who are you, Signora?"

She was incensed as she tried to light a cigarette. "Who am I? Who are you?"

I thought I should make myself scarce, but I also wanted to see how this played out.

He smiled at her and lit her cigarette where she had failed. "I am a Vice Questore di Polizia, Vice Questore Patti. Your turn." There was just the hint of sternness as he finished.

"I am a friend of Silvio's," she said defiantly.

"And your name, Signora Friend of Silvio's?" he smiled again, though she was clearly trying his patience.

"I'm a guest at his home. I'm not sure why you need to know who I am," she was regaining her composure and while she was still a handful, she was losing her rough edge and her obstinance was beginning to seem more like cool entitlement.

But Patti had had enough. "I need to know because his wife, Signora Corini, has just been found murdered, and you are an unknown woman, staying at her house as a guest of her husband."

Her cool composure dropped again. "Elin's dead?! Fek!"

"So, you knew Signora Corini?"

"No, I mean just to hear Silvio talk of her."

"And again, Signora, prego, tell me who you are."

"I'm Silvio's sister," she held out her hand to the Vice Questore. "Aparna."

Just then Sunny walked back up the stairs from Tina's apartment. She looked from the stranger to the Vice Questore and then back to her husband and us. "What'd I miss?"

CHAPTER 7

Mike and I took that as our cue to go to bed.

We slept terribly, finally actually dozing off around sunrise. We know that Silvio must have arrived within the hour of us retiring to our room, but we never heard him. He evidently did not have the flare for drama that his alleged sister had.

Cars started pulling up the gravel driveway around seven. It was a small town; news was going to travel fast. We knew we'd never sleep through all of that, and as we had to pack and find new digs anyway, we decided it was best to get up and get going. We could sleep at the next place—providing no one got murdered there.

Quickly, we showered and packed our things. Initially we both agreed that it was best if we stayed out of the way, but the Wi-fi was better in the main house, and as we were going to need to get online to find a hotel, we reluctantly headed out of our room, past the pool and up the hill to the house.

Tina was coping with her grief by cooking. Clearly. It was barely after eight in the morning, but the dining room table was filled with fresh bread, muffins, and a coffee cake. There was a bowl of fruit from the garden, and a pitcher of juice. I could smell bacon coming from the kitchen.

"This answers the question, 'Who do you have to kill to get a decent breakfast in Italy?'" remarked The Husband. The Italians weren't particularly known for their first meal of the day, which seems a small price to pay for being known for every other meal of the day.

Sunny was coming out of the kitchen as we entered. "Morning! I can't believe you're up. Do you want coffee?"

"That's not necessary," I answered at the same time The Husband said, "Sure!"

I gave him a look before continuing. "You don't have to do that after everything you've been through. We can go up to town."

"I've already made coffee for Nino, Paola, Antonio, Silvio, and three Carabinieri. What's two more? Besides," she admitted, "it helps to have something to do."

"Did you sleep at all?" I asked her.

"Not really. After the bombshell of Silvio's sister, the Vice Questore interviewed Tina, then Renato, then Silvio showed up, then he was interviewed, then Antonio called. Assunta and Immacolata like to go to the sunrise service at church sometimes, and news had already spread. It's been a goddamn zoo here and that's coming from me, who's one of seven kids. Speaking of, I told Paola and Antonio to leave the kids with me today, and Nino's getting ready to take all four boys to the beach so they can be savages away from people who are grieving. You guys are welcome to ride with him if you want to get away from all this," she waved her hand around, like "all this" was an untidy house and not the death of her friend.

Mike and I looked at each other. He spoke first. "Thanks so much, but we're actually going to get out of your hair."

"Yeah," I continued. "We just came up here so we could get on the internet and find a place to stay."

"Stay here," she uttered nonchalantly, like it was late and we needed a place to crash.

"Sunny, that's fucking crazy. The woman who invited us has been murdered and her husband, whose house this is, is either

47

grieving or a suspect or both."

But Sunny dismissed my argument. "No, it was Silvio who insisted. If you ask me, he doesn't want to be alone."

"He's got family here," pointed out Mike.

"Family he hates. I mean he likes Paola fine, but Elin's body isn't even cold, and Antonio wants to talk about selling the villa again. Plus, there's this new wrinkle with the bastard sister."

"And I want to get back to that, because that's delicious..." I began.

"Yes," interrupted Mike, "but we really can't stay. We can't impose upon this poor man."

"It's no imposition."

Everyone jumped a little. Standing in the doorway behind us all was Silvio himself. I hoped he hadn't heard that comment about the bastard sister. Or the one about maybe killing his wife.

He was the same handsome man from the wedding photo, but his dark hair was even wavier and more unkempt. He had circles under his eyes and stubble appearing over the scars that I knew were there from the fire. My God, he'd already been through so much.

"My wife, she loved company. We both grew up with no family: I, with just my brother and father; she, with just her mother. She always loved having people around her and when I met her, I saw the life I had been missing for so long. Even more tragedy will come from this, if her friends get sent away because someone took her from us."

I wanted to point out that we had never met poor Elin, God rest and all that, but if it got me free a room in paradise and helped this poor widower to grieve, who was I to say "No?" I also wanted to point out to The Husband how eloquent Silvio was in talking about his wife, despite his grief, and ask him why he never talked about me like that. But Silvio spoke again before I had the chance.

"Besides, the Vice Questore would like you all to stay."

At first, I was confused because it almost sounded like it was the Vice Questore's home too, and he had invited us. Then I understood. We were all suspects.

"He said that he would prefer if everyone stay close and not go anywhere for a few days in case he has any further questions. He asked if I would mind and I said anything I could do to help catch Elin's killer."

At this, his voice broke a little, and he looked away, trying to compose himself. He took a handkerchief out of his pocket and not only wiped his tears, but mopped his face, as well. It was already nearing ninety degrees outside, or whatever they call it in Celsius.

"We are so sorry for your loss," I offered when I thought enough time had passed. "If we can be of service and do anything for you or your family while we're here..."

"Yes," Mike agreed. "Thank you so much for your hospitality. I wish it was under better circumstances."

"Thank you," he nodded. "Be a good friend to Sunny. She loved my wife very much, too."

A short, muscular man silently walked into the room behind Silvio. He looked to be in his late forties, with a face that had seen a lot of sun, and hair that was mostly grey. He nodded at Silvio as he placed a cell phone back in his shirt pocket.

At that Silvio turned to Sunny. "I came in to tell you the boys can stay here. I'm going over to Antonio's to discuss some family business before he has to return to Rome this evening." He was displaying a remarkable amount of composure, despite the circumstances. It was sort of admirable, but also somewhat disconcerting. Should he even be up to discussing business with his idiot brother if his wife had just been killed? Wouldn't that be the perfect excuse not to have to?

Silvio turned to the man behind him, saying something in Italian before nodding towards us and Sunny. Then he addressed Sunny once more. "Sunny, you remember Enzo, yes?"

"Sì," she said and proceeded to speak to Enzo in Italian.

So, this was the butler. Despite the title, he was not wearing a morning coat with a grey ascot, or anything close to what Carson would have found appropriate on *Downton Abbey*. In fact, he was dressed very similarly to Silvio, in cotton trousers and a button-down shirt. Perhaps this was what modern butlers wore in the summer. I made a mental note to google it when I had decent Wi-fi again.

 Silvio was still speaking with Sunny. "I've given Tina the day off. She's quite upset. Enzo is going to run some errands for me and then be around the rest of the day. I want someone to look after the house, with the circus in town and whoever did this still out there."

Sunny nodded and followed Silvio and Enzo out, presumably to tell Nino he no longer had to wrangle four kids at the beach.

Mike and I just looked at each other.

"Well, this is weird."

"Yeah," he agreed, moving towards the kitchen. "Whatever happened to that coffee?"

CHAPTER 8

As Sunny hadn't made our coffee yet, and we still didn't feel one hundred percent comfortable about hanging out at a dead woman's house—even if it was police mandated—we walked back up the hill towards town to get a cappuccino at a café. The view was more spectacular in daylight, even marred as it was by the images of the night before.

We went to a small bar that had an outdoor patio overlooking the valley below and approached the register to order. The woman behind the counter looked to be in her fifties, with reddish hair and even redder lipstick. "State alla casa di Corini?" she asked me. Yes, I told her in Italian. We are their guests.

At that, she waved me off, saying she would bring our coffees outside. I had a feeling I knew why. A few minutes later she came out with two beautiful cappuccinos and a plate of cookies, which I hoped was just Italian hospitality and actually may have been. But she also had questions.

"Che è successo?" What happened? She wanted to know. As much as it made me happy that I actually understood someone for once, I didn't know what to say, what I should or even could say. Having recently been the subject of gossip myself, it felt wrong to discuss Elin's murder with a total stranger, even if poor Elin was no longer here to be harmed by it.

"La Signora è morta." I figured everyone knew she was dead. I didn't want to announce that she had been murdered. Also, I couldn't remember the verb for "to kill."

She blessed herself and I thought that was the end of it. But then she asked, quieter this time, "Qualcuno l'ha ucciso" Someone killed her? That's it. Uccidere.

I nodded solemnly, thinking surely that would be the end of it. But she kept going.

"Ormai è anziano, Fellegi," she practically spat, her distaste for this old man, Fellegi, clear. "Lui vuole la loro terra. Lui ha voluto l'olive. Ma la Signora Corini, non le voleva venderla."

She then rattled off a bunch of other stuff, but frankly I was exhausted, and I really needed the coffee if I was going to do any more translating. I quickly filled in Mike. "She said this old man did it. He wanted the land, the olive trees, and Elin wouldn't sell."

"I kind of picked that up." I don't know how he does it. Maybe it's all the Latin he studied, or maybe he's just lying to me.

Not wanting to be the source of small-town gossip, potentially derail a murder investigation, and burn my bridge to a fantastic Tuscan villa, I quickly finished my coffee, imploring Mike with my eyes to do the same. As we got up to leave, he stuck a cookie in his mouth and four more in his pocket. "What?" he asked off my look. "You made me miss that breakfast."

We headed back down the hill.

"So what are we supposed to do now?" I wondered.

My husband looked at me. "What do you mean?"

"It's barely ten a.m. We can't sleep. It's too early for lunch. It's too early to drink," I paused. "It is too early to drink, right?"

He gave me a questioning look. "Is it?"

"Yeah..." I said reluctantly. "Even on vacation." I continued reviewing our options. "We can go swim at the dead woman's beach club, where we can be "gli ospiti della morta Signora Corini" or we can go hang out at the pool with four boys and wish we were the dead ones."

We walked in silence for a moment and I thought about nearly twenty-four hours before when we had arrived at the beach and how it seemed like nothing could ruin this trip.

"Hey, speaking of the beach. Do you think we should have told the Vice Questore about the man who was looking for Elin?"

Mike shrugged. "Sunny probably already told him."

"What if she didn't? She had a lot on her mind. She was probably in shock."

"In any event," he continued, "she was probably already dead."

"Well, we don't know she was already dead."

"She looked like she had been dead awhile."

"And you're basing that on how many other dead bodies you've seen?"

"She was pretty dirty. You saw her. It didn't look like she had been freshly rolled down the hillside. Why would her killer show up looking for her if he already killed her?"

"Because that's the perfect alibi!"

"Most killers aren't that smart, and I definitely don't think that guy was."

"How do we know how smart killers are? The really smart ones are too smart to get caught, so we don't even know they're killers," I finished triumphantly.

The Husband gave me a tired look. "I've decided that it's definitely not too early to drink."

Back at the villa, it appeared that Sunny had thought the same.

Nino had decided to take the boys to the beach anyway, so when we returned, she was sitting out by the pool by herself, a cold glass of Falanghina on the side table next to her.

We greeted her and Mike announced to the both of us, "I'm going to try to go back to sleep for a little while."

"But you just had coffee," I protested.

"Not a problem." He grabbed an empty glass, poured himself some wine, and went off towards the guest house. "Wake me for lunch!"

I sat down in the lounge chair next to Sunny's and she poured me a glass. She smiled sadly. "I figure it's not every day that your friend is murdered while you're a guest in her home, so it's like a special occasion, only the exact opposite." She clinked her glass on mine. "To Elin."

"To Elin," I repeated. "She sounds like a remarkable person, a wonderful friend, and I'm sorry I never got to meet her."

She took a healthy sip and then, as if to excuse her morning drinking, said, "I'll take a nap later."

I turned over on my side and looked at her. "OK, I have two questions. One, did you tell the cop about the creepy ponytail guy at the beach?"

"No," she said suddenly remembering the incident. "I totally forgot! We can tell him later. He said he'd be back later today for follow up."

"I told you to just drop it," said an exasperated voice. Mike had returned.

"I thought you were taking a nap?"

"You have the room key. I don't know why you bothered locking it."

"You heard everyone, there's a circus in town," I said as I handed him the key and sent him back to bed, adding, "and a murderer." I turned back to Sunny. "OK, and my second question, speaking of suspicious characters who suddenly showed up yesterday..." I looked around to make sure the one in question wasn't lurking anywhere. "What's the deal with the sister? I thought there were only two brothers. And why is she English?"

"OK, so after you guys went to bed last night, the Vice Questore wanted to ask Aparna more questions—hell, we all wanted to ask Aparna more questions—but she wanted to wait until Silvio got there and the Vice Questore wanted to interview Tina and Renato anyway. You know what's weird?" she started to digress. "No one can remember Elin leaving. I had gone back to Rome on Monday morning to take care of some business and didn't drive back up until Wednesday. Plus, Monday and Tuesday are Tina and Renato's days off. Elin was supposed to leave Monday morning, too, but no one can say for sure she was even here Sunday. Nino and the kids and I were gone all day at his cousin's on the Argentario, and she told Tina not to worry about her for dinner. Tina thinks she saw her for breakfast, but when no guests are here, Elin tends to fend for herself with just a quick coffee in the morning. So she doesn't even remember if that was Sunday or some other day."

"Wow. That's going to make it really hard to establish a timeline before her death," I said.

"Who's a smart girl who watches too many procedurals on TV?" she teased in the same tone of voice a mother uses on a toddler. "Anyway, back to the paternity claim, when Silvio arrived, he confirmed that Aparna may be his sister. The father, Silvio Sr., made a fair amount of business trips to England in the early '80s—something about a car company or something—and supposedly there's some evidence to back up her claim that he had an affair with her mother, but they haven't done a DNA test yet."

"Why not? Wouldn't a DNA test be the first thing you do before you invite someone who might be a con artist to your Tuscan villa?" I paused. "Although to be fair, no one asked me for a DNA test before they invited me and for all they know I might be a con artist."

"True enough," admitted Sunny, toasting my glass again. "Having a successful career in Hollywood is kind of a long con."

"Well, that may be over," I muttered ruefully.

"No, it's not. You're great at what you do! You got fired from one job, big deal. Everyone does and frankly it sounds like a shitty job anyway."

"It was a shitty job," I agreed. No one likes it when their contributions get ignored, or when their talents are undervalued, but that's what the salary is there to make up for. But when you add to that a head writer who seems to not respond to you just because you're a woman, and one creepy, alcoholic producer who shows way too much interest in you because you are one, it makes for an untenable work environment. It's hard to make yourself "one of the guys" when you're afraid to be alone with your boss and trying to deflect his sexual comments every day.

And then there's the question of what to do about it. We're supposed to be able to speak out. Why, we had a whole hashtag! Companies are woke now! But when you're in a work situation you don't feel comfortable in to begin with, it's hard to feel like you'll be taken seriously if you say something about it. "They won't believe me. They'll say it's in my head. They'll say I have an axe to grind. They'll call me the 'c-word'—crazy." This is the inner monologue that keeps you up at four a.m. But then I did say something; quietly, to a higher-up who I believed was a friend and who legally had an obligation to report it. None of which stopped him from telling me that if I wasn't going to say anything to anyone else, there was nothing he could do, and this was why these things kept happening to "you women" because "you don't do anything." And three weeks later I was fired.

I worked hard to be a TV writer. I sent out endless samples that I doubt were ever read. I wrote scripts that were only performed by friends in my home or at writers' groups. I went to countless meetings and drinks with people who probably never had a writing job to offer me, but always promised to keep me in mind. And while this is all challenging and time consuming, none of it is as hard as just keeping yourself going; ignoring all of the inner voices that are telling you to quit and go to law school.

And that's just trying to get the job. Once you have one, you're thrilled as hell to be working—for about three minutes, until the anxiety sets in that you have to actually keep this job now. And that entails more than just being good at your job, which is hard enough. You're also playing a political game. For example, whose side do you take when your host and your head writer are disagreeing about something and both look to you for back up? (ANSWER: Neither. Loyalty is never rewarded in this business.)

I worked hard at my job. I worked hard to earn the privilege to work for ten straight years. And I knew I was good at it. I wasn't a novice anymore; I had earned the right to my confidence. When you're a woman succeeding in a male-dominated profession, you wear it like a badge of honor. You feel empowered, succeeding in this man's world. As a woman, I had avoided all of the nightmare scenarios that so many female writers before me had found themselves in. Maybe it's changed, I thought. Maybe they're a thing of the past.

Nope. I had just been lucky.

I had worked really hard to get there. And no matter how much I enjoyed never having to see the vacant expression that always adorned the head writer's doughy face ever again, it was still hard to accept losing something you had fought this hard for. Of course, it makes my life better not to be there. But that doesn't make it fair. And that's the part that's hard to accept.

"I'm going to keep pouring wine down your throat until you lose that look on your face. It's just going to give you wrinkles," Sunny cautioned me as she topped off my glass, which really didn't need topping off.

"Sorry."

Of course, it's hard to care about any of that when you're drinking wine poolside at an Italian villa, even if you may be a murder suspect. Also, I'm working really hard to try to be positive even if I feel like my entire world has just ended in the last six months. So I pulled out of my downward facing spiral and turned to Sunny.

"You know, I think about Elin and Silvio and how you can have everything and it's still not enough to keep you out of harm's way. And I think of that, and how short life is, and I realize that I won, because I no longer have to waste my short life at a place like that." I took a sip of wine, and grinned. "And then I look at this villa and I really miss the paycheck."

We both laughed hard, but then Sunny's face grew sadder and more serious. "There's something else I haven't told the Vice Questore yet that maybe I should. In fact, I haven't told anyone. Elin was pregnant."

CHAPTER 9

"Not even Silvio knew?" I asked.

"I don't think so. Maybe?" Sunny answered, confused.

"How is it not even her husband knew?"

"She told me on Saturday, but said she wanted to tell him in person."

I understood that. When I found out I was pregnant a few months before, I had waited up until almost midnight, waiting for Mike to come home. He was shooting a show that night and I knew it was going to be a late one but sending him a text just seemed in poor form.

Sunny continued, "He was supposed to be here that weekend, to see her before she left." Her voice cracked as she tried unsuccessfully to hold back the tears, and it was a few moments before she could go on. "But at the last minute something came up for him in Rome, something important, and he said he wasn't going to make it up that weekend."

I knew Silvio would never be able to forgive himself for whatever it was. Unless he was the killer. "I wonder if it was Aparna?"

"Maybe. Elin was leaving Monday, so she said that if she didn't get to see him, she'd have to wait until she got back from the Lakes this weekend to tell him and she didn't know if she could wait that long."

"Maybe she just called him," I suggested.

"Or maybe that's why I didn't see her on Sunday. Maybe at the last minute she decided to drive down to Rome."

It was possible; we were only ninety minutes north of the city. "Where she saw Silvio with Aparna and thought he was having an affair and—"

"And what?" Sunny interrupted. "Drove herself back up to Tuscany and shot herself?"

I laughed. "You have a point. Maybe she did drive to Rome, though." I thought it over for a moment. "But then why wouldn't Silvio have mentioned it to the Vice Questore?"

"We don't know that he didn't."

"Sure we do. You said so yourself no one can establish seeing her after Saturday night. If she had driven to Rome, Silvio would be able to." Unless he didn't want us to know that, I thought.

"Good point," Sunny conceded.

"You know what else I don't understand," I began, ready to test out my same question that Mike kept shooting down. "Why did none of her friends up north call here or call Silvio in Rome when she failed to show up this week?"

"That's a really good question."

"Thank you. Mike keeps telling me it's not a big deal."

"That's because he's a man. They never get concerned about anything except whether or not their penis is going to fall off." Sunny topped off both our glasses. "Let's go find out why no one called."

And with that she started walking back up towards the main house. Sunny and I are a lot alike in that neither one of us can sit still and wait for a situation to resolve itself without thinking that there's something we could be doing. In LA, we were always coming up with ideas that we thought we could pursue: A two-woman show, a documentary, a web series, a burlesque troupe. Few came to fruition for one reason or another, but it always helped to temporarily relieve the anxiety to feel like we were doing something. I followed her into the house and up to the second floor where Elin had a small study. Sunny quickly sat behind the desk and turned on the computer.

"Elin's been letting me use the desktop all summer. It's the only computer here with a hardwired internet connection, so it's the only one that's actually reliable and I've had to send new drafts of the script I've been working on." Sunny had found a niche as a writer who could also translate into both Italian and English and was currently collaborating with an Italian director who desperately wanted his script made with an English company. Unfortunately, he didn't speak any English.

She expertly entered Elin's password and continued as she clicked on her contacts, "I know she was definitely going to meet her old agent, Nadia." She did a quick search on the name. "This must be her."

She picked up the phone on the desk and started to dial.

"Wait a second," I stopped her. "What are you going to say?"

"That I'm a friend of Elin's and I know they were supposed to get together this past week and I was concerned and wanted to know if she had heard from her."

I thought about it for a minute. "Yeah, that sounds about right. You're really good at this."

"I told you I was a co-star on *Law & Order*."

Sunny dialed again and after a moment, greeted someone in Italian. I heard her begin, "Sono un amici di Elin Corini..." and then launch into her story. I was actually proud that I understood quite a lot of what Sunny was saying and this was after two glasses of breakfast wine. Then Sunny appeared to be listening for awhile. "Sì," she agreed at one point, "È molto strano." Something was very strange and the confused look on Sunny's face confirmed it. Then she bit her lip and looked at me, took a swig from her glass, and said, "Mi dispiace, Signora, ma ti devo dire qualcosa."

I'm sorry, Signora, but I have to tell you something.

I could hear the woman's cries through the phone. She seemed to be telling Sunny something, and Sunny could be heard trying to console her periodically. "Sì, Sì, Signora. Anch'io." Yes, yes, me too.

I turned my attention away from the call, feeling a strange need to give the friend the privacy of her grief. I picked up a photo album from the bookshelf and lay down on the sofa across from the desk, idly flipping through the pictures. It was practically porn for me: Glamorous vintage pictures of the stylish family throughout Italy in better times. A wedding photo of Silvio Sr. and his wife from the late '60s, she in a white mini dress and he in a stylish navy suit; the two of them standing in front of a sculpture at the Guggenheim in Venice for what looked like a fancy party; Silvio underneath an umbrella on the beach in Capalbio with his mother sporting big sunglasses and a large hat. There was one photo of the four of them that must have been from before Silvio was kidnapped. His mother was holding Antonio, who was just a baby. Silvio was seated at the table coloring, his face free from scars, his father seated next to him, teaching him to write. His hair was much lighter, and those dark eyes were less troubled.

I heard Sunny say her goodbyes and put down the phone.

"That poor woman," she lamented. "I just felt someone should tell her. Elin's married to a wealthy man. It's bound to make the papers."

"You did the right thing. She shouldn't have to read it."

"I should probably ask Silvio if he wants me to call people for him, now that I think about it. He shouldn't have to do this over and over." She paused. "No one should."

I nodded and waited for her to tell me what she had learned.

"So," she started, switching tones, "this is interesting. Nadia got a call from Elin's personal secretary who said she wouldn't be making it."

"Who's her personal secretary?"

"She doesn't have one. Nadia said the voice was definitely male, Italian, and that she thought it was strange that Elin wouldn't call herself, but he gave her some story about how she had had to go out of town in a hurry for an emergency. She also said something else that was interesting. A few days before Elin was supposed to leave, she called Nadia to say that she wanted to discuss some opportunities when they were together. According-ing to Nadia, Elin wanted to go back to work and she wanted Nadia to look into hosting gigs for her. She said she saw former models on TV all the time and was interested in doing that."

"Maybe that's why Creepy Ponytail Guy was looking for her."

"Maybe, but it just doesn't make sense. She didn't need to work, and she hated being in the public eye. She was so thrilled to be out of modeling you had to twist her arm to get her to come out of the dressing room and show you what she was trying on."

"Unless she needed the money…" I started. "Was she thinking of leaving Silvio?"

"She loved him. She was thrilled they were going to have a baby."

"Then maybe Silvio's money was gone?" I suggested.

"Antonio does seem to be worried about money, always wanting to sell..." she trailed off, thinking.

"Speaking of selling, the lady at the bar thinks some old man named Fellegi killed her for olive trees, like this is Scooby Doo or something."

I explained my exchange with the woman in the café that morning, proud to point out how well I navigated the Italian language on my own, without Sunny there to help me.

"The family could be having money problems, but I thought Silvio was doing well on his own. He has his own law practice and was doing so well, he started doing charity work. He rarely takes a case for money anymore."

"Well, that'll do it." I paused, thinking back to last night at the restaurant when we were still all laughing, untroubled because Elin was still alive, or at least that's what we thought. "Didn't you say last night that he takes on major corporations and they sometimes threaten his life?"

"Nino did, but he's dramatic. He also thinks the Romani can actually put a hex on you when they steal your shit. The bad luck is that you got your shit stolen. That's the hex."

"Still..." I tried to gently point out the obvious. "Elin is dead."

Sunny just looked at me. The only thing stranger than her husband being right was that someone had killed her friend and that we had to actually consider it a possibility.

"Was Silvio ever worried about it?"

"He told her they were just trying to intimidate him, but," she stopped abruptly here, a guilty look on her face.

"But?"

"It scared Elin. She didn't like it. I think that's why she preferred to be here."

I looked at Sunny. "How can anyone who was actually the victim in a kidnapping think anything is an empty threat?"

"Right?" she agreed. "Maybe he just figured once you've been kidnapped, what are the odds that you'll be the victim of a second violent crime?"

Maybe not you, I thought, but what about your wife?

"We should google some of Silvio's old cases," Sunny suggested.

"Yes, or maybe ask Enzo. He doesn't speak English, but you could talk to him."

"That's a good idea."

"Maybe we should ask around about Old Man Fellegi, too?"

"Really?" Sunny asked in a way that made me wonder if I was getting carried away, the way I usually do when I have two glasses of wine for breakfast.

"Isn't there usually a lot of truth to small-town gossip?" I then added in my head, "As opposed to big-city gossip," which I was becoming an expert on being the subject of.

"You're right, it couldn't hurt," she agreed.

But we didn't get to do any of it because just then, the doorbell rang. We ran to the french windows in Sunny's study to look out and see who it was. Waving up at us was a freshly shaved Vice Questore Patti. We went down to greet him.

Perhaps it was the wine that made us a little too enthusiastic to tell the Vice Questore we'd been doing his job for him. In retrospect, it was probably poor judgment to interfere in a police investigation and then tell said police about it, but for the first time in a while, I actually felt interested in something. Something was able to hold my attention for longer than three minutes, without my mind wandering off into sadness and despair, replaying the last few months, wishing moments had turned out differently, still shocked that they hadn't and that this is where I had ended up. (Although, yes, technically where I had ended up in this moment was an Italian villa—albeit one at the center of a murder investigation—so yes, things could have turned out worse.) I just wish I could have ended up in the Italian villa without having to lose what felt like everything else, first.

Sunny and I sat down at the dining room table with the Vice Questore. Tina brought us all some aqua frizzante, which frankly I was in dire need of after all that wine, and Sunny and I filled Patti in on all that we had remembered and learned: Pietro on the beach, the woman at the bar, old man Fellegi, and everything Nadia had told us. Sunny paused and looked at me. I squeezed her hand. "There's one more thing, Vice Questore. Elin was pregnant."

The Vice Questore nodded and Sunny continued filling him in on everything she had told me, while he made a few notes. When she was finished, he looked up at us both and smiled. "Le signore, I want to thank you for bringing all of this to me. But I have to ask you to not contact anyone else who may be connected with this case and I would prefer you not to discuss it with anyone else either. You don't know who may be involved and what information you may be giving them that could impede our investigation."

As previously said, Sunny and I watched a lot of Law & Order, so we knew this talk was coming. We nodded appropriately.

"Of course you both have my card, and should any other information come your way, please contact me. I want to know whatever you hear. It could be important."

"We will let you know everything we manage to learn without talking to anyone or calling anyone," Sunny confirmed.

"Exactly," Patti smiled, biting into the muffin from the plate Tina had just brought out. Apparently she had decided that the day off Silvio had given her was not conducive to her grieving process.

I wanted to enter Patti's number into my contacts—something about having the number of an Italian police detective at the ready seemed kind of cool—only I had left my phone in Elin's study, so I ran back up to get it. When I got there, I saw that I had left the album out, which I thought was just rude of me. I wanted to be a good guest whether or not my host was dead, so I started to put it back on the shelf. Only I grabbed it by the spine, holding it so that it was facing down, and when I did some photos fell out and scattered down to the floor, a few sliding under the sofa as they landed. "Fuck," I said, probably too loudly to be considered a good guest, which was frankly turning into more trouble than it was worth. Nevertheless, I reached under the sofa for the photos, only with them came a few papers that must have been forgotten under there. I wouldn't have looked at them at all, it was none of my business, even if my host was dead so who could it harm, but it was really hard to miss the piece of paper with the large letters spread out horizontally in a rather large bold font: TI UCCIDEREMO.

That time I had no problem remembering the verb for "to kill."

CHAPTER 10

I carefully laid the piece of paper threatening "We will kill you" on top of the album, so I could carry it downstairs without touching it any more than I already had. Then I grabbed the other papers that had fallen out along with it by the skirt of my dress and placed them on top. I slowly made my way down the steps so that nothing would fall off and placed the album with its stack of papers on the table in front of Sunny and Patti, asking, "Do we have any gloves?"

Tina quickly found the Vice Questore some dishwashing gloves, not that he needed them to see the same words I did. There was more to the note, but not written as boldly: Lascia cadere la querela. I didn't immediately understand the translation, whether because of the wine or my own normal lack of understanding.

"Where did you find this?" Patti asked me. For the first time he looked actually surprised.

"It was under the sofa," I explained. "Along with the rest of the papers. I don't know if they're connected or not. I didn't look at them because I didn't want to get my prints on them."

"Brava," the Vice Questore said to me.

"What's the first part say?" I felt my excellent detective skills with the whole fingerprints issue had earned me the right to know.

This time it was Sunny who answered. "It says, 'Drop the case.'"

I was confused. "Really? I thought, 'cadere' meant to fall?"

"It does," said Sunny. "But here it also means 'to drop.'"

"Oh, good, so it wasn't the wine."

"What?"

"Never mind."

"So, maybe Elin was killed by someone Silvio sued?" Sunny said urgently.

I quickly tried to catch the Vice Questore up. "He's taking all these pro bono cases. Taking on major corporations and getting threats. You know how it is. Poor people taking on international conglomerates— "

"Or whistleblowers!" Sunny added.

"Yes! Like *Silkwood*!"

"Or *Erin Brockovich*!"

"Or *the Informant*!"

"Or the one with fat Russell Crowe!"

"Signore..." Patti interrupted. "Prego, please, leave the police work to the police."

It must have been clear that Sunny and I were way too enthusiastic to do any such thing, because his tone changed and he got very serious. "This is not a movie or a TV show. One woman is already dead. Someone killed your friend and whoever did so is still out there. They have killed once and will think nothing of killing again. Please, leave this alone."

But I had drifted off, wondering as I was whether or not court records were made public in Italy and whether or not I could read them if they were. I think Patti could tell I wasn't listening to him, and probably would have reproached me for it, but just then we heard a crunch on the gravel driveway and a few seconds later a black Mercedes was pulling up in front of the large picture window.

Patti turned to Sunny. "Are you expecting anyone?"

Sunny started to shake her head, which must have jogged her memory because suddenly her face winced in a mixture of alarm and dread. "Oh Shit! My fucking sister!"

Patti just shook his head. "You people have a lot of sisters."

Jennifer Sullivan was an ambitious corporate attorney who never made a goal she couldn't meet, whether it was the Harvard Law Review, making partner at her Manhattan firm, or owning her own vacation home on Martha's Vineyard. She had now thrown the same Type-A, overachiever determination into parenting her only child, a five-year-old girl named Sage who might be evil.

In Sage's defense, Jen had made a fair amount of deals with the devil over the years, making a name for herself helping scumbag corporations poison poor people, and if you had told her she had to have unprotected sex with the devil in order to do it, she would have spread her legs in a heartbeat. So maybe it wasn't Sage's fault that she was going to end up like Keanu Reeves in *The Devil's Advocate*.

Sage loved negative attention. I had met her once before, briefly, when our stays at Sunny's in Rome had overlapped for the night. Not quite three years old yet, I watched her spend the entire evening doing things she knew she shouldn't be doing, but only if she thought someone was watching. She would start to draw on the wall, look around, and if no one was watching she'd give up, only to go back to it when she had someone's attention. This was repeated throughout the night as she stood on the cocktail table, turned on the stove, and walked out the door and onto the streets of Rome.

(Perhaps you're wondering why I didn't stop her myself in any of these endeavors, but like Sage, I waited until someone was watching her. Disciplining other people's children is not something I enjoy doing. Parents have all their own rules about how they like their children to be talked to and disciplined and I'm not getting in the middle of that. Plus, Jen has a completely contradictory set of rules and boundaries for her daughter all laid out according to whatever bullshit parenting books she's reading at the moment in an effort to raise "a strong, independent female," as she keeps insisting to Sage that she is, which may be why Sage thinks it's perfectly safe to wander the streets of Rome alone.)

But perhaps the creepiest thing about Sage was how she stared you down if you had her mother's attention and she didn't. If you were talking to Jen (something I try to avoid at all costs anyway) and Sage came over, she would stare at you until the conversation was over. Jen herself was oblivious. But Sage would just lock her unsmiling eyes on you until you wrapped it up, which as I said, wasn't such a bad thing to have to do. In a way the spooky kid was doing me a solid.

Jen was out of the car and inside the door without even knocking or ringing the doorbell. "Sunny, I need cash! You didn't tell me the car service didn't take credit cards!"

"I think what you meant to say was, 'Thanks for booking my car on such short notice, Sunny, even though I've practiced law all over the world and therefore should be more than capable of booking my own car service and asking if they take American Express. I'm sorry I switched plans on you and gave you no notice that I was coming.'"

"I told Nino," she said, showing no remorse.

"Nino barely speaks any English!" Sunny yelled back at her sister. "You could tell him you were serving him a dinner of cooked children and he would just smile and say, 'Yes, is very good.'"

Jen fired back childishly, "His English is a lot better than yours! Where are you going?"

"To get my wallet! Or did you expect me to pay the driver in blow jobs?"

The Vice Questore decided now was a good time to take his leave and I thought I should probably follow, before Sage got out of the car and stole my soul.

I walked across the lawn and past the pool to the guest house. The heat outside was already reaching an unbearable level and I was grateful for the cool dark of our room, even if Mike was snoring. Have I mentioned they have the world's best shutters in Italy? They're these aluminum affairs that seem better suited to tornado country, and they shut out all light as if it's a nation of vampires. They're perfect if you're jetlagged, have a cocaine problem, or have just been drinking at ten a.m. because you practically witnessed a murder the night before. I lay down on the bed next to Mike and shut my eyes just in time for him to roll over and say, "What's for lunch?"

CHAPTER 11

Not wanting to bother Sunny any more—and also not wanting to get in the middle of her and Jen—we decided to head out to the beach club on our own. I'm the type of person for whom the phase "resort wear" sends chills of excitement down their spine so I was thrilled to have an occasion to wear a different caftan, this time a simple white-and-navy linen number, as well as enjoy some relaxation by the sea, and also some more of that delicious bottarga. We were in luck: They also had fresh oysters that day.

I felt like the biggest impostor when we pulled into the covered parking, but when I told the man in my best Italian, "Siamo gli ospiti di Signora Corini," he nodded, even though Signora Corini was no longer among us and therefore not in a position to have guests. Perhaps the news hadn't reached the beach yet.

We were halfway across the lot when The Husband realized he left his hat in the car and started to go back for it. "You're going to need the keys," I reminded him.

"I didn't lock the car."

"No, but I did."

"Why'd you do that? There's nothing in the car."

"Technically there's your hat."

He sighed an exasperated sigh but knew he had never won this argument and never would.

We opted to sit at the restaurant this time, instead of heading straight to the cabana. Mike said he thought it would be quicker, and when I looked over to the Corini's spot and saw Aparna lying face down on a lounge chair, the ties on her top undone to avoid tan lines, I didn't argue.

We ordered a dozen oysters, a linguini with clams and bottarga, another bottle of the Vermentino from the day before, and some fried anchovies and vegetables, too. The Italians do the most amazing things with fried food. They have this way of delicately battering things so that they come out so light and crisp the food almost tastes healthy when you eat it. Mike orders as much as he can in Italy and then talks about it the rest of the year back in LA, like it's the girl who got away.

The waitress brought us a large bottle of acqua minerale which we quickly drank, the humidity becoming oppressive and depleting, despite the sea breeze. I started to fill Mike in on what he had missed that morning: The call to Elin's agent, our talk with Vice Questore Patti, and finding the threatening note. For the second time that day, my husband said, "Maybe we should go."

"You heard Silvio: The Vice Questore doesn't want us to."

"I know, but maybe as soon as he says it's OK, we should get the fuck out of here. This is getting weird. It's one thing if Elin was the victim of a mugging, a random act of violence. That's terrible, of course. But if she was killed on purpose, for some other reason…? Who knows if we're safe?" he pointed out.

"No one wants to kill us," I waved his concern away with an empty oyster shell. "No one in this country anyway."

"No one wants to kill us in America either. Then, what would everyone have to talk about at dinner parties?" I appreciated the joke and even more so appreciated that it was my husband making it. For one of the funniest people I know, he doesn't joke around nearly enough, and neither one of us had much to laugh about these last few months. The reminder gave me pause and I felt of wave of sadness off in the distance, like I was standing on the shore looking out at a storm front that might come this way or might just blow out to sea.

In an effort to distract myself, I ate another oyster, letting the briny liquid mix with the creamy flesh and the cold acidity of the wine. Stay in the moment. Focus on the trip. I closed my eyes, so the culinary perfection of that moment could wash over me before I continued. "Besides," I said, returning to the original topic. "It looks like whoever killed Elin was doing it to get at Silvio over a legal case or something."

"We don't know that. We don't have a lot of facts." He looked me right in the eyes before continuing, "And I think it's best if we try not to get them either."

"What's that mean?"

"Don't get involved. We came here to get away from drama. As far as I'm concerned, we're still on vacation and we should just enjoy it. OK?" He smiled and held up his glass for a toast.

"Agreed." We clinked glasses and he added, in that grouchy way I must find irresistible, "I spent a lot of money to come here so we could relax and have fun, not so you could chase a murderer like you're in some Lifetime Movie."

With that we finished our lunch, a remarkable mix of the salt and the sea along with the earthy richness of the pasta and oil, all of it united perfectly with the crisp white wine. We topped it off with an affogato, an espresso with a scoop of gelato, the only way to drink espresso in this sticky heat. We then headed to the cabana, as I was now significantly buzzed enough to make small talk with the stranger who may or may not be the murdering sister of the stranger whose house I was staying at.

Only when I started heading in that direction, I saw something that made me stop suddenly. Aparna was talking to a man and it was none other than the Creepy Ponytail Guy, Pietro, whose outfit was no less put together than yesterday.

"Mike!"

"What?" he asked annoyed, as my sudden stop had caused him to smack right into me.

"It's Aparna. Talking to the creepy guy from yesterday."

"So?" he replied, indifferent. "He's probably still looking for Elin."

"Don't you think she would have told him Elin's dead?" I looked at their body language. She appeared to be laughing flirtatiously and he was smiling.

My husband, on the other hand, was growing exasperated. "I don't know. I don't know this person. No one does."

"Exactly."

"I told you, don't get involved."

"I'm not involved. I'm just thinking," I protested.

"Well stop. I'm not paying for us to think. Have another drink."

We continued towards the cabana, trying to act like none of this was any big deal, like we used a dead woman's cabana along with her maybe-fake sister-in-law and her definitely freeloading ex-boyfriend all the time. I put down my bag on another lounge chair and approached Pietro with my hand out.

"Pietro, sì?" He nodded and shook my hand as I continued, "Sono Kat. Ci siamo incontrati ieri. Lui è il mio marito, Michele." I motioned towards Mike before turning to Aparna. "I don't think we formally met last night. We're Kat and Mike. We're friends of Sunny, who I think you did get to meet last night?"

Aparna nodded. "She was very helpful to me. Under the circumstances."

"Yes," I agreed. "It's just awful about Elin, isn't it?"

"I know." She looked down, going for an air of solemnity. Pietro, too, looked down and nodded.

"So," I started, looking between the two, "how do you two know each other?"

They exchanged a glance that I wish I could say was a precursor to a confession, but I can't really say what was behind it. And it only lasted seconds before Aparna said, "Oh, we just met. He came by looking for Elin." She looked at me with a serious face. "I had to tell him what happened."

Then why did it look like you were flirting, I wanted to ask. Of course, I was married, so maybe I had just forgotten what flirting looked like.

At the mention of Elin's name, Pietro again nodded gravely and said, in Italian, how sorry he was. He then gave a slight bow in Aparna's direction and muttered, "Grazie, Signora," before heading off across the beach.

I thought it was weird that Pietro would once again come to the beach looking for Elin, especially after Sunny had told him that she was out of town. I also thought it was weird that Aparna and Pietro would spend so much time talking if they didn't know each other, especially when I had never heard Pietro speak a word of English or Aparna speak a word of Italian.

CHAPTER 12

After that exchange, Aparna went back to getting her line-free tan and not talking to us. I encouraged this by taking out my Kindle as Mike went off for a walk to get some pictures. But eventually I got aggravated with my vacation read; it seems every protagonist is effortlessly finding herself pregnant or tragically finding herself barren, as if those are the only plot points open to women, or at least the only ones society values. Was it any wonder that losing a pregnancy was devastating, when the rest of the world told you that no matter what else you achieved in life, this was the only thing that mattered? Although it wasn't like I had a career at the moment either to be proud of. Why don't women in books effortlessly find themselves promoted to CEO or discovering a cure for cancer? Why are our heroines never "tragically" childless and rich, vacationing on an island somewhere? And why did I never notice this before? What if I was never able to feel happy again, at least in my real life, the one I was going to have to go back to? I was going to have to go back to it, right?

I had no answers, easy or otherwise. So it was out of desperation that I tried to strike up a conversation with Aparna. "I hope Pietro wasn't bothering you, was he?" I tried to draw her out. "I've heard he can be a little unsavory." Unsavory? Since when did I use that word? Was it because I was talking to a British person? Would I be going to the "loo" next?

"Him? I've handled worse," she shrugged, reaching into her bag and grabbing a cigarette. "Did you see the way he was dressed? He wouldn't want to get his pants dirty."

I laughed in agreement. "He does dress well. And he's easy on the eyes, too."

"Yeah, if you like that sort of thing," she muttered.

"What sort of thing?" Keep 'em talking. That's what the cops always say.

"Soft guys who care more about their clothes than you do."

"I thought that was all Italian men?" I joked.

"Exactly," she exhaled a long puff of smoke. "It's why I hated living in this country. I had to leave just to get laid."

"You used to live here?" Now this was interesting. "When?"

"Yeah," she said, starting to seem evasive. "For a little bit, when I was younger. What about you? You speak very well. Did you live here?"

I was torn. As a narcissist I wanted to take the compliment. But as a skeptic, I thought she was just trying to get me off the subject. Also, there was a third part of me who kind of liked Aparna in spite of everything. She seemed fun and she was making me laugh.

"Should we get a bottle of wine?" I asked, as I saw the waitress was walking past the cabana again.

"Sure!" she answered. The waitress came around to take our order and there was a pause before I realized Aparna was waiting for me to order with the waitress. I allowed the waitress to reply to me in Italian, before turning to Aparna and asking, "Does that sound OK to you?"

"Oh, I didn't understand a word," she explained. "I swear the only word I know is 'Sì.'"

I smiled and wondered if that was true. I started devising tricks in my head. Maybe Sunny and I could say something terrible about Aparna in Italian and see if she picked up on it or not. I made a mental note to revisit that later.

"How old were you when you lived here?" I started to ask, only just as I did, Mike came back with Nino and the four boys: Marco, Luca, and Paola's sons.

"We're going to get a beer back at the bar," Mike announced.

"Sì," explained Nino. "Sunny is on her way with Jen."

"We have wine coming," I suggested. But they both shook their heads.

"Io lo capisco," I smiled. I understood. No one wanted to be here for the carnage that would be Sunny and her sister. "I can keep an eye on the boys until she gets here."

"I can help," Aparna surprised us all by offering. "I used to be a nanny."

I made a mental note of this as well. "Is that why you lived in Italy?"

"No," was all she said. I gave up and decided to focus on making sure Sunny's kids didn't drown.

Fifteen minutes later I had safely delivered them into the custody of Sunny, who was already so annoyed by her sister, I'm not sure she was a fit parent at that moment. As if to prove my point, she sat down, poured herself a glass of wine, and when Jen said, "Sunny, should we be drinking if the kids are in the water?" she responded with, "Let that lifeguard work off some of that pasta he eats all day."

"Have you slept at all?" I leaned over and asked her.

"A bit. Sage needs a nap at the exact same time every day, which is why we missed lunch." I looked at her knowingly, so she knew that I heard what she was really saying: Her sister was a controlling bitch.

Sage, meanwhile, had run straight to the water as there was now an audience of adults to tell her not to, and Jen soon chased after her, after explaining that she likes for her to be independent and make her own decisions.

Sunny gave her the finger as she ran down the beach, and then turned to me. "So, I was thinking we should go out to dinner tonight and leave Silvio some privacy at home."

"Yes, please."

Sunny looked to where Aparna was lying and looked to me, tilting her head in a question. I answered by shrugging my shoulders and nodding.

"Aparna," she called. "Do you want to go to dinner with us tonight?"

"Holy Christ, I'd love to! I want to give poor Silvio his space, and Antonio is not exactly thrilled by my presence. You should have seen him when Silvio told him. He's got some temper." She turned to us then, as if wanting to confess something. "It wasn't my idea to come here. I'm really not a bad person. But Silvio, he wanted me—" she paused here searching for the right word, and hesitated, as if she couldn't believe it herself. "Well, at first I thought he wanted me out of the way—you know, to hide me —but then it seemed like he wanted me away because he was, well, concerned for me."

"Well," I offered, "he was kidnapped. Maybe he was worried that if someone found out you were a Corini, they would come after you, too."

Sunny nodded. "Nothing like being kidnapped and almost murdered as a child to make you a little paranoid."

Aparna lit a cigarette. Something was bothering her. "You don't really think someone may be coming after me too, do you?"

Not just someone, I thought, but your new half-brother, Antonio.

"Of course not," Sunny lied, pouring Aparna what was left of the wine. "I'm going to make a reservation for us at the farm tonight. You'll love it. It's illegal."

CHAPTER 13

On the way back to the villa, Sunny explained that the farm served a delightful outdoor meal of food that they cooked and raised and grew themselves, but we had to call them a few hours early so they knew how many chickens to roast. Of course, as this was an under-the-table enterprise—as many were in Italy—you couldn't just google the number, but rather the cell number of a guy got passed around among friends. This was exactly the kind of Tuscan experience Mike and I were looking for.

When we arrived, Paola's Audi was in the driveway, Fabrizio the driver standing outside of it, having a cigarette. Paola was stationed again on the patio, cigarette and drink in hand. This time when she offered me a drink, I declined. Instead I grabbed a glass of water and headed back to my room to nap off the day's excessive drinking and drama and wash off the heat. As I walked away, I heard Sunny invite Paola and the kids to the farm for dinner. Unlike the night before, Paola accepted and said she was going to send Fabrizio home.

I still didn't know what to make of Aparna. As I showered, I went over what I knew. She had lived in Italy, but didn't say when. Said she didn't know Pietro, but seemed to talk to him for an awfully long time. Was she really Silvio's sister, or was she some con artist? And if she was a con artist, did that have anything to do with Elin's murder? She did seem genuine when she said it wasn't her idea to intrude up here, which made me want to believe she was Silvio's sister, or that she believed she was. Was it possible someone was trying to kidnap Aparna and killed Elin instead? But why kidnap Aparna and not Antonio if you wanted

Silvio to pay a ransom? Wouldn't he be far more motivated to pay for the sibling he'd known all his life and not the one he just met? I then remembered what Sunny had said the night before about no one liking Antonio and thought of her own relationship with Jen. Maybe not.

And maybe you would want to kidnap Aparna instead of Antonio if you were Antonio and wanted her out of the way....

I kept forgetting that given the information we had, Antonio had the most to gain from Elin being dead: his brother wouldn't be as reluctant to sell off their properties. And Antonio also had the most to gain from Aparna being out of the picture. No matter who the target was, I kept coming back to Antonio.

I got out of the shower and wrapped my hair in a towel before taking advantage of the most awesome shutters in the world and drifting off almost immediately to sleep.

I woke up an hour later and dressed, trying to find something that was appropriate for dinner at a farm. Pants were out of the question; it was still far too hot. I settled on a cotton dress with a bold geometric print. The heels were probably overkill, but flip-flops would have ruined the line of the dress.

Sunny and Nino had to take Jen, Sage, and Aparna in their car, so it was decided that Paola would ride with us along with all four boys squished into the back seat, which never would have passed American safety standards, but I had a feeling neither would the place where we were going to eat. That didn't mean it wasn't absolutely fine.

Right as we were getting into our cars, we saw Enzo coming down the hill from the olive grove. I thought he seemed worried about something, and a second later I felt stupid for even thinking that. Of course, he must be worried about everything! One of the people he had worked for had just been murdered and the killer was still out there. Plus, I was sure the presence of all these people, foreigners no less, speaking English with their screaming children, was probably unnerving to him. This was undoubtedly a terrible time for him, too; he must have been as fond of Elin as everyone else. It wouldn't have been unheard of if he was just in shock to begin with, but he seemed particularly surprised to see Paola there and the two exchanged a few words as she got into the car.

"I guess he saw Fabrizio leave and thought we had gone, too." At that, all four boys started fighting over who should sit on whose lap, and Paola yelled something to her own two boys in Albanian. "Maybe I should have kept Fabrizio and had him drive us," she apologized, "but I wanted to give him the night off."

"What about the aunts?" I asked. "Don't they hate to eat alone?"

Paola smiled and shook her head at the thought of the old ladies' eccentricities. "They've been on sedatives all day, after they heard the news about Elin. They are convinced there is a curse and Silvio Sr.'s spirit is not at rest." She made a tired face. "I do not understand all this superstition. In Albania we were communist country, so we have no religion."

"Another benefit of communism," I joked, like an entitled American asshole who really doesn't understand anything.

"The only one," Paola said more seriously.

After only five minutes in the car, we followed Nino as he turned down a dirt road and parked in front of a barn, next to half a dozen other cars. It was still light out; the sun had not quite set yet and as we walked behind the barn, we could see light the color of an egg yolk as it descended over a large green field, turning to red as it did. Red sky at night: Tomorrow was going to be another hot day. Sunny's oldest son, Luca, carried a ball as he ran with Paola's two boys towards the grass where two soccer goals had been set up. Marco followed behind them, but Sage hung back.

"Sage," Jen started, "don't you want to play with the boys?"

Sage just fixed her eyes on Jen and said in her dispassionate yet somehow demanding voice, "I want you to play. I don't want to be the only girl."

Jen knelt down in front of her daughter. "Lots of times in life we are the only girl, but we can't afford to walk away. You know who Hillary Clinton is, right? Remember how we had a lemonade stand to support her campaign...?"

Sunny looked at the rest of us and said, "Jesus Christ, I need some wine."

Alongside the soccer field was a patio with a dozen tables of varying length, covered with mismatched tablecloths and napkins. We sat down and were offered a small wine list of only local wines. Sunny yelled across the table to her husband. "Nino, pick a red and a white. And don't worry about what we're having. Tonight, we're eating everything."

She wasn't wrong.

The night started with a plate of house-cured meats and local cheeses. A basket of fresh baked bread came out. As there were twelve of us, several dishes of each were served to our table which we then passed around family style, or as they just call it in Italy, dinner. After the salumi came a bucatini in a simple wild boar ragù, followed by those chickens we had to call about. They'd been cooking on the rotisserie for hours; the meat was moist and tender and as it was placed in front of you, a perfume of rosemary and garlic greeted you. After that came a plate of grilled sausages, all "fatto in casa"—made in house. They passed around contorni—side dishes—of stuffed zucchini flowers, which were in season, and the most amazing roasted potatoes I have ever had in my life. I don't know what it is with the Italian potato. Maybe it's all the volcanic soil. But I've never had potatoes cooked quite like this. They're so simple. Just

Yukon gold potatoes roasted in the oven with salt, pepper, olive oil. Sometimes rosemary, but not even that every time. They are browned just perfectly, and the taste is out of this world. I can't explain it and I can't replicate it at home, and I'm a good cook. But my potatoes just taste like air compared to theirs. I don't know how they do it.

The kids had run back to the field to kick around the ball some more and Nino had joined them, teasing Sunny as he went that he was going to cheat on her with his "first love."

"This mistress doesn't just break your heart," she said to me. "Last year she also broke his ankle and he was in a cast for months. It was like I had three kids."

At the mention of kids, she looked at me, then looked around. Mike had just gone out to take photos of Nino and the boys on the soccer field, and the potential sisters-in-law, Paola and Aparna, were making awkward conversation across from us— although it seemed to be getting somewhat less awkward since they had just refilled their glasses.

"I feel bad that I haven't asked how you're doing."

"Please, Sunny, you have so much going on right now."

"So do you," she smiled kindly.

I didn't know what to say so I stalled. "You know…"

I knew Sunny did know, both from her own experience and from being the person I could FaceTime with when I was awake and tearful at three o'clock in the morning, the nine-hour time difference between Rome and LA being our friend in those moments. But at some point, what's left to say? Or rather, what can you say that you haven't been saying for the last couple of months? I was like a political candidate, repeating the same talking points over and over, with nothing actually changing. The only difference was that I was *trying* to change: Get a new job, replace the baby I lost, or just get over the one I did. But nothing was actually changing.

"You're going back into a shoulder stand after sex, right?" she asked.

Just then Paola sat down and joined the conversation. "Yes, you totally have to do this. You will get pregnant like that." She snapped her fingers.

"And Paola only has one ovary," Sunny pointed out.

Paola nodded in confirmation while I looked around for Aparna who had disappeared and wondered why it was Paola already knew what we were talking about. I mean, she knew because Sunny had told her obviously, and I tried to figure out why I minded. I liked Paola, and I appreciated her directness. Plus it felt good to be open with people for once. And it was Sunny's openness about everything that made her such a good friend. But the last time I had chosen to let friends in about my pain it hadn't gone so well, and I think that's why I felt wary when Paola started discussing it.

"How many kids do you want?" she asked me.

I didn't know. We hadn't wanted "kids," that abstract concept that people think it's perfectly acceptable to ask you about at dinner parties; that major life decision that you're supposed to be able to make even though it's absolutely irreversible and you lack the necessary information to make the choice until it's too late and you've already made it. We hadn't wanted "kids." But we had wanted that one.

No doubt feeling left out, Jen moved herself down from the other end of the table, where she had been watching Sage break down gender barriers on the soccer field.

"What are you guys talking about?"

"Best ways to get pregnant."

"Oh, you just gotta do IVF," said the woman with the salary in the high six figures. "Trust me, I had like three miscarriages trying to do it on my own."

And there it is. Jen continued but I had stopped listening. Because this is why I don't like to discuss it, this is what happens. Everyone wants to share their inspirational story. I get it; I did it, too. You want to tell the person not to despair. Your friend had a miscarriage and three months later she's pregnant again. You ask if they've tried acupuncture, or giving up gluten. You just want to help. But it's no help if they try acupuncture and give up gluten and three months later they're not pregnant again. Or six months. Or more.

I gave Sunny a look and being the solid friend she is, she handled it... in her way.

"Jen, no one wants to hear about your three miscarriages. Maybe you shouldn't have spent your twenties with anorexia and a coke habit."

"I was studying!" said Jen, who didn't deny it.

Luckily the men and Aparna were returning so that line of discussion ended, and the waitress brought over the final course: A large, uncooked T-bone steak that had been cut up and sliced thin. They then brought a hot stone to the table and left it there. I looked from the plate of raw meat to the still hissing stone, but before I could ask, Paola stood up and expertly started grilling the meat on the stone, passing around red and pink pieces to the people who liked theirs medium rare, leaving other cuts on to cook longer for those who didn't.

With all of the meat cooked, Paola finally sat down to enjoy hers.

"It's nice to be out enjoying dinner with adults." She smiled, and I could see why she had been crowned Miss Albania. "It's usually just me and the boys with le vecchie," she lamented, referring to the old women.

"What about Antonio?" I asked, although I was hesitant to do so. Knowing what I did, that she hated her husband, it felt a little like prying. But if I hadn't known that she hated her husband, it would have been the next logical question to ask, so I thought it would have seemed weird if I didn't. Sometimes it's tiring to be in my brain.

"He is always in Rome for business." I wanted to ask what business he had, considering it was universally agreed he fucked up everything, but she continued. "Even weekends. I thought we'd spend last weekend together, but then all of a sudden on Sunday he gets phone call and says he has to leave, and then I get a call from him saying he has to stay in Rome and won't come back that night." She smiled again and shrugged. "My mother always said, 'Keep them working. This way they won't get into trouble.'"

I thought it would have been rude to point out to her he might very well be getting into trouble and just telling her he was working. And besides that, another thought crossed my mind: Antonio was missing the night Elin disappeared. He had gotten called out of the house suddenly and then at the last minute didn't return that night. Nadia had said a man called to tell her Elin wasn't coming. And Antonio was a man. The person with the most to gain.

Just then dessert came to the table: A bottle of Amaro. We all sat back to sip the bitter, herbal digestif and talk. The kids would run in from the field, cry about what one or the other had done to them, grab a biscotti, and then run back.

I don't want to say we forgot about the fact that we were staying at a murdered woman's house for awhile, but we kind of did. Especially when a white horse wandered out of the stable and started walking from table to table, eating scraps if the patrons weren't quick enough. This was probably the part that wouldn't have passed American safety standards. It was perfect.

Mike and I smiled at each other as the kids squealed and ran over to the horse, wanting their pictures taken with the ghostly equine. It was almost magical, its paleness practically glowing against the sky, which had grown pitch black over the course of the meal. I guess it sticks with me because it's the last thing I remember before learning someone else had died.

CHAPTER 14

It was when Silvio came around the barn from the direction of the parking lot that we knew something was wrong. It wasn't that he looked grief stricken; we expected that. It was more that he was there at all, the tragic widower, a sign of misfortune.

"I'm sorry for interrupting everyone's dinner," he started regretfully as soon as he reached the table. "But I need to talk to Paola."

"Oh my God! Is it Antonio?" the poor woman exclaimed in fear. For a second, it seemed like she liked her husband.

"No, no, Antonio is fine," her brother-in-law reassured her. "But I'm afraid there's been an accident. It was Fabrizio. He was in your car." He paused. "And he didn't make it, I'm sorry to have to tell you."

Paola's face fell. It was obvious she was fond of the young driver. "We just saw him a few hours ago! When did this happen?"

"It looks like he never made it back to the vineyard from my house, but we're not sure. The car went off the road leading to town. It was a while before he was found. The Carabinieri recognized that it was your car, but they couldn't reach anyone at your house. Imma and Assunta were asleep—"

"Thank God," Paola interrupted.

"Yes," Silvio agreed before going on. "Antonio, of course, was already on his way back to Rome. Finally, someone contacted me at the house."

Tears were now running down Paola's face. "Does his mother

know?"

Silvio nodded. "She's at the hospital."

"I should go offer her my condolences," Paola said, getting up.

"Tomorrow," Silvio insisted, placing his right arm on her shoulder. "Tonight, I want everyone at the villa. I already spoke to Antonio. He agrees with me and he says he will return as soon as possible."

Just then a waiter brought a check and handed it to Silvio. Without taking his arm from Paola, he reached out with his left hand and quickly signed it.

Nino spoke up. "Silvio, prego, please let us pay for this."

But Silvio waved him away. "Fa niente. I want us all home as soon as possible."

"But why?" asked Paola. "If Fabrizio was in a car accident, why do we all need to spend the night in the villa?"

Silvio put on a weak smile, as if he was trying not to look as concerned as he was. He looked Paola in the eyes. "Indulge me. Last night I lost my wife. Tonight, a car that could have been carrying my nephews and my sister-in-law was in a deadly accident. I want to go to sleep tonight knowing we're all safe."

"What about the aunts?" I asked, as I thought someone should.

"Enzo will look after them tonight," Silvio explained.

"Besides," Paola said under her breath, "Death himself is scared of those two."

CHAPTER 15

Once again we were back at the villa at night, the specter of death hanging over us. I looked at Aparna, who was sitting on the patio, smoking. She had a look of concern on her face that didn't seem to lessen when the hunting dogs started howling. All of a sudden she got up, said she was tired and going to sleep.

I wondered if she thought she was next.

"There's no reason to think any of these things are connected," Mike insisted on the car ride back to the villa. Silvio insisted on driving his brother's family, so it was just the two of us. "Fabrizio had a car accident. I'm ready to have one right now. Look at these roads. They're narrow, poorly lit—"

"It was still light out when he crashed. If he crashed."

"He crashed. Look, there's no guardrail, no shoulder, zero visibility around these switchbacks, people zipping around corners, coming from the opposite direction..."

"He's been driving these roads all his life," I protested.

"So had Ted Kennedy. Shit happens," my husband argued back.

Unlike the night before however, no one seemed wired from the night's events. Rather, we were all worn out. Sunny was getting Jen and the kids settled, while Paola had just returned from putting the boys to bed in a guest room in the main house. She was having a cigarette before going off to make calls to Fabrizio's family. Nino had poured us all a glass of wine, but after two sips, my heart wasn't in it and so I said my good nights and went back to the guest house.

I got ready for bed. I took off the heels I had stubbornly worn to the farm and put on my PJs. I washed my face and hung up some of the clothes that I had packed that morning when I thought we were going to leave. My bathing suit was still sitting in a corner of the bathroom. Because of the air conditioning it hadn't dried at all, so I opened the balcony door and went outside to hang it on the chair on the deck.

That's when I heard Aparna yelling in Italian.

To be fair, it wasn't yelling so much as stage whispering. She was trying to convey anger, while also not allowing a lot of people hear her. But I could tell she was angry. I could also tell she had picked up more than just, "Sì."

She was below the balcony, her back towards me, facing the valley and I could see through the slats in the flooring that she was on the phone. She must have figured she'd have privacy out here. I wondered why she wasn't making the call from her room, but then remembered the spotty cell reception and made a note to myself that the area under our balcony was a good spot, if not altogether private.

I wanted to know what she was saying. But the anger was making her speak rapidly. I wished Sunny could hear this. And then I realized she could. I quickly tiptoed back into the room, grabbed my phone and hit record, lying down on my belly so I could keep an eye on her through the slats while I held my hand out over the side of the balcony as far out as I dared. I hoped I hadn't missed too much of the conversation.

"What are you doing?!"

Mike was standing in the doorway from the bedroom to the balcony, a glass of wine in his hand. He startled me so much I almost dropped my phone. I made the universal sign for "Shut the fuck up:" One finger angrily placed in front of my mouth while my eyes went wide and shot daggers at him. But it was too late. Aparna had gotten spooked and was walking back to her room.

"Do you want to get me killed?"

"No one wants to kill you," he insisted, lying back on the bed and taking out his iPad.

"Just this afternoon you thought our lives might be in danger."

The Husband shrugged. "I was drinking."

"You're drinking now!" I pointed out.

"What's your point?"

I then told him about the conversation I had overheard Aparna having.

"So?"

"So, she told me she doesn't speak Italian."

"Maybe she's just not that comfortable speaking it with others?"

"She seemed pretty comfortable with whoever she was yelling at."

"Aparna is harmless."

"We don't know that. What about her and Pietro on the beach?"

"That guy is too pretty to murder someone. He'd get his clothes dirty. My money is on Enzo."

"Why Enzo?" I asked suddenly intrigued. Maybe he had been doing some investigating of his own.

"Eh, I just don't like how he looks at me," he yawned.

"That's not exactly evidence," I chided him.

"Well, I'm not exactly a cop. And neither are you," he added.

"Fine. Want to have sex?"

He looked at the clock. "OK. Make it quick."

CHAPTER 16

I clearly needed the sleep because I closed my eyes after our quickie, and it was daylight when I next opened them. And Sage was staring right into them.

"Why are you sleeping so much?"

I picked up my phone off the nightstand. It was a little after ten.

"My mommy's been up since six. She runs. Every day. You don't run, do you?"

I tried to remember if I had any clothes on.

"How did you get in, Sage?"

"The door was open. Your husband probably left it open. My mommy says men don't pay attention."

I couldn't argue with the kid or her crazy mom there. "Why are you here?"

"I'm bored. Everyone just wants to talk about dead people. Who cares? It's not like we can see their bodies."

I forced myself to wake up, if for no other reason than to keep this kid from killing me in my sleep, just so she could see a dead body. "OK, Sage, I have to get dressed. I'll see you at breakfast."

"I already ate. And we don't eat between meals."

"Super. Can I have some privacy?"

I tried to find the perfect outfit to have breakfast in after a second homicide and decided on a short cotton shift dress that I had bought in Rome at a festa on our first night. I brushed my teeth and tried to make my face presentable for breakfast. All of these people were getting to be a drag; I was practically putting on a full face of makeup before coffee. If it had just been Sunny and Nino I wouldn't have bothered, but for some reason I felt compelled to make a good impression on the people who were potential murderers and who I would probably never see again.

I walked out of the guest house, past the pool where the kids were already playing, and up the hill to the patio where the adults were.

The presence of so many people seemed to bring Tina out of her grief, and she was serving breakfast on the patio as if she was running a bed-and-breakfast. She had Renato running cappuccinos out, and she seemed to be handing out eggs made to order.

Mike and Nino (a true Renaissance man who knew almost as much about photography as he knew about wine) were looking at photos on their laptops that they must have taken the day before. I know Mike had gotten some of the Ghost Pony that he was really happy with. Paola was smoking and deep in conversation with Sunny, who was nodding sympathetically. They greeted me as I sat down.

"Am I the last one up?" I asked.

"Aparna is still sleeping," Sunny explained.

At the mention of Aparna, I remembered the recording from the night before and made a note that I had to get Sunny alone to tell her about it.

"And Antonio is still dressing." Paola exhaled a puff of smoke with a huff. "He's like a woman, honestly."

"Sì, amore mia, but I'm worth the wait," Antonio announced, crossing to where his wife was seated and kissing her on the head. He was tall, tan, and slim, with bone structure that belonged on a Roman coin. He looked much more Northern Italian than his brother: His hair was a light brown, bleached almost blonde by the sun in places, and he had blue-grey eyes. His angular jaw was rimmed by a slight beard that had the casual air of being more stubble than deliberate grooming, and his hair was cut short, but full on top, and it fell across his forehead in a boyish way.

He shook Sunny's hand, pulling her in for a kiss on each cheek as he did so, and then did the same to me when we were introduced. I saw what Paola saw in him. I would have married him, too, even if he was a fucking idiot. As it was, I knew there was a good chance he was a murderer and yet in that moment all I could think about was what he looked like naked. I laughed, imagining Sunny's voice responding in my head: "Like a fuck-up who's naked."

I managed to stop looking at his full lips long enough to remember why we were all having breakfast there. I looked him in the eye, because that view was nice, too, and offered my condolences. "I'm sorry for your loss."

"Grazie," he replied, looking down, which gave me a glimpse at just how long his lashes were. I had to look away at something —anything—to not make a fucking idiot of myself. I looked to the other side of the table where The Husband was salting his bacon. Problem solved.

Also, just then, Silvio arrived to take my mind off of wanting to have sex with his brother. And then he punched his brother in that beautiful face.

Looking back on it now, we all should have been more shocked than we were. But he was grieving, and they were Italian. I think in a way Silvio had been holding it together so well for the last day—too well, really—that we all expected something like this to happen.

Antonio, to his credit, did not fight back immediately, but rather moved a safe distance away from his brother to the lawn and started shouting in Italian. Following him to the lawn, Silvio didn't wait for him to finish, but started yelling over him, also in Italian, "Quanto hai messo? Quanto?" Which I knew was "How much?" but it was soon followed by a bunch of other stuff I didn't understand.

Paola stood up and started yelling at them both to stop. "I ragazzi!" she pleaded. "The children." But the brothers didn't stop and only continued yelling.

I turned to Sunny. "What are they saying?"

"How much did you bet to get my wife killed?"

"Holy shit!" exclaimed Mike, finally looking up from his camera. "Does Antonio have a gambling problem?"

"Probably," answered Nino. "He has every other kind of problem."

Paola was now in the middle of her husband and his brother, and she looked a little more sympathetic to the latter.

I remarked on this to Sunny. "She looks like she's rooting for Silvio."

Sunny smirked. "Can you blame her given the circumstances? Besides, it's not that surprising. She used to date Silvio."

"She did?" This was a new and interesting detail in the Corini family tree.

"Yeah. It's how she met Antonio. What can I say? Rich guys and models, right?"

"I wouldn't know anything about either," I sighed.

"Yeah, well looking at this clusterfuck, that may not be such a bad thing," The Husband pointed out, nodding in the direction of the brothers' fight.

Enzo had just run out of the house and was trying to get in the middle, imploring them in Italian.

"What is he saying?"

Nino translated. "He's telling them they are family. And that you must be loyal to family. And that it would break Elin's heart to see this."

"Which is hilarious, because Elin hated Antonio and would have loved this," Sunny whispered.

"Still, Enzo looks like he's going to cry," I observed.

"He loved Elin. And he loves Silvio. Elin always said he was like a father to him."

But despite the intervention, Silvio and Antonio continued their fight, which the four young boys were now trying to participate in.

Sunny called to her children to stop what they were doing; Luca was trying to join the fight and Marco had his penis out again. And Sage picked that moment to announce, blood on both palms like some toddler stigmata, that she had cut herself and Sunny should really watch where she leaves her corkscrew when she's been drinking.

Nino turned to us, no longer interested in the drama of Cain and Abel or the children. "So, my friends. I was thinking now would be nice to do some wine tasting, yes?"

CHAPTER 17

Sunny wanted to get as far away from the madhouse as possible, too, but considering half of the inmates were her family it was going to be a little trickier.

"Normally, I'd leave the kids with Paola, she's cool about watching them, especially after we took her boys all day yesterday. But I know she's so upset about Fabrizio."

"Plus, now there's this thing with her ex-lover and his brother, her husband," I added, a little more salacious than sympathetic. I then felt like a hypocrite and realized I needed to be more careful about that in the future.

We were now sitting by the pool, watching her boys and Sage, whose wounds had turned out to be scratches at best. Mike and Nino were changing clothes and then we'd be off on a wine tour. Sunny and I were desperate to figure out a way that she could go with us.

"Why can't Jen do it?" I paused before adding, "Where is Jen? Because I know she's not watching her daughter who just woke me up."

"She went looking for a decent cell signal. She had to check in with the office."

At the mention of bad cell reception, I remembered Aparna's conversation from the night before. I lowered my voice in case Aparna—who still had not been seen—left her room at any moment.

"That is weird," Sunny admitted. "Get your phone. Let me see if I can understand it."

A moment later I was back with my phone and headphones so that Sunny could have a chance of hearing it over the kids' screams. She played it back a few times, scrunching her face as she did, which wouldn't help her ears at all, but we all do it to help us concentrate anyway.

"It sounds like she's saying, 'I have to come home. I could be in danger.'" She was hesitant. "I think she argues why after that but with those goddamn hounds it was hard to hear anything specific. I thought I heard 'This isn't worth it. We'll find another way,' right before Mike came in."

"This isn't worth it?" Was she thinking about the inheritance? Was she just some con artist pulling the plug on her scam? I was thinking over everything I knew about Aparna when it hit me.

"Sunny! That's it!"

"What's it?"

"The solution. Aparna says she used to nanny. Let's see if she wants to watch your kids."

"You want me to leave my kids with a woman we don't know, who lies about what languages she can speak and may be connected to a murder, so I can go wine tasting?"

"Yes."

"Well, it couldn't hurt to ask."

We walked over to Aparna's door and knocked. No one answered, but instead the door did that thing that you only see in the movies where when someone knocks, the door just gives way and opens, because it was never locked to begin with. Sunny and I looked at each other. We knew this wasn't a good sign. It was usually followed by the discovery of a body. Not another one. Goddammit, there goes our wine tasting!

"Aparna?" we tentatively called, knowing full well that no one was going to answer.

We slowly walked into the room to find to our relief that while Aparna wasn't there, neither was a body—hers or anyone else's. In fact, there didn't look like much of anything; it looked like Aparna had cleared out.

Sunny sighed. "Let me see if I can't throw Tina some extra cash to watch the kids."

On our way back up to the main house, we ran into the Vice Questore Patti walking across the driveway from his car.

"What brings you here, Vice Questore?" I have to admit, I was kind of excited to see him. If he was here it meant there was either new information—or he needed some. "Is it because Fabrizio's car accident wasn't really an accident?"

"Or is it because Aparna just took off which is totally suspicious?" Sunny chimed in.

"Signore, I have cautioned you both to stay out of it." He smiled when he said this, but his voice was wary.

"How are we not staying out of it?" Sunny was getting indignant. "Are we just not supposed to notice when someone disappears without giving anyone a heads up?"

"Leaving them stranded for a sitter?" I added.

"Yes, and leaving me totally stranded for a sitter," Sunny concurred.

I continued, sounding a big indignant myself, "Are we not supposed to know that there's no way Fabrizio would have had an accident in broad daylight on roads that he's driven his whole life, or that everyone knows Paola goes home to eat dinner with the aunts and should have been in that car—along with her children—and that just the other day Fabrizio was complaining that the car wasn't driving right? Are we just not supposed to know that?"

The Vice Questore nodded. "I understand your point. And that is all valuable information. Anything else?"

Sunny and I looked at each other and shrugged.

"Well, Vice Questore, while minding my own business at the beach yesterday I saw Aparna talking with Pietro Romano, although I've never seen him speak English…"

"And she claimed to not speak Italian, although we have a recording of her doing just that," Sunny finished.

"Very well. I will make a note of all of this. In the meantime, I'm here to speak to Antonio."

Sunny answered him first. "You'll find him in the main house. He's just been punched in the face."

"Gambling problems," I concluded.

Did I see the Vice Questore faintly smile at us both before walking towards the villa? Frankly, it would stand to reason. For all his cautioning us to stay out of things, we were really doing a lot of the leg work for him and he should be thanking us.

I looked at Sunny. "Here's the question…"

"Will Tina watch my kids so I can get drunk?"

"That, too, but also, who would want both Elin and Paola dead?"

"Their husbands who were sick of them trying to solve a murder on their very expensive Italian vacation?" Mike, freshly showered and ready to drink Tuscan wines, was standing behind the both of us, shaking his head.

"Aparna left," I announced a little defiantly, as if it somehow justified my getting involved.

"Good for her. She's the smart one. What do you say you and I follow in her footsteps?"

I acquiesced. "OK, fine, I will go wine tasting with you instead of trying to solve a double homicide." We started to walk up to the main house.

"Did you lock the door?"

He moaned. "Yes... Stop asking me that. What's the big deal?"

"For starters, there's a murderer on the loose because you'd rather go wine tasting."

CHAPTER 18

Thirty minutes and a hundred Euros in childcare later, Mike, Nino, Sunny, Jen, and I were all in a car on our way to our first winery. I was a little surprised that Jen would leave Sage with a relative stranger for the afternoon, but I suppose if it was a choice between helicoptering her "strong, independent female" daughter and ruining the afternoon of her "strong, independent female" sister, she couldn't resist the latter.

Nino had taken us back down the hill, away from the town center, through the country roads that divided the vineyards and farmland. But where we normally would have driven straight to go to the beach, we turned off the main thruway instead, taking a dirt road. We drove down the narrow road and pulled up to a wrought iron gate with an intercom. Nino pressed the buzzer, said something in Italian, and the gates opened.

"To start, we will begin at one of the newer, more expensive vineyards," Nino explained. "And then we will go to a family who has been making wine many, many years, that is not so fancy."

We drove up a driveway that cut between two vineyards. Is there anything more beautiful than vines in summertime? Nothing but rows of grapes, the clusters of foliage a vibrant green, highlighted by rays of sunlight. The alternating colors of green vines and brown earth, green vines, brown earth, creating the striped panels on the countryside's quilt. I wanted to look at just such a vista every day and I was going to make it my life's mission to see that that happened. I just had to figure out how to get my cats on a plane.

At the top of the driveway was a large terracotta building with a tiled roof and a gigantic wrap-around patio that provided the most stunning view of the vineyards below and the sea just beyond them. Our guide was already waiting for us outside, which was impressive as once again, the heat and the humidity were stifling. I couldn't imagine drinking red wine in this weather, but somehow I would have to persevere.

Nino greeted the guide, a petite woman in her early thirties with a jet-black bob. She introduced herself as "Francesca" in perfect English and then apologized, saying her English was not that good. Francesca led us back down the driveway briefly, in order to point out the various vineyards and which grapes grew there. She then brought us back up to the house and around the back, where two large, barn-sized doors stood open. Explaining this was where the trucks brought the grapes to be crushed after vendemmia, the harvest, she led us through the open doors into a large garage-like space filled with machinery, and past that into a cool dark hallway which I assumed would lead to the cellar.

The slight chill was welcome after the heat of the vineyard, and my attention started to drift off as we passed through one tiled room after another containing large stainless-steel vats. As Francesca explained the fermentation process to us, Nino was still nodding sagely, but Mike moved away to take photographs and Jen very unabashedly took out her phone.

"Oooh, Wi-fi!" she squealed. "Holy shit, I have four bars!"

Sunny shushed her but I could tell her heart wasn't in it and that deep down she, too, would be thrilled to find such a strong signal after putting up with the unreliable service at the villa.

We went through the barrel rooms, hearing the differences between Slovenian oak and French, barrels and barriques, all while Jen answered work emails. Finally we started going up again, and Francesca led us into a sunny tasting room with a large oak table that stretched the length of it. One side of the room was a balcony that looked out over into the barrel room we had just come from. The opposite side was a large picture window that overlooked the estate. The table had been set for us, with five wine glasses set out at every place setting and a large platter of charcuterie in the middle. Jen, Sunny, and I sat on one side with Nino and Mike on the other.

Francesca poured us a very generous tasting of each wine, explaining what we would be tasting, and then invited us to try them for ourselves side by side and explore how they changed when mixed with the fattiness of the meats and cheeses. We were eager to oblige.

After a few minutes, she said something to Nino in Italian, and I could tell talk had turned towards Elin's murder. I tried to feel better about it by telling myself that it was in the public interest to want to discuss a murderer at large, and not just people rubbernecking through the tragedy of others. It dawned on me that we must be celebrities in a small town like this: A high-profile murder had happened, and we were close enough to it to have information, but not so close that it would be in poor form to ask. And then I realized that we weren't celebrities so much as Kato Kaelin, the freeloading hangers-on, and that sad truth almost killed my nascent buzz.

With Nino talking to Francesca and, more importantly, Mike distracted by taking copious notes on the wine as well as copious pictures of it, I used the opportunity to turn the talk on my side of the table to the murder, too. Specifically, Aparna's recent disappearance.

"Do you think she thought she was going to be the killer's next target?" I asked Sunny. "I mean first Elin gets killed, then someone comes after Paola... It could have been Antonio, you know, who wanted all of them dead. Elin and Paola. Maybe he has life insurance on her. Do they have that in Italy?"

"Yes," answered Jen.

"They do? Then why don't Nino and I have it?" Sunny wondered.

"Well, at least you know he'll never try to kill you," I reassured her.

"I don't know that Antonio would try to kill anybody. He's really not that much of a go-getter," Sunny vacillated. "But he does have money problems, and you heard Aparna say he wasn't thrilled about the idea of her."

I agreed with her. "But why is he so threatened? I mean what can she really do about it? Think about it, just because she's Silvio Sr.'s daughter doesn't mean anything if he left everything specifically in Silvio and Antonio's names. Then Aparna is pretty much screwed, right?"

"Before a few years ago, maybe," Jen began, in what was turning out to be the most interesting conversation I had ever had with her thus far and probably ever would. "Italian estate law guarantees that the deceased's heirs will receive a portion of the inheritance, even if the deceased tried to will it away from them."

Sunny looked at her sister, incredulous. "So no matter how many times I tell Marco not to take his penis out in school and he does it anyway, I can't disinherit him?"

"Nope," Jen finished her Vermentino and moved on to the first of her four reds before continuing. "Also, a few years ago, Aparna wouldn't have had any claim being born out of wedlock, but that law changed. Which may be why they haven't seen her until now."

"So is this what you've learned in international law? I just always thought you were taking advantage of poor people," Sunny stated bluntly, well into her third wine.

Jen ignored the comment. "There's quite a few people bene-fitting right now from these murders. One of the firm's group emails that just went out was about a class action suit being a postponed because the attorney, one Silvio Corini, is on grief leave. But they can't postpone too long or else the statute of limitations will run out."

"Oh, my God, that's just like that note you found before Jen got here yesterday!" Sunny exclaimed, as she smacked my shoulder and then quickly filled Jen in on what had happened. Jen lis-tened but only said, "Maybe I need to recuse myself from this conversation."

"You did have motive and opportunity, Jen," Sunny told her sis-ter. "And you did change your plans awfully last minute."

"Jesus Christ, you are never going to let me forget that," Jen re-sponded, which wasn't a denial.

The five wines I was tasting were catching up with me, and one sister accusing the other of murder seemed like the perfect time to go to the bathroom, even if it probably wouldn't be the last time today that happened. I left the tasting room and walked down the hall, taking out my phone and checking email as I did because I needed to see if my Instagram photos had received any likes from people who used to be my friends and could now see how well my life was getting on without them.

The Wi-fi signal here *was* really good.

I know the Vice Questore had told us not to contact anyone in-volved in this case, but he didn't say anything about googling.

The first person I wanted to search was Aparna, but I never got her last name. I did, however, know Pietro's last name, and as it seemed they were chummy that might lead me somewhere. I opened Safari and typed in "Pietro Romano photographer Italy."

I only had a few minutes before everyone was going to think

I had some sort of major intestinal upset, and I didn't want people thinking that: I could hold my wine. But I got lucky. The first half dozen results were for an actual town named Castel San Pietro Romano, which immediately made me suspicious that the name was some sort of alias. But frankly, given everything I knew about Pietro, I shouldn't have needed an excuse to think he was using a fake name. The next result after that was for the Facebook page of a nineteen-year-old gamer. But right after that was a Wikipedia page for a Pietro Romano and I clicked on it.

I was both relieved to find it was the same Pietro Romano, and also put out that this freeloading charlatan had a Wikipedia page and I didn't. I had to remember get my agent on that if I ever decided to go back to my old life. I also had to remember to get an agent. My old one had stopped returning my calls after I lost my last gig, another thing lost. My year so far had a body count.

I wondered why an unsuccessful photographer would have a Wikipedia page even if he did date some famous women, but the sub-topic "Football Betting Scandal and Suspension," answered that question for me. It seems Pietro, just as Sunny said all Italian men would tell you, had played for a Lega Pro team, whatever that meant, but was convicted of match fixing and suspended, which subsequently ended his career. I wasn't surprised that he would be caught up in something of this nature, but at the same time it led me no closer to anything related to Aparna or the Corinis. I made a last-ditch attempt to google "Pietro Romano and Aparna" but only found a bridge in the town of Pietro Romano.

Defeated, I made my way back to the tasting room where what remained of my flight awaited me as a consolation prize. Sunny seemed to have dropped the murder accusations—for now—and Nino and Mike were talking about whether or not to use a flash on a shot Mike was trying to take.

I wondered if the next vineyard would have Wi-fi. I needed to know more.

CHAPTER 19

We drove back through town for lunch before the second tasting. Nino picked a place where the menu was handwritten in the window, an excellent sign. There were only half a dozen or so small tables in the tiny establishment, another good sign. We fortified our stomachs for the next tasting with a gnocchetti with summer truffles and a pappardelle in a wild boar ragù, which we complemented with a Rosso from nearby Montalcino.

There are so many good wines in Italy, it's hard to pick a favorite. I favor reds in general, but they do some amazing things with white wines, too, that can really dazzle the palate on a hot day or while eating oysters or anchovies. But even if I narrow it to reds, I can't talk about why I love one without talking about why I love another. It's like trying to name your favorite band. What genre are we talking about? And what kind of day am I having?

Barolo is like the Beatles. And again, I don't mean that it's the best. It just has staying power and never disappoints. It's a classic. You'd be hard pressed to find someone who doesn't like the Beatles and the same goes for Barolo. And if someone tells you they don't like either, you should definitely ask yourself what is wrong with them.

When asked my favorite wine though, my mind almost always first goes to the Rossos and Brunellos of Montalcino. The first time I drank one it was like the first time I heard David Bowie: This was everything I wanted my music to sound like. This was what I had been waiting for. There's so much going on! The wine has an elegance that is layered with tannins and the taste of raw earth, like Bowie's voice, smooth and velvety against the backdrop of the raw guitar riffs. It's one grape, the Sangiovese, and yet it can be a chameleon, taking on the characteristics of that year's soil and climate. I once did a barrel tasting at a vineyard of that same grape planted in different terroirs: Clay, mineral, volcanic soil, that were all subject to different amounts of wind and sunlight and sea. Each barrel was unique to its conditions, like each Bowie persona was to its era.

Although as soon as that answer comes to mind, I immediately think of the Aglianicos from down south. Bold, big, dirty and tasting of tannins, I once joked that I saw the face of God when I drank one particularly stellar vintage. It's not unlike when I listened to the Doors as a teen and heard Jim Morrison's voice alongside the erotic bass line and sensed there was something sexy and dangerous—which is even more sexy. But you can't discount the indy upstarts, the wines you drink that few people have heard of that make you feel just a little bit cooler for knowing them: The Negroamaro and Malvasia Nera of Puglia; the Nero d'Avola and Nerello Mascalese of Etna Rosso; and the Cannonau of Sardegna.

Of course, your palate and ear may vary.

And to answer your question, I have listened to music recorded after 1990. But everything that's come out in recent years is too much like California wines: Trying too hard to make sure everyone likes it.

Regardless, it was safe to say the red wines from Montalcino were among my top three Italian wines, and I was enjoying both the quality and the price point that being so close afforded us.

Meanwhile, Sunny was checking her phone. "Paola's just invited us to stop by their vineyard on the way back for a drink. She says that she can meet us there with the kids, if we want. I should tell her I want to meet her there without the kids. Why do I want to see them?"

"Is their wine good?" Mike asked.

I could see Nino weighing how to answer that. He finally said, "They just bottle for themselves. They don't make any to sell."

"Why not?"

Nino again weighed what to say, but Sunny beat him to it with her usual honesty. "Because that would require Antonio to plan and follow through on something."

Nino prevaricated. "Ma Sunny, the wine business, it's very hard." He turned back to the rest of us. "Do you know how you make a small fortune in wine? Start with a large one."

At the mention of Antonio's name, our waitress, a young woman in her early twenties with curly, dark hair pulled back in a pony-tail, stopped clearing our plates and instead turned to Sunny, speaking to her in an agitated, rapid-fire Italian. I was happy I followed none of it when I saw Sunny's face fall, a chastened expression spreading across it. Nino, too, was subdued and nod-ded at the woman whose anger turned into tears as she abruptly left our table, the plates still on it.

The restaurant was silent as people looked from us to the wait-ress. One of the cooks called back into the kitchen for help. She had been the only waitress and I wasn't sure she was returning.

"What the fuck was that about?" a now-buzzed Jen broke the silence.

"Here is not the place," was all Nino said. He took out his wallet and we all quickly followed suit, leaving cash on the table and leaving as respectfully as we could.

In silence we walked back down the narrow streets to the car. When we were all finally in and the doors were shut, Sunny filled us in. "That was Fabrizio's cousin. And she does not like Antonio. She called him a bastard who owed Fabrizio money and got him killed."

"See, I told you it wasn't an accident!" I said to The Husband.

"Why did she say that?" he wanted to know.

"She had many ideas," Nino equivocated. "She said Antonio was too poor to keep the car in good condition. That Fabrizio told him it needed work and he refused to have it done."

"That's not murder," Mike cut him off, looking at me.

"It is if Antonio did it on purpose so that his wife would die and he could get the insurance money!" I fired back.

Nino waited patiently for us to finish our marital squabble and then resumed talking. "She also said very bad men were after Antonio. That he had asked Fabrizio to start carrying a gun."

"That's not good." Jen finally spoke. "Of course, it does leave plenty of room for reasonable doubt with your corporate espionage theory, Sunny."

"Jesus Christ, are you planning on being indicted for murder, Jen?"

Jen shrugged her sister's accusations off. "No one plans to be indicted for murder. But a good attorney is always prepared."

"No, that's the Boy Scouts."

I interrupted the sisters impatiently. "What else did she say?"

"That's basically it," Sunny finished. "It wasn't a long conversation and she was mostly upset, saying Antonio would get his."

This exasperated The Husband. "Great! Can we get the hell out of this paradise before the honor killings start?"

Nino turned to him and smiled. "So, my friend, you do not want me to take you to the next winery then?"

Mike answered quickly. "Look, as long as we're already here…"

CHAPTER 20

We were sitting in the modest dining room of an elderly couple, and they were showing us pictures of their grandchildren while we tasted their wine that retails for seventy-five dollars a bottle in the States.

"I thought you said this wasn't so fancy?" Mike asked Nino when he heard this.

Nino looked around at the plastic covering the couch, the homemade chicken-liver crostini in front of us, and the cat who had made himself at home on Mike's lap before responding. "In America, it's expensive, yes. But here it's very affordable... maybe twenty Euros a bottle. And if you have cash, even less!"

The Husband shrewdly did some math in his head while stroking the cat. "I mean, we're going to need wine for the villa anyway, and they've been so hospitable, it would be rude not to buy anything..."

One purchased case of wine later, we were all back in the car, enjoying the scenery as we winded our way through the Tuscan countryside; up a hill, around a corner, and then down around the valley again on our way to Antonio and Paola's. And that's when Jen got sick.

"Nino, can you drive a little slower?" Jen asked resting her forehead on the seat back in front of her. "I'm getting nauseous."

"You're just drunk," Sunny dismissed her.

"I am not! I'm a Sullivan. I can hold my booze."

Nino tried to comfort his sister-in-law. "Jen, it's very, very hot and we drank a lot, plus we are in the car and these roads are very," he paused searching for the English. He finally gave up and muddled on. "These roads are very up and down and side to side."

At the mention of the side-to-side roads, Jen moaned and said she was getting dizzy.

"Not to worry, Jen, we're almost there. I myself lost my senses the other day when I was driving the motorino through Rome in this heat," he reassured her. "I almost had a crash and had to stop at the side of the road."

We pulled off the main road onto a long driveway, which soon divided into a circular drive, in the center of which was a small vineyard. Nino turned to the right, driving the remaining quarter of a mile up to the front of the house, where we could see the driveway turned back around down the other side of the vineyard, leading back out to the main road. It was clearly Antonio's house: In addition to a Mercedes sedan parked in front was a vintage white Ferrari and a Jaguar convertible. He was the only one in all of Europe who hadn't heard of austerity measures.

The house was two stories and made of stone, with a pair of twin archways on both the bottom and top floor, the bottom ones leading to a loggia, the top ones framing a balcony. Behind the villa I could make out a lawn to the right where I could see a converted barn that must have been one of the three houses. Both the lawn and the house were on the edge of even more vines.

As we pulled up front, Sunny spoke in what for her passed as a soothing tone of voice. "Come on, we're here, Jen. Paola can get you some ice water and let you lie down."

But that's when Jen shrieked, "Hives!" and held out her hands. Up and down her hands and arms were red welts. She took a few swallows. "Oh no!" She was full-on panicking now. "Was there fish in that pâté?"

Sunny looked to Nino. "I don't know," he answered uncertainly. "I think sometimes people put anchovies in the fegatini, sometimes they put pork."

"What?!" Jen looked at her sister and screamed, "You're trying to kill me!"

"You'll know when I'm trying to kill you," Sunny said very matter-of-factly back. Up until this point, she was doing a pretty good job of remaining calm. "Where's your Epipen?"

"I left it at the villa."

Sunny was no longer calm. "Why the hell did you do that?!"

"Because I'm a grown woman who knows not to eat fish because this will happen!" Jen argued back.

"Nino, call an ambulance!" Sunny yelled as Jen started hyperventilating, or perhaps losing consciousness. Her husband quickly obliged. At this point Mike had gotten out of the car and gone to get Paola, who came back in a hurry and asked what the problem was.

"It's no problem," she soothed. "We have a kit for the bees. Assunta is allergic, not that she's been outdoors in fifty years." She rolled her eyes as she ran back into the house. She came back a few moments later with a zippered case, which she quickly opened up. "Uno momento, Jen."

Only when she opened the case, nothing was there.

Paola's face was shocked. "I don't understand. It's always here. No one uses this."

At that, Jen started to really gasp. "Benadryl!" I exclaimed, remembering the stash I kept in case the magnificent Italian flora brought on less-than-magnificent hay fever.

"Great idea!" agreed Sunny. I only had a couple of them in my purse, but I handed her what I had. "We need more."

She turned to Paola. "Antihistamico?"

Paola nodded and ran back into the house, while we tried to get Jen to crush the pills we had, in order to enter her system quicker. I thought about snorting a few myself just to relax with all this drama. Paola ran back out with a bottle of cherry-colored liquid, offering it apologetically. "All I had was for the kids." We got Jen to take a couple of generous shots and hoped it would be enough until the ambulance got here.

Whether it was Pavlovian or for real, her breathing did seem to settle down after taking the medication. Knowing how Type A Jen was, all she probably really needed was to feel that she was being proactive about the problem in order to calm down. But whatever it was worked. While still looking nervous, and with a rash now spreading up her neck, she was able to remain conscious until the ambulance arrived.

Once it did, a medic got out to attend to Jen, and Paola greeted the driver.

"He's also the Mayor," Sunny explained.

"Does the honor of driving the ambulance come with the gig, or does being Mayor pay so little he has to take a side gig?" I asked.

"Everyone here in Italy has four jobs." Nino shook his head. "Even our elected officials."

Paola invited all of us inside for a drink, even the Mayor, who hesitated, but then looking back to the ambulance said he should probably go and maybe on the way back. She kissed him goodbye on both cheeks and then told Mike and me that we could have a drink out back where the children were playing. Holy Hell, I had totally forgotten there were children here! I felt so bad for Sunny. I knew she'd want a drink more than ever now, but that she would have to ride in the ambulance with her sister. Sure enough, Nino came in just then and said that Sunny was going with her sister to the hospital to make sure she didn't die, and that Nino was going with the both of them so that Sunny didn't kill her. Because of the space in the ambulance, he was taking the car but would be back for us and the kids.

"Don't be silly," Paola assured him. "Antonio can drive them all."

I wasn't sure I wanted to be in a car with a man who had a price on his head and was most likely a killer, but then she handed me a glass of wine, so I quickly forgot my concern. I also realized that my time being stranded at Paola's could be a perfect opportunity to find more evidence against her husband.

We had gone through the archway and past the loggia, entering the house and a large foyer with exposed wooden beams and a floor of brightly colored majolica tile. To the right was a wide staircase that probably had been very grand, the once-ornate runner down the middle now worn and faded in places. After all the wine and excitement, Mike needed to use the bathroom, so Paola pointed him towards a powder room to the left of the foyer and told Mike and me to meet her out back.

As I waited for The Husband, I examined the photos that adorned the walls of the room. There were gorgeous old black-and-white photos of the vineyard at the turn of the century—the last turn of the century, that is. There was the same photo of the Corini family before the kidnapping that I had seen in Elin's study. There were more modern ones, too: Some formal pictures of Silvio and Antonio as teens, a few modeling shots of Paola, even a picture of Antonio's soccer team. I looked closely at it, one player in particular catching my eye.

It was Pietro Romano.

The photo was from a number of years before, but he looked just as handsome and put together in his jersey and shorts. And he still had that creepy ponytail.

"Juve Stabia," I read off the jerseys. "It even sounds deadly."

"What's that?" The Husband inquired, sneaking up on me for the second time that day.

"Antonio played on the same soccer team as Creepy Ponytail Guy, Pietro. Until, that is, Pietro was suspended for trying to fix the matches in a betting scandal."

"You got all that from a photo?"

"No. Wikipedia. I googled Pietro while we were at the vineyard today."

"I thought we agreed no more Nancy Drew-ing?" He seemed a little put out which was very disappointing as I really thought I was onto something and he should be more impressed.

"No one ever got killed for googling," I protested. "Or for saying it's quite a coincidence that a man with gambling debts and a man who used to fix soccer games played on the same team once and are now in the same town where two murders have occurred."

"Actually, someone could get killed for that," he pointed out.

He wasn't wrong about that and we started down a hallway, off of which was a spacious but darkened living room, a formal dining room, and the kitchen.

"But that does seem highly coincidental..." he granted me. "I mean, I'm not saying that had anything to do with anyone's death or that I think that poor bastard Fabrizio was anything more than an accident..." he started. This was perfect. I knew The Husband well enough to know that anything that was my idea was quickly discouraged, but if it became his idea instead... "But I'd bet good money they were both involved in the game fixing. Rich guy probably just got away with it as always."

"That makes a lot a sense," I nodded, as if it wasn't my idea.

We had come to the end of the hallway, which spilled out into a sitting room with four sets of French doors that opened onto a terrazza where Paola was sitting, smoking and watching the children play.

"I'm so sorry about the Epipen," she reiterated as soon as she saw that we had joined her. "I am sitting here thinking, wondering what could have happened to it. I always make sure to keep it up to date and no one here would have use for it."

"Maybe Assunta took it?" Mike offered.

Paola shook her head. "She's afraid of it. It's why I keep it."

"Well, don't worry about it. It's all fine now. Besides, you've had a tough enough day. A tough enough couple of days really." I added, remembering that she had lost her sister-in-law two days ago, her driver yesterday, and had just, over breakfast, watched her ex-lover punch her husband because he was a degenerate gambler.

Paola must have realized she hadn't seen either of us since that morning and felt she had to address it. "Silvio took off after the fight. He got in his car and drove away. It's understandable. He needs to cool down. He and Antonio, they've done this since they were boys. Antonio gets in trouble. Silvio yells at him. And then Silvio fixes it." For the second time that day she seemed to have more sympathy for her brother-in-law, but who could blame her?

"How did Silvio find out about..." I tried to think of the best way to put it. "...Antonio's current problem?"

"Enzo. It is always Enzo. He is Silvio's informant. You might think it was Enzo's money the way he acts." She exhaled a puff of smoke ruefully. Everyone else adored Enzo, but Paola clearly didn't. It made me wonder if maybe Enzo had informed on Paola about some things, too. Maybe she had as much to hide as her husband. After all, she had a lot to lose, too, if Antonio lost everything. I liked Paola, but as recent events had shown me, my taste in friends could be shit.

Paola looked out to the lawn where her husband had now appeared, walking from the direction of the vineyard with a much older man, dressed in tan slacks and a white undershirt. He took a handkerchief out of his pocket and wiped at his balding head, looking up at the terrazza as he did so. Smiling, he lifted his arm to wave at Paola, which caused Antonio to look up towards us, too. Only he wasn't smiling. Or rather his smile seemed to quickly disappear when he saw us sitting next to his wife. Was that my imagination? Or was Antonio merely embarrassed after that morning's confrontation?

Paola wasn't smiling either. Instead she just shook her head disapprovingly.

"Who is that?" I asked.

"Some old farmer who fills Antonio's head with fantasies. Tells him this land is worth millions of dollars and they are missing out on a terrific opportunity. Antonio thinks he can get rich listening to Signore Fellegi." She shook her head again. "Signore Fellegi, cazzo!" she practically spat.

At the mention of the name "Fellegi" I looked at my husband who returned my look by rolling his eyes and shaking his head.

Meanwhile, Paola was also looking at her husband, her expression a mixture of sad and wistful. "The one thing he doesn't do is cheat on me. Isn't that funny? He cheats at everything else. But I told him I would shoot him if he ever did and I think he believes me. I keep a gun in the bedroom just in case."

Mike looked at her. "You might want to make sure it is where you think it is, just in case you ever have to go for it."

127

CHAPTER 21

It struck me as odd that after insisting we all be together last night, Silvio just let his family scatter to the wind where anyone could have done anything to them. Maybe, now that he thought he knew what the real threat was, he believed he could solve the problem—or maybe he no longer cared what happened to any of them. There was still a third option: That he was so consumed with grief he wasn't thinking clearly about any of it.

I take that back. There was a fourth. Silvio was the murderer and was not concerned because he knew exactly who was in danger and from whom, and last night had been some act.

This was the thought process I was struggling with as I sat in the front seat of the Mercedes in which Antonio, a potential murderer and potential target, was driving me, my husband, and three innocent children home. Well, two innocent children and Sage. OK, one innocent child, Sage, and the little pervert who had taken his penis out right as Assunta and Immacolata were coming down for dinner.

That's when Antonio thought it was best that we all leave. Frankly, I think he saw us as his way out. It turns out, I was right in more ways than one.

He was asking us a lot of questions about what we did for a living, a thing I was always told Europeans never ask.

"Sunny says you guys work in Hollywood," he began.

"Technically it's usually the valley," I corrected him.

Not understanding the nuance, he kept going. "You write for television? How do you like it?"

"If it was awesome, we wouldn't be here," Mike said bluntly.

Antonio took his eyes off the road, which was really gambling all things considered, and turned around to look at him. "You should buy a place here!"

And there it is.

I put him off. "We have a rule: We don't have more houses than jobs. And right now, we have zero of the latter."

"My mother has a second house. She says it's a great investment," Sage chimed in.

"You guys know so much about food and wine, you could buy a vineyard for nothing. Niente. All of these old properties have been in our families, but we don't have enough money to keep them. You could get something for a steal."

I had watched enough *House Hunters International* to know that you couldn't get a vineyard for niente, but Antonio kept going. "Maybe you have some Hollywood friends, you make an investment."

At the mention of Hollywood friends, I caught Mike's eye in the rear-view mirror and we both shared the same cynical laugh. Right now, we couldn't raise enough money to invest in a lemonade stand.

When you find yourself pregnant, everyone tells you not to tell people in case something happens to the pregnancy, which is the most useless piece of advice I have ever heard because if something happens to the pregnancy you have to tell everybody anyway. There's missed work, missed social engagements, and after a while you're too consumed by your own drama to keep creatively inventing lies. The good news is that when you tell a lot of people, they end up surprising you with how loving and supportive they can be.

Those are your real friends.

Then there are those friends who also surprise you with how unbelievably callous and mean spirited they can be. It's not an unusual phenomenon. I've heard more than one story of a person getting life-threatening cancer only to have someone make it all about them and say to their sick friend, "I just don't think I can handle this," or something equally rude. When I finally told my best friend—who I will just refer to from here on out as Cruella (and not only because of her penchant for animal prints)—when I had finally told her what had happened in an email that I still can't read without crying, she responded with a meme that said, "So boring!"

As previously stated, I am a fan of gallows humor. However, as a comedy writer I also know the secret is timing and her timing sucked. I knew it was a joke, but it still hurt my feelings and I said as much. And it just seemed so... childish. Not the response of a forty-something woman whose wedding you had been in. All I wanted was an apology. Instead, I never heard from her again... at least not directly. Instead she started taking every one of my friends to lunch, telling anyone who would listen for the price of free sushi what had happened and how I had "lost it." How she didn't know what to do. It never occurred to her that the thing to do would have been to say she was sorry. And even when that was suggested to her, she decided that she'd rather tell them why I didn't deserve it.

You can say you don't need friends like that, and it's all valid and true. But sometimes I am still shocked by how cold and hateful a person you thought you knew can be, especially when you needed them the most. I suspect I always will be. And I also have to wonder what it says about me. Did I not deserve better? Or were my instincts of who to trust just that bad?

Just then my phone dinged. I was excited to both have a new message and to have a decent signal again, and I got hopeful that it was one of the google alerts I set up at the vineyard for Silvio or Pietro. However, my excitement quickly turned to confusion when I saw it was just a text from my husband in the back seat:

"THIS FUCKING GUY"

I laughed, catching his eye again in the rear-view mirror. He smiled back at me.

And then sometimes all the other conflict falls away and you know what really matters.

Maybe that's why I was so consumed with Elin's murder. Here was this stranger who had opened her home to us when one of our closest friends had let us down. Maybe now I just valued the friends who mattered even more—like Sunny, who had always been there for me, and I'm not just saying that because she also gives me a free place to stay in Italy. I had learned the hard way that not all friends are created equal, and friends like Sunny were invaluable. I wanted to help her if I could to find justice for Elin, an invaluable friend of hers.

"Antonio, you used to play football, right?"

"Sì, senora, but I injured my knee and I had to retire."

I wondered if his knee had been injured accidentally or by some-one else on purpose.

"Did you know Pietro Romano?"

At the mention of Pietro's name Antonio's head turned sharply and abruptly towards me. Unfortunately, the steering wheel also followed suit and for a second we dipped down over the side of the road. Mike kicked the back of my seat. Marco and Luca cheered, "Do it again!" while Sage said coldly, "Perhaps you shouldn't have had so much to drink at lunch."

Antonio righted the car, formulating an answer. "Yes, I think so," he tried to affect a casual vagueness. "I think we played on Juve together very briefly."

I made a mental note to check on how briefly they played together. Providing I could get a Wi-fi signal again.

"Why do you ask?"

I also tried for a casual vagueness. "Oh, we met him on the beach our first day here. He was looking for Elin. Paola says they used to date."

"He is here?! Pietro? In Capalbio?" Antonio seemed not only shocked to hear his old teammate was in town, but also alarmed.

"Sì. I don't know if he's still here. But he was yesterday."

"So, Antonio," The Husband interrupted, trying to change the subject, "where do you recommend for dinner tonight?"

But I wouldn't let him win so easily. "We had lunch in the best place today. Osteria Antica Mura?"

I watched him to see if he would react.

"Do you know it?"

"Sì, it's very good." He paused, no doubt wondering how much to say before deciding to make his handsome face go sad and those eyes mournful. "It is the restaurant of the uncle of our driver, Fabrizio."

I matched his expression. "Oh. Poor Fabrizio. Do they know what happened to him?"

"Nothing happened, it was just an accident, right?" Mike insisted.

I pushed back. "Of course, but do they know what caused it?"

Antonio seemed distracted for a moment but then quickly said, "I think maybe he stopped off for a grappa on the way home. He was a young man and sadly I think he liked to drink too much. He was known to do this, yes."

And yet you let him drive your wife and kids around, I wanted to say.

We turned off into the villa's driveway, noticing that Nino's car was there, which meant that Sunny and Jen must be back from the hospital. Antonio stopped the car, his charming smile back on his face. "Here you are, my friends. I think tonight I do not come in and say 'Hello' to my brother. He has much on his mind." A purple blotch had formed on Antonio's cheekbone since that morning, the physical proof of everything on Silvio's mind, and a reminder of the unspoken reason for his haste to go.

We got out of the car with all three kids who ran immediately to the pool, one of them taking his pants off on the way. I'll let you guess who. Meanwhile Sunny and Nino had come out of the villa to thank Antonio for his help, which I imagined was one of the first times someone had actual cause to do that. Then Marco came back crying, saying that Sage had hit him for sexually assaulting her and he didn't know what that meant. So that's what it looked like when Antonio started to back out of the driveway, almost running into one of the three police cars that were speeding into it, lights flashing, blocking his exit: The five of us standing in the driveway, mouths open, one of us holding his penis.

CHAPTER 22

They had come to arrest Silvio.

I don't know that the three cars were necessary, except that as a man of means they might have thought he'd try to flee. He could have; the olive grove was on several acres of hillside and he probably could have made a run for it for a while before they caught up with him. But Silvio was a lawyer and he knew the best thing would be to comply. He let them lead him down the driveway, calmly making requests to us as he did so.

"Nino, please get Sunny's sister."

As Nino ran towards the guest house, Silvio turned to Sunny. "Sunny, please stay on here, help coordinate for Tina and Renato. They will all be upset but tell them I need them here. The circus is still in town and reporters will be asking questions. Please tell Enzo to keep an eye on Paola and the kids and help Antonio with that thing we discussed."

Nino was now back with Jen, who looked haggard after her ordeal that day. Silvio looked at her. "I'm going to need an avvocatessa." He smiled. "You have not lost your credentials since we took you to court for poisoning my clients' water?" Jen shook her head. "Good. I know you don't normally represent innocent people," again he tried to smile at Jen and keep things light, "but it is a Saturday during summer and I was hoping you could come with me and handle some things until my own lawyer can join us? I'm afraid he is vacationing on Sardegna and won't be able to make it until tomorrow."

"Absolutely. Let me grab my bag."

"And Kat, I want you to find the real killer and get me out of jail," Silvio didn't say to me, though I was really hoping he would. That didn't stop me from trying however; while the polizie were getting him situated in the back seat, I approached Patti, who was having a cigarette.

"I have some more information for you."

"You have not been still getting involved, have you?" I have to say he sounded a little fed up with me. It's a tone I'm familiar with—I'm married.

I decided to call his bluff. "You already caught your killer, so what danger am I in? I just thought you should have all the facts. It might help your case."

"OK, well what new things have you learned, Signora?"

"Well, Fabrizio's cousin thinks Antonio got him killed."

"Sì, sì, we already spoke with her. She is very upset and would probably blame the Pope if it would make her feel better. Anything else?"

I wanted to tell him that A., I didn't appreciate his tone, and B. ,There was a multitude of things to blame the Pope for and I wouldn't be surprised if Fabrizio's death was somehow one of them, but I knew I had to speak quickly as The Husband had just noticed I was talking to the Vice Questore.

"Pietro, the creepy ponytail guy from the beach?"

He nodded impatiently, making the universal sign for me to get on with it.

"He used to play for Juve Stabia, with Antonio. But Pietro was convicted of match fixing and Antonio later got a 'knee injury.'" I made sure to put that last part in air quotes and hoped Italians knew what air quotes were. "Antonio was shocked, and if you ask me a little worried, that his former teammate was in town."

"OK, well thank you very much, Signora. And now that we have apprehended Signora Corini's murderer, please don't feel you have to stay around any longer."

He might as well have just said, don't let the door hit your culatello on the way out of the country. He had cut me off before I could mention seeing Il Vecchio Fellegi with Antonio that day, but frankly with his attitude, I didn't think he deserved to know.

Besides, Patti thought he had his killer. I looked to where Silvio was seated in the back of the car, quiet now that he had made his arrangements. Had he been too calm? Too pragmatic? I tried to think how Mike would react if I had been murdered and he was arrested for it, but all I saw was him being annoyed that I had gone and gotten myself murdered, probably doing something he told me not to do, and now they were blaming him. So I tried to picture myself if I was arrested for Mike's murder, or any murder really, and I realized that I would not be so composed. I would be distraught, railing against the injustice of it all, screaming to the world that I was innocent, and probably requiring a sedative. I shuddered. It sounded so terrible, except for that last part about the sedative, which sounded great after the year I'd had. But my potential pharmaceutical abuse aside, I had to admit to myself as I watched Silvio do none of those things, that he didn't seem like a man who had been unfairly accused. And then I remembered that he had just lost everything and probably didn't care what happened to him, and I knew that feeling all too well, too.

Having gotten her things and made herself somewhat more presentable, Jen was now being seated in a car for the ride back to the station. Antonio had disappeared in all of this: He must have gotten one of the polizia cars to move and returned home. I was not surprised to find out that he didn't wait to accompany his brother to the station. Instead, I wondered what it would mean for their estate if Silvio was convicted of murder. Who would be in control of the decisions?

We stood there silently watching all three cars back down the driveway and turn to leave. It was as the last car pulled away that Luca shouted, "That was AWESOME!"

CHAPTER 23

"It's not him. They've made a mistake," Sunny insisted as we walked back towards the house. We followed the kids back to the pool. Nino joined us a moment later with a bottle of Gavi and we sat on the edge with our feet in, sipping our wine, all of us still stunned. "It's not him," Sunny repeated.

I didn't want to argue with my friend and tell her that her friend might be a murderer. For one thing, I don't know that I believed he was: There were just way too many other things going on here to believe that it was all just Silvio. But still, I knew from watching *How to Get Away with Murder* that it was often the spouse or lover. And as much as I believed Sunny that they were in love and happy, there were a few things that didn't add up. For one thing, why was Elin looking for work if she had a husband who was rich? Why was her freeloading ex-boyfriend looking for her? Maybe she was having an affair with him and planning to leave Silvio. Maybe the baby wasn't even his, but Pietro's.

Nino offered to cook. It seemed like the smart decision given that anywhere we went the talk would be of Silvio's arrest. Plus we had a case of wine we had to drink before we flew back to the states. Sunny said she needed to do something to take her mind off of things and went to bathe the kids, so I decided to take one last swim since it was now a water-gun-and-child-penis-free environment.

Once it was just Mike and me alone, he said, "I know he's her friend and I feel really bad for these guys, but I'm glad they made an arrest so we can get on with things."

"You mean now that they've arrested the man whose house we're staying in for free, you're relieved we can get on with our vacation of staying in his house for free?" I asked.

"It's not ideal, I'll give you that." He drank some more wine before continuing, "But I'm glad that you can focus on our vacation and not on trying to solve a murder."

"Two. Two murders."

"Would you let it go?"

"Would you rather I talked about losing my job? Or the baby? Or what happened the night before we left?"

"I'd rather you let all of it go and enjoy your trip."

"Why do you think I'm not? I'm having a fabulous time. I've been to the beach; went wine tasting; met a former Miss Albania. I've had truffles at practically every meal. I'm having a fantastic vacation. You're the one who seems to think I'm not."

"Just don't get obsessed."

"I'm not!"

I was desperate to get on the internet. But I wasn't about to prove my husband right. I hate that. So I sat on a lounge chair, pretending to read my Kindle, until he announced that he was going to shower before dinner. It was a good call; our bodies had been slick with humidity all day.

He headed off to our room and I ran up to the main house to Elin's study. I turned on her computer and the password prompt came up. Shit. I should have paid more attention when I was watching Sunny yesterday, but I didn't quite think I'd be trying to hack a computer in order to solve a murder then. I typed "S-i-l-v-i-o" on a whim and it started to boot up. Well, that was a good sign. At least the password wasn't "P-i-e-t-r-o."

I started at the beginning. I googled "Silvio Corini kidnapping" and up popped dozens of photos of the young boy, so heavily bandaged you could barely see his face: Being carried by polizia; being handed over to his parents; in the hospital. I then checked his Wikipedia page, scrolled through the kidnapping. It was mostly exactly as Nino had said, and so I focused on the section titled "Later Life."

Silvio went to college and then received his law degree and went to work for a couple of very big firms, was courted for a political career, and finally, "Mr. Corini later started his own practice taking on several controversial cases including the Nostri Salumi lawsuit, Laura Caruso vs. Basel Pharmaceuticals, and the Royal Motors emissions test fraud."

Wait! Silvio sued a car company. In fact, he sued *that* car company! The Royal Motors case was so huge we knew about it in the United States, and as a people we are almost as willfully ignorant about European cars as we are about soccer. The suit was worth billions and alleged that they had lied on all of their emissions tests over the years, basically poisoning us. Their CEO was currently in prison awaiting appeal based on information that had come to light during Silvio's case. The stock took a dive, the company had to shut down and a lot of people lost a lot of money.

It was also a British company, which made me think of Aparna again. Could she be an angry stockholder looking for revenge? Aparna did not seem the type to have a financial portfolio, but maybe she had a mum or dad back in England who had spent their life working at the company, only to be fired when Royal Motors met financial ruin, and their pensions went with it? Do British companies have pensions? While I googled that, I thought that if that didn't pan out, maybe Aparna was the hired assassin of the jailed CEO or some other bigwig. Of course, she didn't keep a very low profile for a hit person, but maybe that was part of her strategy. Maybe that was why she was good.

I then realized that none of this explained Fabrizio's death, or why anyone would try to target Paola and the boys. Maybe Mike was right, and the two were unrelated. Or maybe Paola still meant as much to Silvio as when they were dating, and someone knew that.

Putting aside the "business revenge" theory for a moment, I kept reading. But when I scrolled through the rest it was mostly personal life stuff that I already knew. Married Elin... father and brother in near fatal boating accident (no mention that it was Antonio's fault)... father Silvio Sr. died of a heart attack last year... younger brother owner of a Serie B football team. I didn't realize Antonio owned a team. *And* he has gambling problems. That seemed convenient if you wanted to fix matches. Or had an old teammate who wanted to.

I hated myself for doing what I did next, but I googled Paola. With suspicions raised again about Antonio, my thoughts turned back to his wife and what sort of stuff she might be hiding, especially if she was so resentful of Enzo. I told myself that I owed no loyalty to the woman who had thus far only provided me a couple glasses of wine and a ride home in her husband's mobile timeshare presentation.

I was inundated with thousands of photos of Paola: magazine covers, runway shows, and even some tabloid shots of her wedding and pictures with the kids. There were a few YouTube videos of her on what I can only assume were Albanian talk shows; thanks to the day's wine tasting I hadn't bothered to consider that most of the searches for Paola were going to come back in Albanian. I was just about to give up when I found one video whose description was in English. It appeared to be from a BBC program that was profiling some third-tier royal with his own country home. Wondering what it had to do with Paola, I clicked on it.

It must have been at least ten years old. The duke or baron or whoever he is was running for Parliament, and already people were talking Prime Minister someday, all with his gorgeous fiancée by his side. Paola. Rich guys and models, right? The narrator highlighted Paola's modeling career before saying she was planning to give it up to raise their children, and then the gorgeous couple took us on a tour of his family's ancestral estate as they prepared for the annual hunting party. It seems Paola was an excellent shot.

"I keep a gun in the bedroom just in case."

Where else did Paola keep a gun?

Now I was interested. I hit the back button and started it all over. The pasty beau wasn't a duke at all, but actually a viscount. I wonder how he messed up with Paola so that she preferred her fuck-up of a husband to the future Prime Minister of England. She could be a viscountess right now, and then when his father died and he became the eighth Earl Stafford, she'd be Lady Paola Stafford.

Wait.

I hit the back button on the browser. I knew I had seen that name before during my search. Click. Click. Click. I kept going back until I got to the page on Royal Motors. The CEO who was currently in prison was Andrew Charles Randolph Stafford, the seventh Earl Stafford.

Paola had dated both the son of the man in prison and the lawyer who put him there.

Only that was as far as I got because I looked out the window and saw that Mike was at the front door. He came in and asked Nino if he had seen me.

"Sì, I think she went upstairs."

That rat! I could hear him coming up the stairs, so I quickly grabbed my wine, snatched a photo album off the bookshelf, and jumped onto the sofa, trying to land in a leisurely pose.

"I just wanted to say I'm sorry." He leaned over and kissed me. "What are you up to?"

Exactly what you don't want me to be doing.

"Oh, I'm just looking at some old family photos of the Corinis." I had grabbed the same album from the day before and had flipped to the photo of the four of them, the Signora holding Antonio as an infant and Silvio Sr. teaching Junior to write. And then I realized, Silvio Jr. was writing with his right hand.

But Silvio was left-handed.

I had seen him sign for the check just last night. He had his right arm around his sister-in-law and wrote with the other. And I remembered thinking that Assunta and Immacolata must have thought he was from the devil. But here he was writing with his right hand as a small child.

The Husband could see something had suddenly bothered me. "What is it?"

"You're going to think I'm crazy."

"That's crazy," he said two minutes later when I had explained it to him.

"I told you you would say that!"

"Well, congratulations! You were right. And I know how important that is to you." He paused, hopefully to take the sarcasm out of his voice, which I didn't appreciate. "Look, there's a thousand reasonable explanations for that."

"Uh-huh," I said, unconvinced.

"OK, fine then," he relented. "What's your theory?"

143

I had to admit, I didn't have one. It just seemed strange: Children have the left-handedness beaten out of them, not the other way around. I also had to admit that I smelled and was also probably dehydrated. I really needed a shower.

Plus, I had a lot of other information floating around in my head. There was Antonio and his football team; his wife the excellent shot; and the many corporations who would want revenge on Silvio, one of which was run by the father of the man Paola used to date. And what had happened to Aparna?

But I had forgotten that we were not alone in the house. On my way to the stairs I saw Enzo disappear down the hallway into another room. I wondered how long he'd been there and how much he'd heard. And if I would be the next person whose behavior he would report to Silvio. And despite the heat, I suddenly had the chills.

CHAPTER 24

Nino made us an extraordinary meal. We had burrata and anchovy bruschetta; mussels in a white wine garlic sauce; a spaghetti carbonara and grilled wild boar sausage. Sunny had put all three kids to bed, so the four of us stood in the kitchen, keeping Nino company as he prepared it, eating each course as it was served, pairing a separate wine to each course. I had no idea how the Italians did it. I watched him put olive oil, garlic and white wine in a pot, steam the mussels for a few minutes, and then produce a broth of such an amazing flavor, I used my weight in bread to sop up the sauce. Yet, whenever I go home and try to reproduce this simple alchemy, it never tastes quite the same.

Jen returned to the villa while we were eating the sausage, which was lucky for all of us as she might not appreciate all the fish we were eating, given her earlier troubles. That seemed forever ago, however, as she sat down and began to fill us in on what had happed to Silvio since we had last seen him being arrested for his wife's murder.

Nino made his sister-in-law a plate of the food that wouldn't kill her as she started to explain. She looked haggard after the various ordeals of the day, not the least of which was the wine tasting that we had done that morning, but she was all business as she patiently laid out the facts. "The majority of their case seems to hang on the fact that they can prove through cell phone records that Elin was at their apartment in Rome—or at least the vicinity—on Sunday night. But Silvio is denying that he ever saw her, which looks suspicious. They keep asking, 'How could he not know that his own wife was in town?'"

"Haven't those cops ever been married?" I asked. "Mike is often unaware of what I'm doing for days at a time."

"Because I trust you."

"Because you don't remember a thing I told you I was doing."

"That, too."

"Wait a minute!" Sunny interrupted, agitated. "How is this even possible? I thought Silvio had an alibi!"

"Sort of," Jen said gently, but in a way that didn't hold out a lot of hope for her sister. She swallowed a bite of sausage before continuing. "His alibi is Aparna, who no one can find now. And the fact that she just sort of appeared out of thin air and then disappeared again seems suspicious."

Sunny knew that didn't look good, yet still protested further. "But what motive could he possibly have? He loved her!"

"They think she told him about the baby, and he got angry. That Silvio was planning to leave her before that. Why else would she be asking her old agent for work? At least that's what they think," she added hastily when she saw how upset Sunny was getting.

Sunny slammed down her glass of wine. "I knew I shouldn't have told that cop that she was pregnant."

"Don't beat yourself up about it," her sister said compassionately—a little too compassionately given their relationship. I started to wonder what was behind it, but then I could see Jen weighing something in her mind and I knew she had more information than she was sharing.

Sunny could sense it, too. "What?"

"What what?"

"Jen, you know something. What else is there?"

"Sunny, it's nothing."

"Jen, it's going to be all over the papers. I'm going to find out anyway."

"Look, I don't want you to shoot the messenger. This is all just shit the cops say to intimidate Silvio. I have nothing to do with it."

"So then tell me!"

Like the rest of us, Jen knew that Sunny wasn't going to rest until she had all the details, so she gave in, however hesitantly she did so. "Again, this is just what the polizie are saying. I'm just relaying information. But it appears that Silvio recently bought some property—"

Sunny cut her off. "So? He's rich. That's what rich people do."

"Do you want to argue the case with me, or do you want to hear the part that landed your friend in jail?" Jen's sudden compassion was in danger of disappearing again. She took a deep breath and exhaled. "Yes, that's what rich people do, but Silvio bought the land with money from his business account, not any of their personal accounts. So they think he didn't want her to know."

Sunny stubbornly shook her head. "It's just not true. They don't know these two." Still, I could tell she was grateful to her sister for telling her everything as she laid out a plate of biscotti for her and made her a cup of tea.

"How was Silvio?" Nino asked, after he had given her some time to eat.

Jen thought about it for a moment. "I'd say good, all things considered, but I don't think that's it. It's like after everything he's been through: Losing his father, his wife, and of course, the kidnapping, he just doesn't give a damn what happens to him anymore."

Jen's words echoed the exact same thoughts I had had earlier, only now I wasn't so sure that either of us were correct. I had to agree with the cops: It was suspicious that Silvio's wife was near their apartment on Sunday night and he claimed he had no knowledge. Also, it seemed strange that he would buy property out of his business account, although given the way Italians hated to pay taxes, maybe there was some loophole where that made sense.

But if Jen had doubts, she wasn't expressing them as she further described Silvio's state of mind. "Even when Antonio— who managed to find an attorney on a Saturday night to draft paperwork giving him control over their estate—even when he showed up, it didn't seem to matter to Silvio one way or another if Antonio just plunged them all into ruin."

"What?!" Sunny was incensed. "Are you kidding me?! That's like letting a priest take the altar boys camping."

"It's not a good idea this, no," Nino agreed.

"Don't worry, I wasn't about to let that happen," Jen assured them, showing the legal tenacity that earned her salary. "It took some balls, though, I'll give him that. It also makes him look like he had a motive, which could be good for Silvio in the long run. I know if I was Silvio's defense lawyer, I wouldn't mind casting some suspicion on Antonio. I managed to shut it down, but still, I'll be relieved when Silvio's real attorney arrives tomorrow. I find it hard enough to navigate the fucked-up Italian legal system, and that's with case law I am familiar with."

"It is not perfect, no," Nino said, which was a gigantic understatement that normally would have caused Sunny to respond with a snort and a tirade, discussing the stories of friends who sued their employers for wages never paid, only to be told by a judge that they had to keep working for free, or some equally inane thing. But she was far too distracted by what she had heard and was working herself up to a tirade on a different matter.

She looked at Jen and started pointing, which was a sign she was getting really fired up. "This is fucked up, is what this is. First Antonio talks about selling the day after Elin died…"

"Then someone tried to kill his wife and kids," I added.

"Yes. Then that."

"Then we find out he's got gambling debts," I went on.

"Exactly," Sunny finished. "Now the minute Silvio gets arrested he tries to get control of their finances?!"

"Plus, it turns out that he and Pietro Romano used to play on the same football team where Pietro was found guilty of match fixing."

"What? When did this happen?"

"I found out while you guys were at the hospital. Also," this was so delicious I couldn't believe I had forgotten to tell Sunny, "while we were at Paola's, Antonio got a visit from Old Man Fellegi."

"Chi é questo Fellegi?" Nino looked from his wife to me, confused.

But it was Mike who answered. "Some lady in a café yesterday told us she thinks he killed Elin, because he wanted the olive grove and Elin wouldn't sell." It was clear from his tone that he thought this was totally ridiculous, but I wasn't going to let it drop that easily.

"And today he was walking with Antonio, and Paola told us he fills his head with fantasies about how they're all going to get rich from this land."

That was all Sunny needed to hear and she turned towards her sister. "Why has no one arrested Antonio?"

"Sunny," Jen began, "Silvio is a very rich man who can afford the best legal counsel. Let them fight his battles for him. I'm sure they'll mention all of this."

But I didn't want to let it go any more than Sunny did. "It just seems strange to me that none of the cops have noticed that Antonio does seem to be benefitting from this situation. It's like they have a vendetta against Silvio," I started to say. But I could see The Husband shooting me a look to cut it out, so I quickly tried to distract him. "If someone murdered me, would you be so distraught that you wouldn't care if you got plunged into financial ruin?"

"No."

He took a drink of wine as if to banish all thoughts of financial ruin from his mind. Mission accomplished.

CHAPTER 25

Jen finished her tea and went to bed. The four of us moved into the living room with our wine, and Mike and Nino, who had once again been discussing photography, suggested that we look at some of the photos from the trip as a distraction. Sunny pointed out that Elin had an Apple TV so Mike could use AirPlay to show them on the very large flat screen on the wall.

While Mike went down to the guest house for his computer, Sunny turned to me. "I really hate to say this, but I think this could all be Antonio. I didn't think he was a murderer either, but he is desperate, and I just know that there's no way Silvio did this. I mean it's more likely that I'd kill Nino."

Nino nodded very seriously in agreement before winking at us both and then leaving to go check on the boys.

"Oh, totally," I agreed. "No one would ever be defending Mike and me like this. It would be like, 'Yeah, he got aggravated with her all the time and frankly she probably had it coming.'" I added emphatically, "Especially now."

Sunny raised an eyebrow at me like she wasn't sure if I had more to say, while I debated for a moment whether or not I did. Seeing me teetering on the edge like that, she poured us both a glass of wine and said, "Spill."

"It all sounds really petty right now."

"Don't be ridiculous. Your whole stay here has been full of our drama. I feel like we haven't had a chance to talk about you at all."

"A murdered friend is not just 'drama,' Sunny."

"Well, then look at it like you're distracting me."

So I confessed, "The night before we left, our house sitter, Edie, came by to pick up the keys. You've met Edie. She was here for our wedding."

"Of course. Loud, opinionated... we got along immediately!"

"Exactly. Well, she told us that the night before she had been invited to dinner at Cruella's house."

Sunny nodded with a sour look on her face; she had heard the tale of Cruella already, and wasn't a fan.

I continued, "Cruella had invited another couple, Jeff and Vanessa, which was weird enough because they've really always been our friends. Cruella always thought Jeff was full of himself, and frankly Jeff always thought Cruella and her husband were shallow—"

"And they'd both be right!" she concluded.

I laughed. "Totally. Yet Edie shows up and all four of them were there for dinner." I paused, took a swig of wine, then looked her in the eye, pointedly though I could tell she already sensed where this was going. "Guess who the main course was?"

"No!" Sunny gasped. "How the fuck old are these people?"

"Older than me and you!" At that, we high fived each other. I'm not above being petty when it suits me.

"So, Edie told them that if they were going to insist on talking about us, she was going to tell us everything that was said."

"Good for her!"

"I know, although, I sort of think that was Cruella's end game all along. One last 'fuck you' to hurt us."

"What did she say?"

"Well, she started out concerned. 'What can we do? We feel so bad…'"

"You can fucking apologize," Sunny interrupted.

"Thank you. But she didn't want to hear that. So it just became about how fucked up we were."

"Why? Fucked-up people don't deserve an apology or something?" Sunny wanted to know.

This made me laugh, which allowed me to continue. "Vanessa kept bringing up the fact that we missed Jeff's birthday, calling it selfish. We told Jeff we had other plans, but the truth was, we were just too depressed…"

"What grown man needs a birthday party so desperately that he wants depressed people to show up?"

"Oh, you know how some people just want you to be an extra in their life? Just sit in the background and go through the motions to make their lives look fuller than they are. They're all a little like that, I suppose, and it's better just to realize all of this." I knew that's how I was supposed to feel, but I said it without any conviction, because not being their friends wasn't really what was hurting me. It was thinking they had been my friends and then hearing what they had said. The betrayal gave me a feeling of raw shock that still didn't feel real at times—and then hurt someplace deep when it did.

"Cruella was relentless, she kept saying wasn't I 'just being dramatic?' 'Women have miscarriages every day.' Why wasn't I over this yet? Believe me, I wish I had the answer to that question, too." At that I could feel the tears start and I paused, because I really didn't want to start crying. I detested crying before all of this happened, and after the last six months I was so very sick of crying. I never wanted to do it again, and yet it felt like I would never stop.

Sunny put a hand on my shoulder and silently waited for me to continue. When I thought I was past it, I did. Unfortunately, the worst was still to come. "She said everything that happened at work had been my fault, too. That I just couldn't hack it. It was no big deal and all women have to deal with it." I paused from recounting her commentary for my own. "All I tried to do was hack it," I pleaded. "It still wasn't good enough."

"No," Sunny agreed. "It never is."

"Then she started attacking our marriage." Moments of our lives were dissected; things that you tell friends that you never think are going to be recounted and analyzed and used against you.

"How could she?! That goes against girl code!" Sunny was incensed. "I have to be honest, I always thought she was cold," she began.

"It's the Botox," I interrupted.

"What?"

"Too much Botox can inhibit your ability to feel compassion for others. I saw that on Facebook."

"Good to know," she said, unconsciously checking her forehead in the reflection of the coffee table. "Botox or not, I didn't think she was capable of being this big of a bitch. And I'm so sorry. You guys have been through enough. You're already feeling vulnerable and exposed. Someone who would put you through this, too, isn't your friend."

I smiled warmly to try to show her my appreciation for her being such a good one and then I remembered one of my favorite awful parts. "Oh! At one point she asked if it bothered anyone else that we seemed to be always having problems and then all of a sudden were acting so in love?"

"What?! Have they met married people?"

"Exactly."

"That's the craziest fucking thing I've ever heard. I woke up this morning wanting to kick Nino in the balls. And then we had sex. And it was great. But I still want to kick him in the balls. I don't even know why anymore."

I laughed, but just then we heard the front door open and I knew Mike must be coming back. I shook my head at her to indicate we should stop talking about it.

"He's livid about this," I quickly whispered to Sunny. "He can't even talk about it." She nodded as Mike walked in the room.

"You guys talking about the murder again?" he asked, exasperated.

"Sorry," I apologized. Sunny and I exchanged a smile.

Nino returned saying the boys were sound asleep, and he and Mike went about setting up the Apple TV. A few minutes and a few swears later, we were watching photos from the last few days. Mike started with the most recent ones: There were shots of the kids playing soccer at Paola and Antonio's; some gorgeous shots of the tasting room and cellar at the vineyard that morning; and even a few pictures of all of us at breakfast before the fisticuffs. I couldn't believe that was only this morning. We moved on to the shots from the farm the night before, the ghost horse and the sunset, before seeing some stunning shots he had managed to get of the beach. For the first time all day, I stopped thinking of the murder and became lost in how beautiful my vacation memories already were. I wasn't lying to him earlier: I was truly having a remarkable time.

It was unfortunate that it took a couple thousand dollars and travelling six thousand miles away to forget my troubles, or maybe it was fortunate that at least there was something that allowed me to do just that. Travel has always been an antidote for me. People will say that you take your problems with you wherever you go. And I say, fuck those people. Don't believe them. Whatever worries plague you in your daily life melt away when you're standing in front of the Coliseum or Pompeii. It's hard to be upset about what job you didn't get when you're standing in front of something that's two thousand years old. Next to such permanence, your own life feels transitory and insignificant, which sounds depressing but is actually quite freeing. It makes you realize there are grander, more wondrous things in the world than whether or not your "friends" are spilling your most intimate secrets at a dinner party. There is a whole astonishing world out there to explore, far bigger than four petty people in a living room in Los Angeles. And much of it has beaches to sit on and wine to enjoy!

After going through those photos, Mike moved on to the album from our first day in Rome, where he had gotten some amazing shots at twilight. We hadn't had any time to look at these yet and it was nice to revisit the beginning of our trip in our favorite city.

There is nothing in the world quite like landing in Rome. We had touched down around seven in the evening, and by the time we got our luggage and got to the hotel it was almost nine, which in Rome is still plenty of time to change and head out to an amazing meal. We were giddy to be out in the ancient city again, walking among the ruins that were placed throughout the city as casually as you would find a gas station or bus stop bench in Los Angeles.

After twenty hours of travel and a late-night meal, we had slept in until almost noon, had a quick cappuccino standing up at a café in the piazza, then made a trek to the outskirts of town to try a new place for lunch, because we read in a magazine they had amazing fried zucchini flowers and The Husband would happily walk across Rome for amazing fried zucchini flowers.

We were delighted with our choice as it seemed off the beaten tourist track: All of the nearby businesses had iron shutters pulled down over their windows signifying the lunch hour and there was nary a cab in sight. The restaurant itself was not at all air conditioned and was populated almost solely by men only speaking Italian, another sign that we were at a place frequented by locals and not people who were carrying the latest copy of Rick Steves. One whole table was taken up by porcinis, drying out for the dinner service that evening. We cooled down with acqua frizzante, drank Greco di Tufo, and snacked on arancini and fried anchovies.

As there was nary a cab in sight, we headed back towards the centro on foot, stopping to visit the Borghese and admire the so-very-life-like Berninis. I could spend all day looking at a foot he sculpted, the way it arches so that you can see every tendon and muscle. Or the way the hand presses into the flesh, dimpling it, like in "Pluto and Proserpina." You can feel the force of Pluto grabbing her, just looking at it. That one man can convey all of this out of a slab of marble is astounding to me. Her flesh looks pliant. Her hair has movement. And it's all marble. It's one of those things about Italy that gives me that much needed perspective: It's breathtaking and old and bigger than all of us.

Afterwards we walked through Piazza Del Popolo, past the Spanish Steps, through all the high-end shops on Via Condotti, ending up at the Pantheon. Once at the world's oldest continually used church, we had granita con panna from Tazza d'Oro while sitting in the piazza watching the crowds and all of the musicians as they played the three songs they play in every piazza: The theme to *The Godfather*, "That's Amore" and "Volare." Afterwards we went back to the hotel for a drink on the rooftop bar overlooking Campo de Fiori and then headed out to one of our favorite restaurants for a dinner of truffle potatoes, more zucchini flowers, and cacio e pepe in the city where they cook it the best. Cacio e pepe: It's pasta with pepper and a salty pecorino cheese. Cook it yourself at home, and it's a congealed mess of cheese on pasta. Have it cooked in Italy and it's the perfect meal, at once comforting but also sharp.

Afterwards we went for gelato and then headed over to Trastevere, where they have an outdoor festival all summer along the banks of the Tiber. Even at eleven o'clock at night the heat was still inescapable, but I love that about Rome in the summer. It's so hot and so close and it's clear: Everyone is there for sex. It's on everyone's mind, whether walking down the street in the afternoon or sitting in the Campo de Fiori at almost two in the morning, every café still crowded with people drinking and smoking and thinking about sex.

I was enchanted by the memories of all of it when we were all suddenly brought back to reality by the crime scene photos of Elin's body.

"Oh my god, I'm so sorry!" Mike immediately uttered, jumping up to get his computer.

"It's my fault," I hurriedly explained. "I thought the police might find them useful later."

"No, it was smart," Sunny said simply.

Mike was trying to close out of the album and fiddling with his computer, which had picked that moment to hang. More furious and desperate swears followed. I, however, couldn't look away from the image, which, at over four feet across, was almost life size. I studied everything I had seen that night: Elin, shoes cast off, her head lying sideways across her bottom arm, her other arm lying limp at her side. Only...

"Wait a minute!" I jumped off the sofa and ran towards the television.

"No," The husband told me emphatically.

"Yes, hold on. What is that in her hand?"

"Nothing the cops didn't find I'm sure."

"No, look, it's a yellow ticket."

Sunny approached the TV and stood next to me. "I can see it, too."

Nino joined us and squinted. "It looks like the biglietto from the Autostrada."

"Yes! That's exactly what that is!" I confirmed. The Autostrada is a toll road, and so when you get on it you take a ticket showing which exit you entered at. Then when you reach your exit to leave, you put your ticket back in the machine, then you swipe your credit card and pay and then the machine says, "Arrivederci!" and Mike and I always say, "Arrivederci" back, and we laugh, and the gate goes up and you go on your way. But you don't get your ticket back.

"If she drove into Rome that night, why does she still have the ticket?" I wanted to know. "She would have needed it to get off the Autostrada."

"Unless she never made it to Rome," suggested Sunny.

"Exactly. Not if she was intercepted on the highway." Suddenly a thought occurred to me. "What happened to her car?"

The Husband interrupted. "These are all answers the cops have I'm sure. Or at least questions they've asked. And who knows how old the ticket is or if it's even hers? She might have found it on the ground."

Sunny ignored my husband, something I wish I could do more often. "I think we should call the Vice Questore."

"I still have his number in my phone. I'll go get it."

"You want to call him now?!" A vein was now standing out in the middle of The Husband's balding head.

"An innocent man is sitting in prison right now," Sunny protested. "Besides, he told us to call with anything and this might very well be something."

Nino gave Mike a look like, "Women, amiright?" before asserting, "What harm could it do? Maybe it's nothing, maybe it's something."

"All right," conceded The Husband, pouring himself another glass of wine.

I ran out of the house and down the lawn. I was almost to the pool when I looked behind me, in order to see the silhouette of the hill town at night. Only what caught my eye was one of the second-floor windows. I could see the silhouette of someone standing in it. Staring at me.

Or maybe they were just staring out admiring the view. It was unmistakably the silhouette of Enzo; Tina wasn't nearly that stocky, and I had never seen her husband, Renato, inside the house. This is why the staff always blackmails rich people, I thought, this is why they know all of their secrets. Because it was so easy to forget that they were there. I reminded myself to be more vigilant in remembering that we were not alone in the house, but then I asked myself, "Why?" Why should we worry about what was said around Enzo or Tina? Wouldn't they want the person who killed Elin brought to justice? According to everyone they were loyal to the family. What was it Paola said? Enzo treated Silvio's money like it was his.

I looked back at the window. I knew it was the one for Elin's study because it was only yesterday that Sunny and I had stood in it, saying hello to Vice Questore Patti. For a moment I forgot that I was forgetting my suspicion and I worried that I hadn't shut down Elin's computer earlier; I hadn't had time before Mike had come up. Anyone could check my browser history if they were so inclined. I tried to think if there was anything incriminating in it. Did Enzo know? Was he standing in the window to intimidate me? To send me a message?

Other than a few lights in the house and the stars, it was pitch black. And silent. You had that feeling that you were all alone on the planet. It was a feeling that usually made me anxious. Like you could hurtle off this planet into some abyss and no one would ever know you were here.

Only I wasn't alone. To my left, on the other side of the lawn, I heard the unmistakable sounds of footsteps walking into the olive grove. I looked over to where the acres of olive groves became threatening shadows that could have hidden anything—or anyone—and I instinctively started walking towards it.

I told myself there was nothing to be afraid of. We were in the country, on the estate of rich people. What were the odds it was going to be a stranger on the Corini's land? It was probably just Renato or Tina. But I had to admit I didn't want it to be Renato or Tina. I wanted it to be someone else. Someone unexpected, but who would somehow make everything that happened in the last few days make sense. After the last few months, I desperately wanted something to make sense.

When I was working, my life made sense. When I had friends that I thought I could trust to not air my private moments at dinner parties, my life made sense. I was where I was supposed to be in the world, living the life I wanted and that I worked hard to create. This sense of equilibrium was disturbed when I lost my job. Only as soon as that happened, I found out, quite unexpectedly and not unlike those female protagonists in books that I hate, that I was pregnant. But for a short while, it seemed maybe that was the new place I was supposed to be. For a moment, things still made sense. Despite being fiercely pro-choice my entire life there was never a question about keeping it; at almost forty I knew that this could very likely be my last and only shot, and the writer in me was drawn to the plot twist. Maybe this was the next chapter. But then the pregnancy wasn't viable, the jobs weren't coming, the friends were untrustworthy, and suddenly it felt like the story was over. I didn't know where I was supposed to be in the world and my life no longer made sense. I was just hurtling into the abyss, both figuratively and literally as I continued to walk into the Tuscan darkness.

When I got to the edge of the olive grove, I hesitated briefly, but then I kept going, despite knowing that this was a potentially bad idea. If we assumed that Silvio was innocent, that meant that somewhere out there was a killer. And yet it was hard to connect to the danger that I should have been feeling. Was it because part of me believed Silvio had really done it? It was usually the husband, and his behavior both leading up to the murder and in the wake of it at times seemed unusual.

But there was more to my carelessness. The truth was that over the last few months I had become rather agnostic about whether I lived or died. To be clear I'd rather not feel terror before I die. But when your present is largely nothing but heartbreak and sadness, you can't imagine anything being different in the future and you become less attached to whether or not there is one.

Mentally I marked how far I had come by the number of trees I passed. Just one; I was still feet from the clearing. Now, two, then three; I could still run to the edge. But although I couldn't see them, I knew someone was up ahead; I could hear them crunching twigs and rocks underneath as they went. I quickened my pace as much as I could without making the same telltale noises myself. I had lost count of how many trees I had passed. Was it nineteen? Was it twenty-two? I only knew it had gotten darker; less light was coming in which meant I was definitely much farther into the grove, much further from the entrance.

Just then the hunting dogs started howling, which really

spooked me, and I turned to the noise. My mind caught up to my fear and I reminded myself that we knew what they were and they were no big deal, but my heart was already pounding in my chest from the scare and I felt my hands start to tingle from the adrenaline. The howls died down in moments, although I couldn't say the same for my thumping heart. And that's when I realized the footsteps had stopped. I could no longer hear whoever it was. I thought they must have gone on up ahead, out of earshot, only just then I thought I heard footsteps coming from behind me, further up the hill. I turned to look, but even though I could see no one, I could still hear something. And I realized they could hear me because in all of the excitement, I had stopped being so stealthy and quiet. Then the footsteps stopped, but now I could hear breathing, heavy.

And then, finally, my mind caught up with my bravado and I realized that best case scenario, it was a pervert jerking off. Best case. So I ran towards the edge of the grove as fast as one could on a hillside in flip-flops after a day of drinking. Which is to say, I was an easy target for whoever was following me. But as I reached the safety of the driveway and the lawn without being slashed to bits, I started to wonder if there had been anyone there at all, or if I was just searching for any kind of drama to occupy myself with, to take my mind away from my own mysteries that I couldn't solve.

And it was these thoughts going through my head as I crossed the lawn and saw Enzo had left the window, which left me to think he wasn't trying to send me a message at all but just staring out the window, thinking of his friends who tragically weren't with him tonight. I knew the feeling.

CHAPTER 26

Patti asked us to email him a copy of the photos, urged us once again to not go digging around, and then said if we wouldn't listen to him, at least do what we did tonight and keep him in the loop. He said he believed they had caught the real killer, but that you never knew if there were accomplices and any interfering could put our lives, and the fate of the case, at risk. He seemed just frustrated enough with us to care more about the latter than the former. The Vice Questore said he'd be by in the morning, and then said we should all go to bed now so as to stay out of trouble until he got there.

We immediately ignored his advice because Nino and Mike wanted to try a time-lapse photography thing in order to capture the stars and the night sky over the valley. I didn't quite understand it, but I was happy to stay talking to Sunny while they wandered up and down the hillside looking for the right place to set up Nino's tripod. I thought to warn them about the olive grove but realized it was a lose-lose situation: Mike would be mad at me for going in there at the same time he would tell me it was all nothing and just my imagination.

Sunny and I had just sat down with some gelato when the front door banged open and Nino and Mike walked back into the room, both looking rattled.

"Don't panic, it's OK," Nino tried to assure Sunny and me. Which is the exact wrong thing to say when you don't want someone to panic. I'd blame the language barrier, but Mike always does that, too.

"What happened?"

"Is it the boys?!

"Is someone else dead?"

"Is it Jen?"

Mike interrupted the melee of questions. "No, no, everyone is fine. And we're fine, too, by the way, thanks for asking. But our room was broken into. We've been robbed."

"What did they take? Oh my God, did they take the camera?" I knew if they had taken his camera, and with it whatever photos were on it, it would crush Mike, and I just couldn't bear that.

Mike pointed to where it was hanging around his neck. "Luckily this was in the house with us all night. And so was the computer. But I went back for the monopod and the door was wide open. They grabbed the iPad, the GoPro, and it looks like some cash."

Between us, I wasn't sorry to see the GoPro go. The Husband put that camera on a selfie stick and insisted on doing 360-degree shots of us in every piazza we strolled through, totally oblivious to my embarrassment. And because he's always on the cutting edge of embarrassing-your- wife photo technology, he had a selfie stick way before anyone else, so no one even understood what it was that we were doing for the first two years. Not that the fact that now every sorority girl and midwestern dad was doing it made it any better. Frankly, it would be a relief to not have to do that again this trip.

Something very important dawned on me. "Oh my God, what about our passports?!" While I would not have minded being stranded in Italy indefinitely, I still sensed that replacing my passport while in this country would be an unholy pain in the ass that I'd probably want to avoid in this lifetime.

"They're fine. They were hidden away inside a magazine in an inner compartment of the suitcase. For once your OCD paranoia came in handy. And it looks like this person was in a hurry."

"I was just in the room an hour ago for my phone!"

All of a sudden Enzo was standing in the doorway, placing his ever-present cell phone back in his shirt pocket and rattling off something in very ominous Italian to Nino. Nino turned to us and translated.

"He says that's why it's always important to lock the door. You have to be very careful; the circus people lurk in the shadows and are very sneaky."

"I locked the door," I protested. "I never don't lock the door. I took the keys with me and everything. I grew up on the East Coast, I lived in New York, I'm a very suspicious person." I was really getting agitated, but I didn't want to hear that we had lost our things due to some carelessness on my part, especially when I knew it wasn't true. "Tell him that. He knows." I spoke to Nino, but I looked right at Enzo. "He watched me cross the lawn."

It was then I remembered that if he watched me cross the lawn, he also saw me run into the olive grove to chase what may have been circus people who came back to steal our stuff. I certainly didn't need him getting angry back at me and mentioning that to my husband, so I quickly tried to tone it down and smile at Enzo instead.

But if Enzo was angry, his face didn't show it, but rather remained passive as he said something else, a little friendlier this time. "He says he's sorry, but he doesn't understand English," Nino reported.

I immediately felt bad for snapping at him. He was only trying to help us, strangers who were trying to have a vacation while he was being plunged into grief.

"He also said that he's already called the police."

"How'd he get a signal?" Mike immediately wanted to know.

Nino smiled and shrugged. "Enzo's phone always has a signal."

I wouldn't think they'd send a Vice Questore investigating a homicide to a standard B&E, and the look on Patti's face when he showed up thirty minutes later showed that he wouldn't have thought so either.

"I asked you all to go to bed and stay out of trouble until morning, and you could not even do that," he bemoaned.

"I can't help the circus people," I defended myself. "Besides, why are they sending you out here for a burglary?"

"Signora, it's not just a burglary. It's a burglary at a house where la donna has been murdered and her husband is in jail for the crime," Patti explained. He then asked to see our room, asking a bunch of questions about what was taken as we walked across the driveway and down the lawn. "You are very lucky," he concluded when he heard all it was. But I had questions of my own.

"Any word from Aparna, yet?"

"No, Signora."

"What about Elin's car? Have you found it?"

"No, Signora."

"And the ticket, was it entered into evidence?"

"Signora," he implored, "it is mezzanotte. No one is at work. Except for me that is."

"And the circus people," I added.

"Sì, sfortunatamente for you and your husband," he smiled weakly as he looked around the room. "They wait in the shadows and look for an opportunity. An unlocked door..."

"I always lock the door," I said quickly.

"Signora, it's been a long day. Maybe you had some wine?" He discreetly glanced at the three half-filled glasses around the room. "We all become forgetful. You are in a normally quiet town. It's understandable."

I was really getting tired of being mansplained to about whether or not I locked my door. And another thought had just occurred to me.

"So, I'm telling you that I know I locked the door, and I assume that you keep insisting I didn't because there's no sign of forced entry?" I looked to the pristine doorway, which was absent of any cracks or splinters or signs of a crowbar. Patti did as well, looked back at me, and just nodded.

"Well, then, someone on the inside with a key did this on purpose because I am telling you drunk or not, I locked that door."

Mike had been silent up until this point, and I waited for him to defend Patti, to tell me I was letting my imagination get away from me and then try to convince me of the possibility that I had erred.

But instead he turned towards Patti. "You should listen to her. She's right. This was definitely an inside job. I've never known my wife to not lock a door."

I don't know that I've ever loved him more.

CHAPTER 27

We told Sunny and Nino we were leaving in the morning.

"Oh, please," Sunny pleaded. It seemed she didn't want to be left alone and under the circumstances I couldn't blame her. But we couldn't keep pretending this was just another Italian vacation. "I'm sure it was just the circus people. Who would want your stuff? I mean not that you don't have great stuff. But I just mean I don't think anyone here would have done this on purpose. Who would want you guys to go?"

"I don't know. Antonio might want us gone so he could just sell this land and pay his debts. Silvio? He'd probably like to come home from being indicted on murder charges to a quiet place. Patti definitely wants us gone. Probably broke in himself just to be done with me. Il Vecchio Fellegi, maybe, if la signora in the café is to be believed." Paola, I added in my head, keeping that one to myself. I hadn't told Sunny what I had learned earlier, and it was getting late and didn't seem like the time. Plus, what was it other than one big fat coincidence? It didn't explain why someone targeted the car she was supposed to be traveling in, unless Paola did that herself to throw suspicion off of her. What was it she had said when I had met her? Cunning like a whore?

"Where are you guys going to go?"

"Mike will probably book a hotel on the Argentario." It was a small island off the coast of Tuscany, only thirty minutes away. You might know it as the place the Costa Concordia went down off the coast of in 2012. So that seemed like a good omen.

"Come with us," I suggested.

"I told Silvio I'd look after things," she said weakly.

"Tina and Enzo and Renato can do that. Maybe it'd be best for you guys to go, too. Maybe you really need to get away to grieve your friend." It struck me that we were both grieving the loss of a friend, and I wondered if getting away was really the answer. Had I really come to terms with the betrayal over this trip, or had I just had the luxury to not have to think about it? And were they even two different things?

"I'll think about," she conceded.

"Fair enough." I smiled at her. "I'm going to go pack. I'll see you in the morning." I gave her a hug and tried to think of something to say. I wanted to tell her I loved her, but that seemed too serious. So I just said, "Thank you."

"For what?"

"All of it."

While I was sad to be leaving Sunny and Nino, and a little aggravated that I hadn't managed to solve a double homicide, I had to admit that I was excited to be able to visit another part of the country before we left. Mike had managed to turn the phone into a hot spot long enough to book a room and was eagerly showing me pictures of our view. It looked like the ends of the Earth, a paradise where no one could find us. I was OK with that.

The next morning, we headed up to the main house for our last breakfast at the villa. Silvio's arrest had utterly deflated Tina. Whatever coping she had been previously doing through her work was abandoned. Sunny told her to take some time to herself and had gone out instead for pastries and biscotti. There was a lot of sadness here. It was understandable, but I realized that it was a good thing we were going.

Sunny made us cappuccinos while asking about our next destination. Her oldest, Luca, was distracted by his iPad, but Marco was sitting with us at the table drawing. He told me in English that he was going to draw us a picture of the Argentario, then asked his father a question in Italian. I was amazed by how deftly the children switched back and forth between the two worlds, but I guess they say children are malleable like that.

Our coffees finished, it was time to head out. Mike was getting directions from Nino while Sunny turned to me. "You're staying with us your last night in Rome before you fly out, right?"

"We wouldn't miss it." Sunny and Nino's the night before we left had become one of my favorite traditions of our yearly trip. Sometimes they'd have relatives over for a traditional Roman dinner. Other times we'd all go out to a restaurant that Sunny had just discovered. Even if it had been a year since we had seen each other, we always picked up right where we left off as if no time had passed; Sunny and I talking well past what was advisable given our early flight the next day. It was the perfect last night before starting our twenty-hour journey back home.

Marco announced in English that he was making us a map and then asked me how to spell my name, carefully writing out the letters as he did with his left hand. I remembered what Sunny had said about Assunta and Immacolata and wanted to make the sign of the cross as a joke, but a thought halted me.

"You ready to go?" The Husband asked.

"I have one last stop."

CHAPTER 28

"What?!" He wasn't happy.

"It will only take a minute!"

"We said we were leaving!"

"We are. But we can't even check in until three."

"I don't want to miss lunch."

"We won't miss lunch," I promised The Husband.

"Ok," he grumbled again. "But I don't want to miss lunch."

"I said we wouldn't miss lunch."

"Good. Because I hate to miss—"

"What did I say? Am I speaking Italian?"

I looked at Sunny. "Would you take me to Paola and Antonio's? I need to see the aunts."

Sunny was surprised. "Good God. You must be really desperate not to go." But she agreed to take me.

Sunny called Paola on her way and she was there to greet us at the front door. She told us that Antonio was in Rome on business, which I was glad to hear. I didn't need a repeat of the day-before's car ride. Also, as he had most likely already killed two people and had probably stolen my shit to intimidate me into leaving, I didn't know how he would take to me just showing up at his house the next day. Which is something that should have crossed my mind before I decided to come here. But as I said previously, my survival instincts weren't what they should have been.

I explained, "I want to ask the aunts something, and it would be great if the both of you would be there to help me translate."

"This is all very mysterious," declared Sunny. "I like it."

We went through the loggia into the foyer, and I stopped at the black-and-white photo of the young Corini family. "Permesso?" I asked Paola in Italian, even though I could have asked her in English. But the Italian seemed to lend a flair of the dramatic to the events. She nodded and I carefully took the picture from the wall. Paola then led us into the formal living room decorated with the type of furniture that had been in a family for generations: brocaded couches; high wingback chairs whose fabric was rubbed bare in places; marble-topped tables. To the right of the door was a high shelf with several old ceramic busts, a collection of Venetian glass carafes, and a few marble pillar candleholders that looked like they had been excavated straight out of ancient Rome.

The old women were almost impossible to see with the heavy velvet curtains drawn, and it took Paola opening the curtains for me to see the sisters were sitting on one couch, smoking cigarettes, although I could smell what they were doing long before. I wanted to say, "You know that will kill you," but now was not a time for jokes, especially ones that no one would get. Comedy is about timing, after all, not to mention knowing your audience.

Paola pointed first to Assunta and then to Immacolata, and, in Italian, introduced us and told them I was a friend of Sunny's and staying with Silvio and Elin. At the mention of Elin, they blessed themselves and looked towards the Heavens, exhaling puffs of smoke as they did so. It would have been an ethereal effect if it wasn't so suffocating.

Assunta was smaller and rounder, seeming almost as wide as she was tall. Her feet, shod in the clunky black shoes most popular with nuns, didn't even touch the floor and her white hair was pulled into a knot on top of her head. Imma, meanwhile, was bird boned with a long neck and hair she still died jet black and had set three times a week, I'd guess by the looks of it.

Although different in stature, the two sisters had the same face, and in their face I could see that of Silvio Sr.'s, but with softer, more feminine curves. I noticed their excellent bone structure was still visible despite the sag of age and I could see where Antonio got his beautiful face from....

Focus, Kat! I had a job to do. Or not really. Technically I had no job, neither here nor at home. All I had to do was enjoy my vacation with my husband, who I had abandoned back at the villa where we were sure to be killed if we didn't get out of there immediately. Shit. Well, when you put it like that, what was I doing?

The women both smiled and nodded at me and said something to Paola in Italian, motioning to their aperitif glasses of moscato and the plate of cookies in front of them.

Paola nodded her head in their direction as she asked me, "They'd like to know if you'd like to join them in some moscato?"

Jesus Christ, it was ten a.m.! What the hell is it with this country?

"Sure, that sounds great!" I sat down and Sunny sat next to me. Paola quickly poured us all a glass and sat down across from us. Now I had to begin. But I hadn't really thought that part out.

"Please tell them how much I appreciate their talking to me, and that I have a few questions that I would be very grateful if they could answer. If you like, tell them I'm a writer and this would help me on a project that I'm working on." I don't know why I threw that last part in; it would be obvious that my questions had nothing to do with anything but their family, but it seemed more official to say I was a professional who needed help.

Paola and Sunny took turns communicating this. Both Assunta and Imma nodded so I smiled back and said, "Le ringrazio per l'aiuto."

Assunta leaned over and said something to Paola so low I couldn't hear. "They want to know if you're Italian," she explained.

I responded, "Sì," and the old women's faces lit up.

"Di dove?" asked Immacolata.

"I miei nonni erano di sud di Napoli."

At the mention of my grandparents being from Naples, their faces fell.

"Ahhh... Napolitano," sniffed Assunta. Imma took a sip of moscato and looked away.

"Good luck," Paola cautioned me.

"Sì, ma la mama della mia papa era di Firenze," I lied. My dad's mother was Irish. But at the mention of having a grandparent from the North, both women were smiling again.

I took a deep breath. It was now or never. I placed the photo I had been holding onto the table in front of them and looked to Paola. "Ask them, please, this photo was taken before Silvio Jr. was kidnapped, right?"

Paola translated. The women nodded sadly as they gazed at the photo of the family in happier times.

I continued, "And Silvio Jr., he is writing with his right hand in the photo?"

Paola spoke to the women and they nodded once again.

"So, before the kidnapping he wrote with his right hand? But now he writes with his left?"

The women answered "Sì," again to both questions, but they seemed more cautious, as if they didn't know where it was all going.

"Did he come back from the kidnappers writing with his left hand?"

This time when Paola translated, the women shared a look of concern. Assunta shook her head and looked down and it was only her sister who said quietly, "Sì."

I leaned in to speak to them even though they couldn't understand me. "Why do you think that was?" But before I could get the question out Assunta blurted out hysterically, "Perche era il diavolo che tornata!"

I knew before Paola repeated it back to me that Assunta had said that it was because it was the devil who came back.

CHAPTER 29

I stood up, thanking the aunts and Paola, who seemed shaken by the old woman's outburst. Sunny, too, seemed a little freaked out, downing the rest of her sweet wine before following me into the hall. On my way out, I hung the photo back on the wall. Sunny and I didn't speak until we got in the car. It was she who broke the silence.

"Did you get the answers you came for?"

I thought about it for a minute. "Yes, and more questions. Why would Silvio come back writing with the opposite hand?"

"They used to beat kids for using the wrong hand until they used the right one."

"Yeah, but that was to make them right-handed. No one ever beat a kid to make him left-handed."

"Not that I ever heard of," she conceded.

"Sunny," I started, then stopped. "This is going to sound crazy."

"Crazy ha ha or crazy peculiar?"

"Crazy intervention time."

"My favorite. Go on."

"What if it's not the same kid?"

"Meaning?"

"What if that's not Silvio Jr.? The real one?"

177

She paused, thinking. Finally she said, "Then who is it?"

"I don't know. Doesn't every family have seventeen kids? Someone could have lost one and not known it."

"Not anymore. The birth rate is in serious decline."

"Look, all I know is that the kid who did come back was badly burned, completely bandaged, and writing with the wrong hand. By the time the bandages came off his mother was in a pill stupor and hadn't seen her son's face in years. And look at Silvio next to Antonio. They look nothing alike, and yet Antonio resembles his father and even his aunts."

"I look nothing like two of my sisters. Not that I'm complaining."

"I know," I admitted. "It could all just be a coincidence. But doesn't it seem weird to you? Even the aunts think someone else came back in his place. I mean, sure, they think it's the devil, but still. That must be why they hate going there, by the way."

"But even if this was all true, why would someone send someone back who wasn't Silvio Jr.? And what would it have to do with Elin's murder?"

"Maybe she found out he was an impostor," I posed.

"Maybe," she said sadly. "But that would still mean that Silvio killed her."

"Unless someone else had to benefit from keeping her quiet about it."

"Which leads back to my first question, why would someone send the wrong boy back?"

"What would someone gain from that?" I wondered, too.

As soon as the last questions were out of our mouths, we pulled into the villa driveway one last time. Goddammit! I had pissed off my husband and wasted my morning and I was no closer to understanding anything. Maybe this was all a fantasy. Maybe it was foolishness to think I was going to solve a double homicide. Maybe the actual cops had already solved it.

Sunny and I were still sitting in the car. She had turned the engine off, but still neither of us moved.

"You know, I think I'm being ridiculous," I confessed to Sunny. "My mind just needs something to do, a puzzle to solve and focus on, so that I don't spend my days dwelling on everything I've done with my life. Or not done."

She put her hand on mine and smiled. "It's OK. It makes sense."

"I'm sorry I couldn't help free your friend."

"You did your best," she sighed. "Besides, maybe he's guilty. Sometimes we don't know people as well as we thought we did."

"Ain't that the motherfucking truth," I agreed, feeling about a thousand years old.

Just then I remembered that in all the chaos of the night before I had never told her what I had learned about Paola; that she was an expert shot and used to date the son of a guy that Silvio had imprisoned. And then I realized I wasn't going to tell her now either. Partially because I thought I was just grasping at straws anyway, trying to play the part of this super sleuth. But even more importantly than that, I knew she liked Paola and that once I cast suspicion on her everything would change. Sunny had lost a lot in the last few days. I didn't have the heart to take one more thing from her.

We got out of the car and walked up the driveway towards the rest of my vacation. I was going to go to the Argentario with The Husband, and I was going to have someone bring me drinks while I swam in a cove, and I was going to forget about solving murders.

It almost worked.

CHAPTER 30

I kept my promise: We made it to lunch.

Sunny had called ahead for us to a restaurant on the beach whose carpaccio she had raved about. When we arrived, I had a suspicion it might be good: The waiter wasn't wearing a shirt or shoes. Wearing only a pair of shorts and an apron, he escorted us to a table a mere eight feet from the shoreline. In front of us were families in their bathing suits relaxing on lounge chairs under umbrellas while vendors went from chair to chair, selling everything from jewelry to beach cover-ups to towels. A twelve-year-old kid was parking cars. It all seemed really authentic, very charming and most importantly, like vacation. No polizia. No corpses.

We selected a Greco di Tufo and started to study the list of the day's fresh catches.

Sunny was right: The carpaccio was amazing. They brought the fish to the table, told you the selections that day, and sliced it right there. We chose the tuna: it was a deep reddish purple and the flavor was amazing. We also had anchovies with stracciatella cheese, the best part of the burrata, which I had thought was all of the burrata but I was mistaken. The stracciatella was the creamy inside, like the Oreo filling of Italian cheeses. We finished with grilled prawns. In a million years I never would have thought to grill my prawns with mint, but they did, and it was outstanding.

The beach was looking really inviting, especially as we had been sitting outside for the last ninety minutes in the heat, and we were anxious to get to our own hotel and our own beach. We got back in the car and made our way around the island. A few kilometers down the road from the restaurant was a small port town, after which we turned off and drove inland. We climbed upward and the road got more treacherous; it narrowed, becoming one hairpin turn after another. Often, a car would be coming from the opposite direction and there wasn't enough room for both cars to pass so one of us would have to back up.

"I hope you like the food at the hotel because we won't be driving anywhere for dinner tonight," The Husband declared the second time he had to back up on the narrow roads.

I didn't argue. I wouldn't want to be on these roads at night. Instead I just suggested, "Maybe the hotel can call us a taxi." There was a Michelin-starred restaurant on this island and if I could get in, I wanted to try it.

Finally, after another tight turn, we started descending, eventually seeing both the water and signs for our hotel. A number of switchbacks later and we were pulling into the circular driveway in front of the reception area, where a young man in a tan shirt and pants swooped in to grab our luggage. I would miss the villa, but it was nice to not have to worry that the staff might be trying to kill you.

The Husband had done an amazing job on incredibly short notice. The hotel was situated on a cliff with an outdoor restaurant and bar area perched right at the edge, providing an unobstructed view of the sea and a smaller island across from it. The remains of an old stone tower stood in the middle and was now used as the bar. Mike was already studying the history of the tower, as it was written in the bar menu and allowed him to kill two birds with one stone.

"It says here the tower was used as a lookout, so they could be prepared for attacks by hostile forces."

I snorted. "We need one of those in our house."

And then something magical happened. My husband laughed at one of my jokes. And then he kissed me. "I love you."

"I love you, too."

"I'm really glad I'm here with you." And then to prove it, he grabbed two glasses of Prosecco from the bartender and walked me further along the cliff. A few steps down was an infinity pool, which gave the illusion that the guests were swimming right up to the edge of the world and about to fall off. That sounded pleasant to me.

We checked in at the front desk, providing our credit cards and passports, and I was once again grateful and somewhat amazed that whoever broke in had left those behind. Even if someone had been trying to scare us off, they had certainly been polite about it. Maybe it hadn't been the killer, just someone who thought we were in danger and should go. But the only person I knew who thought that was The Husband, and if had broken into our room himself, it meant that somewhere he still had the GoPro and that was little comfort.

A young woman led us to our room, where we were treated to an even more stunning view. The island was a series of inlets and coves that wove in and out the whole perimeter. Therefore, while we were on top of one cliff, our balcony overlooked the next one down, giving us the vista of both the water in the rocky cove below and the mountainous lush green peak that rose out of it.

"Is it OK?" The Husband wanted to know.

"It's perfect."

"Well, no one's been murdered here, but it will have to do. Should we hit the beach?"

The beach was a kilometer walk down the steep hillside, a trip I was not anxious to take no matter how much burrata and gelato I had eaten. At the bottom was a small beach club where we checked in and were then led out into the cove, flanked on both sides by rocky plateaus that eventually rose up into the green, tree-lined slopes. Up and down the flat parts of the rocks were chairs and umbrellas with a series of steps here and there to help you get up and down. A teenage boy gave us the number for our own chairs and very reluctantly agreed to show us to them, as if we should be able to find them ourselves in the maze of stairs and granite.

Italians lay all over the rocks like lizards in the sun, accumulating a base tan the color of a rich leather, and at the sight of several seventy-year-olds doing just this, I wondered if they ever did any skin cancer studies in this country. Maybe olive oil and wine make you immune. Conversely, my Irish husband coated himself in a thick white suntan lotion before putting on a long-sleeve shirt and an Indiana Jones hat. And he would probably still get burned.

I helped him adjust the umbrella for maximum coverage and then kissed him goodbye, off to the water to test my own genetics in maximum sunlight. There was no easing into this; there was no shallow end or shore. At the bottom of the rocks was a dock with a ladder that you basically climbed down and jettisoned yourself into the cool deep. I followed suit, floating on my back and looking up at the scenery from in between the two peaks. It couldn't be more peaceful.

And yet I couldn't stop my mind from going back to the events of the last few days.

What did I know for sure? Someone had killed Elin and her phone had been in Rome Sunday night. Silvio and Antonio had inherited their father's estate after his sudden death from a heart attack a few months earlier. The brothers fought over what to do with it because Antonio had gambling debts. A car that should have been containing Antonio's wife and children was involved in a fatal accident. And Aparna, the potential sister of Silvio and Antonio, had disappeared. She had been seen talking to Pietro, a former boyfriend of Elin's and former teammate of Antonio's, who had been convicted of match fixing.

And maybe was a hit man?

Elin dead meant Antonio could sell the land. His wife and children dead meant no dependents, and possible life insurance money. Aparna gone meant no third sibling to split the money with. Everyone's death seemed to benefit Antonio, even his father's. It made me wonder if Antonio had fed him fried pork and scared the shit out of him right before he died. And Pietro was a contact of questionable morals who could get close to both his sister-in-law and his alleged sister. And he knew Paola....

Or maybe the aunts were right, and Silvio was the devil who returned. And then he killed his wife.

I then reminded myself that I had no idea what I was doing and should really stop.

"Hey!"

The Husband had decided to join me. He swam over and gave me a kiss.

"It's freezing!" he complained. Mike lacked the enthusiasm I had for refreshing water.

"Check out this view!" We were now treading water side by side in the middle of this Eden.

He looked around at the otherworldly 360 vista. "I really wish I had the GoPro."

I kissed him. "Why don't I make it up to you back in the room?"

He sighed. "OK, but I'm still really bummed it got stolen."

CHAPTER 31

Before we could have "Make up for your stuff getting stolen" sex, we had to stop back at the front desk for our keys, which is a quaint European custom that I don't understand in the least. When you leave the hotel, you leave your key at the front desk. Initially my suspicious American mind worried that someone could steal our stuff that way, forgetting that anyone who worked there already had access to a key to my room and thus could steal my stuff anytime they wanted, as the events of the last twenty-four hours had proven. Eventually I learned to see it as a convenience, as my room key was one less thing I had to worry about losing during my travels.

The concierge told us that there was a last-minute cancellation and she had managed to get us in at the Michelin-starred restaurant that evening at nine o'clock, if we still were interested. I was. I saw the look of hesitation on The Husband's face and asked if she could arrange us a taxi.

I realized as I was getting dressed that as much as I had loved Capalbio, I was happy to be going someplace a little fancier for dinner. I had gotten an unbelievable deal on a Marchesa cocktail dress earlier that year, and it was begging to be returned to its Motherland and worn in Italy. I had since found out that Marchesa wasn't at all an Italian brand, which, while disappointing, did not change the latter half of the statement, or that it should be done with the tan, strappy butterfly-look heels I had gotten in Verona two years before.

We had enough time to catch most of the sunset from the bar

while enjoying another glass of Prosecco before meeting our driver in the lobby. In his mid-forties, he was tall and lanky, with dark hair and a beard. He introduced himself to us as Tommaso.

Tommaso liked to talk. "Where are you from?" he asked in accented English as soon as we got in the car.

"California," we answered.

"California? That's where my girlfriend lives. Un-be-LEEVE-able!" Tommaso liked to accent the third syllable of unbelievable whenever he said it, which turns out was a lot.

"You are going to love the food at this restaurant. Un-be-LEEVE-able!"

"You should see how some people drive on these roads. Un-be-LEEVE-able!"

"You are writers for the television? Un-be-LEEVE-able!"

I was still stuck on the girlfriend in California. What were the logistics of something like that? Was it just some green-card scam Tommaso was working? Or was having a girlfriend in California the Italian equivalent of having "a girlfriend in Canada?"

"Here's what we do," Tommaso said when we reached the restaurant. "I give you my card. Half an hour before you finish your dinner you have the waiter call me up and I come get you. Cool?"

"Unbelievable!"

Equally unbelievable was the restaurant we had arrived at, Stella d'Oro. The maître d' led us out through a large airy dining room, onto a terrace lit with twinkling lights, and straight to a table right up front that overlooked the sea and a garden below. We have learned to tell everyone that we are celebrating our anniversary when we travel, and it is usually true, if not wholly accurate. Does it have to be the exact same calendar date as my marriage for me to celebrate and be grateful for it?

We were immediately handed champagne, which I recognized from the biscuity, dry aroma that you don't find in standard sparkling wines. I breathed deep in the flute. Prosecco was wonderful and I would drink it always, but there was a special place on my palate for the nuance of a good champagne. To complement it, the waiter brought an amuse bouche of caviar crostini, done Italian style with a creamy burrata instead of crème fraiche.

It then occurred to me that this wasn't going to be cheap, and this was on top of the added expense of staying at a hotel. The Husband had booked the room; I had no idea what he was paying last minute during high season. When we had agreed to do this trip, we thought we would be staying for free in a house with a kitchen.

My face must have betrayed my concern because just then he asked me, "What's wrong?"

"I was just thinking about how this trip suddenly got expensive." I took another sip of champagne, relieved that at least we had a driver, and that's when I remembered that we had a driver. Tommaso was another expense.

The Husband grabbed my wrist and looked me in the eye. "Look, I just want to have a good time. I want us to have a good time." He smiled. "Frankly, I'd pay anything to get away from staying at a crime scene."

I laughed, but I was still preoccupied. If I hadn't lost my job, money wouldn't be an issue. Likewise, if I'd been able to get another job. Maybe I'd have another job if I hadn't been so depressed after... all of it. And if I hadn't been so depressed, we wouldn't have needed to come here at all to shake me out of it.

I looked down at my plate so he couldn't see the tears gathering in my eyes, only the moment I blinked, a big fat tear hit the remains of my crostini anyway.

"Listen, we're both going to get jobs again and then we won't have time to come to Italy and get shitfaced."

I admired his optimism. And I desperately wished that I could share it. But I smiled anyway, especially when he said, "So I think we should do the wine pairing, too. Fuck it. That's what Tommaso is for."

And Tommaso was as good as his word. After a dinner of delicate soffitto in brodo, a langoustine risotto, and roast duck, we were back in his car careening around roads made invisible by the lack of natural or unnatural light. But as we had opted for the wine pairing, I was fine with it.

"I was very happy to receive the call from the restaurant to take you back to your hotel. Un-be-LEEVE-able!"

He further explained, "It's all part of my business plan. See, I can take you one way and you pay me and our business, it is done. Who cares?"

Considering the cost of taking us one way was a small ransom, it seemed he should have cared, but I didn't say anything.

"Or, I can be nice and give you my card and you call me again and I take more of the money."

He wasn't wrong about that.

"For years I drive this taxi out here, taking some of the money. And then two years ago I say, "Tommaso, why have some of the money when you can have all of it? And I start my own cab company. Un-be-LEEVE-able!"

We nodded, a little confused at this point, but whether that was from the wine pairing or Tommaso's tenuous command of English was unclear. Overall, he seemed to speak very well, so I was going to guess the wine.

However, whatever our level of impairment, we didn't let that stop us from having a final drink on our balcony. Looking out over the sea it was hard to believe that twenty-four hours ago we were emailing the police crime-scene photos and having our room broken into. For the first night in days, I drifted off to sleep thinking about something other than murder. (Until The Husband started snoring, that is.)

Unfortunately, when I woke, murder was the only thing on everyone's lips.

CHAPTER 32

One of the things I like about staying in a nice hotel is the canvas bag they stick on your outer doorknob in the mornings that contains the morning paper. I rarely read the newspaper, it's far too depressing, and I think we've already established that I struggle with The Sads as it is. But it's a nice touch and lets me know that I'm getting my money's worth, like having those miniature ketchup bottles on the room service cart, or a better class of toiletries in the bathroom. (Both of which I have a compulsive need to always take with me even though I don't even eat ketchup. One time, I didn't have to buy soap for a YEAR.)

The paper that greeted me that morning was in Italian, but the large half-page photo of Silvio and Elin was all I needed to see in order to understand the headline.

Of course, I thought, by the time he was arrested Saturday night and news got out they probably didn't have enough time to make yesterday's paper. But this way, they could start fresh on Monday and if it was anything like America, the story would lead the news all week.

I would have to remember to text Sunny to see how she was doing.

"Did you see this?" I asked Mike when he joined me at cliff's edge for breakfast. I held up the paper for him to see what I, and it appeared every other table out on the lawn, was talking about.

"Yeah, the woman at reception couldn't stop reading it. I have never been more grateful to whoever stole our shit and got us out of that house. It's going to be a madhouse there."

Realizing he was right, I grew worried for Sunny and hoped she had gone. I quickly sent her an email to check in and then went back to reading the article while I drank my cappuccino and The Husband went off in search of bacon at the buffet.

The reading was a little slow going, save for the fact that a lot of the story I already knew and was able to skim over. There wasn't really a lot of new information. It said that Elin's body had been found Thursday night, that she was last known to be in Rome on Sunday, and then talked about her career as a model. As for Silvio, they of course mentioned the kidnapping, striking a tragic tone, and even discussed his career as a lawyer in favorable terms. But then the tone turned dark, even suggesting that the trauma of his past led to a violent impulse that the heir had always tried to repress. Frankly, I was impressed with myself for understanding the nuances of this, even with the help of my Italian dictionary app. There was no real information about the crime since it was all just some wild theory anyway: There were no witnesses, no weapon, no evidence. I went back up to the top, to the part where Elin was last believed to be in Rome and tried to re-read something I had skipped over earlier. It looked like they had found Elin's car parked behind an Autogrill on the highway. I was right! She never made it off the Autostrada—at least not alive.

Oh, Elin, who met you there? Who met you there and killed you?

I read on to a side article about the effect all of the attention was having on the tiny town of Capalbio, now that reporters and news vans were descending on it like trophy wives at a sample sale. Everyone was complaining. News crews reported having equipment and even a van stolen, and the excess traffic was causing problems all over town. They were blaming it for at least one accident, involving a man on a vespa who got run off the road by one of the crews. I read on. He had been taken to the hospital for a concussion, and while not a resident had been vacationing there for the summer....

The Husband had returned while I was reading, and in between bites of bacon and toast was perusing a guidebook of the island, making suggestions for our day. Therefore, the look on his face wasn't pleasant when I said, "We have to go back."

"I've already paid for tonight."

"Nino's in the hospital."

I could see him weighing his finances against his concern for his friend.
"Is he OK? What happened now?"

"According to this, he had a motorino accident yesterday. He's in the hospital with a concussion."

Ding. My phone beeped, letting me know I had an email, which was shocking since last I checked I got zero bars here and the "Free Wi-fi" they promised was also "No Wi-fi." Not that it mattered. If you came all the way here needing internet, then frankly something was wrong with you.

"Hold on. It's Sunny writing me back!"

> OH MY GOD it is so good to hear your voice or see your typing or read your words or whatever the fuck I can no longer think straight. You guys were smart to get out when you did. Paparazzi started showing up yesterday afternoon. We had to stay inside and couldn't swim and the kids were barbarians destroying the house so I sent them back to Rome with Jen, who complained about how hot it was going to be and then said she was anxious to teach Sage about the gladiators in the Coliseum, because that will make for some sweet dreams.

Probably for Sage it would.

Anyway, originally, I had wanted to wait here until Silvio is released, so that I could see him. And now we're stuck here anyway since Nino fainted for real on the motorino yesterday and hit his head and is now in the hospital for observation. He's such a pussy about this heat.

I had to admit, she didn't seem very concerned. And she didn't mention anything about a news crew, unlike the article.

Paola insisted that I stay with her last night so now it's just Enzo at the villa. He refuses to leave. I suppose if he can rescue Silvio from kidnappers and a fire, a few photographers and reporters are no big deal.

She was at Antonio's?! Someone there was most likely a murderer and it was probably Antonio. But I suppose when you grow up with a father in construction, some people are bound to be murderers so maybe it wasn't all that weird for her.

Still, I didn't like the idea of my friend all alone there, with her husband in the hospital and a distractingly handsome, gambling, psychopath on the loose. I decided to not let my husband know that she was OK with all of that.

"It's half an hour away!" I pleaded. "We can go there and come back."

The Husband looked at his watch. "I don't want to miss lunch."

"Great! I just have to go back to the room to change my shoes."

Now I was pushing it. "What?! Why?!"

"These are just my walking-around-the-hotel shoes. If there's paparazzi in Capalbio I want them to see me in heels."

CHAPTER 33

On the way out, me and my vintage Chanel slides with a kitten heel clicked pass Tommaso in the parking lot with some new passengers, on his mission to not just take some of the money, but all of the money. He was clearly doing his best to make sure that happened.

"I'd feel better about this if it were Tommaso driving us back to Capalbio," Mike lamented. He hated to drive roads like these almost as much as he hated being the passenger while I drove roads like these. It was a no-win situation for him when we traveled. When we went to Ireland, he couldn't stand driving on the left side of the road while I really had no problem with it. But being in the passenger seat and having no control bothered him even more and after a day and a half he insisted on driving the whole time, white knuckling it all the way. Meanwhile I drank whiskey and Guinness, figuring I had tried.

"I can't even imagine what something like that costs considering it was a king's ransom to take us fifteen minutes last night," I remarked when something hit me. No articles I had read ever mentioned that they had caught the kidnappers so they must have gotten away with the money. Ransom was a funny negotiation. No one ever asked for all of a person's money. Just a number that was meaningful, but that they felt the person was willing to part with and pay. Why did they never ask for all of it? Surely, the Corini's would have paid anything to get their son back. But there was a certain etiquette to the ransom request. J. Paul Getty had even famously refused to pay the original demand saying he had far too many grandchildren to pay that amount every time one went missing and the kidnappers had accepted less. Granted, they sent his grandson back missing an ear and with enough psychological problems to cause a life-ending drug problem. But as Tommaso had wisely said the night before, why take some of the money when you can take all of it?

I called Sunny to let her know we were on our way to the hospital to see her. She sounded surprised but also relieved, or at least that's what I wanted to believe since I was putting my marriage in further jeopardy with what may have been an impulsive idea. I remembered how sad she had been to see us go the day before and thought she could probably use the company, but never would have asked outright. I was hoping I could get her to come back with us, and Nino, too, if he was OK to travel. This just all seemed like too much. It couldn't be good for her. She had rescued me when I needed it; now I wanted to do the same for her.

Fortunately, the hospital was in Orbetello, a small town on the lagoon between the Argentario and Capalbio, so it was only ten minutes later that we were parking in front of the building and negotiating the crowd of people smoking furiously outside of it. I didn't know if I should be shocked that in Italy so many people were that desperate to smoke that they created an almost human barricade to the front doors, or shocked that at least they forbade you from smoking in a hospital. It was still Italy, after all. Mike and I actually had to push our way through, like we were trying to get backstage at a concert, and there was twice as much smoke. We saw a number of doctors and even a few patients, still in hospital gowns and attached to IV, all lighting up. A gurney with a dying person on it didn't stand a chance.

Soon enough, we were standing in a hallway outside the room were Nino was sleeping.

"We have to keep waking him up every two hours, so he doesn't fall into a coma," she explained. "I should have kept the boys here for that," she joked. "God knows, I haven't gotten more than twenty minutes sleep in a row since they were born."

"What happened?" Mike asked.

"I have no idea. Nino was going to go up to town to pick up some things for lunch. He had to call work first to say that he wouldn't be in today, but my phone overheated in this weather and his had no signal, so on his way out he said he was going downstairs to see if Enzo was in his room and ask if he could use his phone, and I went to take a nap. Next thing I knew Paola had come to get me, hysterical. After Fabrizio's accident earlier this week she was beside herself, and insisted that I not be alone and that Antonio drive me everywhere."

That didn't sound good, but I had more pressing questions. "You said he fainted?" I left out the part where she called him a pussy.

"Yeah, that's what Nino thought might have happened. You heard him say he almost did while driving the scooter the other day. It's got to be a thousand degrees inside that helmet. He can't remember a thing though. The knot on his head is gigantic. The man who called the ambulance says they saw one of those gigantic news vans drive him off the road, but chissà, who knows? Everyone is so angry about the reporters they'll say anything."

I nodded, knowingly rolling my eyes. "Yeah, I read that someone got their van stolen?"

"Yes, and then that turned out to be a false alarm. They just had forgotten where they had parked it or something." She sounded exasperated with the whole thing. "I can't believe I'm saying this, but thank God that pain-in-the-ass sister of mine was in town and had already left with the kids. I don't know how I would handle all of this."

"Well, let us help. What can we do?"

"There's one thing you could do, but I hate to ask."

"Go ahead. You practically planned our wedding. It's the least we can do."

"Would you go by Silvio's and get some of our things? I didn't have time last night and I want to be here when Nino wakes up."

"Of course." I said as I caught The Husband looking at his watch. I quickly elbowed him and muttered, "We're fine for lunch."

CHAPTER 34

"Drive carefully. I don't like our odds these days," I cautioned.

"I just want to make sure we're back in time for lunch."

Sunny had provided me with a set of keys to the villa as well as her room in the guest house, along with a list of the things she and Nino were going to need. When we pulled into the driveway, I expected to see a zombie army of paparazzi, but instead there was one lone photographer, and he was so brazen as to be sitting in the shade of an umbrella by the pool.

He immediately started taking our picture.

"Siamo nessuno!" I asserted. "We are no one." Which for some reason satisfied him and he put the camera down. Or maybe he just wasn't that motivated to do his job. Still, I was glad that I had worn my heels. I also may have unintentionally smiled, but I swear it was just a reflex. Someone puts a camera in your face, you smile.

I asked him where everybody was, and he told me they had gone to the courthouse; they had gotten word that Silvio would be released today. That was quick, I thought. Maybe Jen was right, and he had the best defense money could buy. Or maybe they thought someone else was the killer now. The paparazzo added that "Il maggiordomo" had gone to pick him up. I assumed that was Enzo. I relayed it to Mike as we went to the apartment below ours, which was Sunny and Nino's. Mike fiddled with his phone while I packed their bags.

"Hey, I've actually got a good signal down here."

"I'm not surprised," I recalled. "This is near where I saw Aparna making that phone call the night before she disappeared."

I went into their bathroom to pick up some toiletries.

"Holy shit!" I heard from the next room.

"Did someone else die?" I asked wearily.

"No! My iPad is here!"

"What?!"

The Husband quickly explained. "I totally forgot I had 'Find my iPad' turned on the other night."

"Because you were drinking."

He ignored me and continued, "I guess I just assumed my iPad was long gone and I didn't even think to use it."

"Because you were drinking."

"I thought of it last night, but of course, no signal on the island."

"And you were drink—"

"Shut up! Now that I have a signal, I just turned it on as a goof and it's here."

"That means the person who stole it is here!" I cried out, probably way more excited by this prospect than I should have been.

"Or I left it in the house all along and only thought it was stolen."

"Well, let's go see where it is!" I zipped the two bags closed and we carried them across to the car, following the signal the whole way.

When we got to the house, we could faintly hear the iPad pinging from the basement. I had never been down there and was apprehensive, but reminded myself that we had nothing to be worried about. We were alone in the house, if the man who takes pictures of people against their will for a living was to be believed.

We went down the stairs and found ourselves in a wine cellar. We followed the signal through that into a laundry room. The pinging was coming from beyond that. There were two doors off the laundry room. We opened one; it looked like a storage closet filled with extra linens and lightbulbs and things, but the noise only got fainter when we walked in. So we went to the second door and slowly opened it. It was Enzo's room. And the pinging was coming from inside of it.

Enzo had wanted us to leave. Or someone had ordered him to get us to leave. Was he acting alone, and it was a warning? Or did he hear us casting suspicion on Antonio and do it to protect him? Or maybe someone only wanted to frame Enzo and hid our stuff here.

"I told you that I always lock the door!" I exclaimed when Mike pulled his iPad off of the top of Enzo's armoire. He felt around for a minute before grabbing his GoPro, too.

"And I believed you, remember?"

"You're right. Let's just get the fuck out of here!"

We bounded up the stairs, waved goodbye to the lone paparazzo, got in the car and tore off down the driveway, trying to put as much distance as we could between us and the villa. We were halfway back to the hospital when Sunny texted to say they were releasing Nino, and could we meet her back at Antonio and Paola's? I tried to text back "Sure" but right then my battery died. I had relied heavily on the GPS all morning, and with the lack of a strong signal that had depleted my battery. I tossed it under the seat and told Mike we were going to have to use his phone for the rest of the day.

"Why would Enzo want us gone?" I wondered.

"Because we're loud, freeloading Americans who drink too much?" The Husband answered all too quickly.

"Well, yes, all of that is true and more, but why does he care? It's not his house."

Just then, I remembered what Paola had said: "He acts like it's his money."

Who would act like it was their money?

"Do you think Enzo and Silvio are lovers?"

"What?!" The Husband jerked the wheel he was so surprised, and we briefly drifted into the opposite lane. "Are you out of your mind?"

"Why wouldn't they be?"

"Trust me. I'm a guy. Those two aren't gay."

"That's so homophobic of you. Think about it. Enzo wants us gone. He acts like it's his place, his money. Who acts entitled like that if not a lover?"

"In that family? Everyone. The brother. The bastard British sister. Us, probably, if we had been able to stay two more days."

He had a point there. I was already thinking of the place where we had spent three nights as our room and trying to figure out how to wrangle an invitation for next year. Proving Silvio's innocence would help.

We pulled up at the vineyard, grabbed Sunny and Nino's bags and went to the front door where Paola greeted us with hugs and wine. I really liked her. I really hoped she wasn't the killer.

She invited us out to the back patio. The Husband looked at his watch.

"Still plenty of time," I advised him before following her out. Sunny was already seated at the table.

I smiled at her encouragingly. "I heard while we were getting your things that Silvio is being let go today."

"Sì," Paola confirmed.

Sunny explained that they didn't have bail in Italy, but depending on how much evidence they had against you, they could release you until you were found guilty. Sometimes you were placed on house arrest, "and sometimes you could take a fucking vacation to America if you wanted. This fucking country," she finished, shaking her head.

Paola nodded before adding, "He is on his way here now. His house is molto pazzo, much crazy, too many cameras. But he knows he will be followed, so Enzo is going to pretend he is driving Silvio to the villa and then Silvio will sneak out with Antonio when no one is looking, and Antonio will bring him here."

And if they should get into a car accident, we'll know who to blame, I thought. I had to admit, though, it was a smart plan whether or not you wanted to murder your brother. Because you felt entitled to all the money, I added in my head, thinking. It was like Tommaso said. Why have some of the money when you could have all of the money?

Just then Antonio came out on the patio and I was momentarily distracted by the brilliance of his murderous smile, which was killing me softly.

"Silvio is showering and then will be down shortly for lunch," he announced. "Lui ha molto fame!" He was very hungry, as I can only imagine a person would be after spending two days in jail, although I did wonder if even the prison food in Italy was good. "My friends, would you like to stay and have lunch with us?" he added, looking from Mike to me.

On the one hand, I knew that eating lunch with Antonio was bound to turn into one of those time-share presentations where he tries to sell us on buying a vacation home in Italy with fifty of our closest friends. On the other hand, it was lunch, and I knew that would get The Husband off my back about it. However, as someone here was a murderer, it might be prudent to be on our way—especially as one of the suspects also had a price on his head.

"Sure!" agreed The Husband, refilling his wine glass from the carafe in the center of the table.

"Perfetto! I will let our cook know." He jumped up from his seat and went to leave.

Paola called after him, "Please ask her to pick up another Epipen for Assunta at the farmacia when she runs errands today." She turned to me. "I meant to do it yesterday, but I forgot. I don't like being without one, not after the accident with Jen this week."

"Did you ever figure out where it was?"

"No, it is a mystery. Hopefully my kids didn't take it. Who knows what could happen if they accidentally gave it to themselves?"

I thought of Paola's boys chasing Sunny's around the pool the other day and I couldn't imagine them with any more adrenaline in their systems. It would give them a heart attack, or at least give their mom one trying to watch them.

Because that's what adrenaline does to you.

All of a sudden it added up. At least some of it did. I looked over to where Sunny was sitting and caught her eye, then glanced to the doorway. When she nodded very subtly, I got up and asked where the bathroom was. Then I headed through the doors and back to the darkened sitting room where I had met the aunts the day before. A moment later I heard Sunny say something about checking on Nino and then follow me down the hall.

"Elin wasn't the first murder," I blurted out as soon as she shut the door.

"What? Who?" She sat down next to me on the sofa.

"Silvio Sr. His heart attack was induced by adrenaline. That's where the missing Epipen went."

"But why would someone want him out of the way? Never mind, I know why. He was rich. Oh my God, the old women were right! His spirit wasn't at rest!" We started laughing but then I think we both got a little creeped out sitting in the darkened room by ourselves. Sunny got serious again and asked, "Do you think it was Antonio?"

"Probably. He had the most to gain from all of this." But then why would Enzo want us gone? Maybe Antonio wanted us gone and had Enzo steal our stuff. But Antonio didn't want us gone, he thought we were going to buy the vineyard. And Enzo wouldn't do anything for Antonio. He was always ratting him out, acting *like it was his money.*

Or maybe it would be some day.

But why would he think that? I had to admit, Enzo and Silvio being lovers still seemed like the most likely explanation.

"There's just too many unanswered questions!"

"I know what you mean," Sunny agreed.

I looked down at the table in front of me and my mind went back to the conversation that was had in this room just the day before. Sunny's must have, too, because she said, "I can't stop thinking about what the aunts said yesterday."

Silvio didn't return, the devil did.

Why get some of the money when you could get all of it?

What would you gain from sending another boy back?

I closed my eyes and started to mentally turn things around in my head like when you're trying to put pieces together on a jigsaw puzzle. This looks like it fits. Nope. What about this? Close, but not right. But what about these two? There you go. And next thing you know you have three or four pieces in a row that fit.

"Sunny, what if it's true that Silvio didn't return? What if another boy did?"

As soon as I said it, I felt foolish again. "What am I doing? I said I wasn't going to do this," I lamented, the frustration and self-doubt evident in my voice.

Sunny grabbed me by the shoulders. "Kat, this isn't a pair of shoes or a piece of cake! This is a murder. Now stop criticizing yourself and tell me what you're thinking!"

I took a deep breath and gathered my thoughts. "OK, why kidnap a boy and just get some of the family fortune for the ransom, when you can send your own boy back and get all of it?"

I was worried that Sunny was going to laugh, or worse, look at me with a sad look that said I had tried but I just couldn't do it. Because apparently, there was no way I wouldn't find to make a triple homicide all about me. But instead, she thought about it for a moment, seriously considering it, before admitting, "That's a great idea for a movie. You should totally write that someday. But who would have done that in real life?"

"I wish I knew." The man's voice was coming from a darkened corner of the sitting room. We turned to the source of the voice, barely visible in the dark, although Sunny already knew who it was because she recognized it. It was Silvio. He was seated in a large wingback chair that faced out the window, totally obscured from us between the angle and the poor lighting. He said to us with an apologetic tone, as if to explain his intrusion, "It's the only room in the house where they don't mind smoking." He extinguished his cigarette. "I don't normally, but after the last few days, I really wanted one."

"Silvio, I'm—" sorry, I started to say, which doesn't come easy to me.

Only he finished for me. "Right. You're right." Which I have to admit I liked the sound of a lot better.

"It is true. I am not Silvio Corini. Or so I've been told."

At that bombshell I found myself wishing that I hadn't left my wine on the terrazza. I casually looked around the room to see if the aunts had stashed any of their moscato there. As if he could read my mind, Silvio got up out of his chair and went to an antique sideboard. "I don't know about you ladies, but I could use a drink." He smiled sadly, pouring each of us a glass of Vin Santo, a white dessert wine the color of honey. It also often tastes like medicine, but it would have to do.

He sat down next to us on the sofa and took a sip. "I don't have many memories from before the age of five, as I suppose most of us don't. I've seen the pictures, of course, so sometimes I think I remember things. But I've always been told that with the trauma of the kidnapping and the fire it's not uncommon to block these things out at such a young age."

Sunny and I nodded silently. This was all textbook.

"I do remember thinking I was going to die in the fire, and Enzo saving me. And I had vague memories of people telling me that I wasn't really a Corini, that I would never be one of them. I thought they might be a dream, and I would wake up in the middle of the night afraid that I wasn't really home. But my father always assured me that it was just a bad dream and of course I was home.

"As time went on, the dreams came less frequent and I assumed my father was right; I was just a confused child. Eventually I forgot about the fear altogether. And then when I was eighteen, I started to get letters.

"They told me I was not really a Corini and they demanded money to keep my secret. I ignored them at first. They seemed ludicrous. Although I suppose part of me always wondered. I did have those dreams. What if they were memories? And of course I saw the difference between myself and Antonio, both physically and," here he paused and attempted a smirk of humor, "financially, as well. So perhaps I always wondered a little. And then they began threatening to tell my father. I knew he had a bad heart. I didn't think he could handle revisiting the whole ordeal."

"Why didn't you get a DNA test?" Sunny asked compassionately.

Silvio had clearly spent a lot of time thinking the same thing because he was quick to answer.

"At first, at the time, I told myself they weren't easy to get. But really, I just didn't want to know. If they were right, then what? Was I going to tell my father that his real son was dead, and I was nothing more than a grisly reminder who lived in his home all this time? Also, selfishly, I didn't want to lose my family. I know that makes me cowardly, but even if they no longer loved me, I would always love them."

He paused to take a sip of his wine and perhaps to gain control over his emotions, because his next words sounded more detached. "And so, I started paying. It's what motivated me to go into my own business. I told myself that I was making more than I was paying out. Also, I only had access to so much. The businesses were still in my father's name and some of the money was in trust. So, I felt the bulk of the estate was safe." He paused, angry at himself. "It didn't occur to me that this would only make my entire family a target. But then came the boating accident that almost killed my brother and father. Everyone blamed Antonio, but I suspected otherwise."

"But what changed?" I wondered out loud.

"Scusa?"

"The kidnappers were content to blackmail you from the time you were eighteen until just a few years ago. It's not the most efficient scam there ever was, but it was an arrangement they seemed happy with. Then, all of a sudden, they attempt to murder two people? Why? What changed?"

A weary Silvio shrugged. "To be honest I wasn't around much in the time before the accident. I had a very important case up north against a huge corporation that was also fighting an inheritance claim."

Something about what he said seemed familiar, but I couldn't quite grasp what. I really had to dry out when we got back to the States.

If I was hoping he would elaborate on the case and jar my memory, I was disappointed when he went back to the reason we were all here. "After the death of my father, I reassured myself it was only a heart attack, but I knew I would always have my doubts. I couldn't sleep, I couldn't work. I worried that they wouldn't stop at him. I finally had to confess all of it to Elin. She was the only one I ever told."

He was tearing up now and I could hear Sunny sniffling next to me.

"She was such a remarkable woman." He full-on broke down now. "We agreed, as a couple, that we were going to tell the truth and build our own lives away from the Corinis."

"That's why she was looking for work!" I hadn't meant to interrupt him, but now it all made sense. "That's why you bought the home with your corporate account."

"Yes," he sighed. "We wanted to make sure we took no proceeds from the Corini estate. We wanted to make sure our affairs were in order before we told Antonio and did a DNA test. I also think Elin wanted one last summer here, and I couldn't deny her that." He smiled at the memory of his wife in better times. "She was always so happy here."

Sunny spoke. "And that's why Aparna never had a DNA test."

"I knew she couldn't do it with me," Silvio admitted. "It wouldn't be fair. If it didn't match, we still wouldn't know conclusively."

"So, who are these people?!" Sunny wanted to know.

"I don't know who is behind this. I've never met with anyone face to face. But I do know that they killed my wife and probably tried to kill my brother's family in order to get their hands on all of the Corini's money through me."

"Because you can't disinherit someone under Italian law!" I suddenly remembered. But that wasn't all of it. There was something else I wasn't thinking of.

"Esattamente!" Silvio looked at Sunny breaking the tension. "Your friend is a brava student of law already."

"She remembers everything," Sunny said once again, proudly.

He turned to me and said solemnly, "In that case I am very sorry. Some things in life it is better if we could forget."

He looked at me with sad eyes that I knew would never forget, never unsee the things they had seen, no matter how much he desperately wanted to. I knew that look far too well. I saw it every time I looked in the mirror.

"What do we do now?" Sunny wanted to know.

Silvio stood. "We eat lunch, of course."

CHAPTER 35

Silvio had asked that we not discuss this at the table, as he wanted to find the right time to discuss it with Antonio. I wanted to say that anytime was the right time to tell Antonio that all of his father's fortune would now be his to piss away as he chose, but kept that to myself.

Still, it just seemed weird to sit down to a large meal as if nothing else was happening. "What about the real killer?" I asked.

"Well, I can assure you that no one here is a murderer, so I think we're safe here enjoying our lunch. My brother has an excellent cook. As you can imagine he's spared no expense."

I thought this was a little naïve of Silvio. His story didn't discount Antonio being the killer. He still had plenty of motive to want them out of the way. Maybe he had even caught wind of the whole fake Corini business over the years and was using it to rattle Silvio and force him to admit the truth, thus giving up all rights to the money.

Sunny quickly ran to the guest house to actually check on her husband this time, leaving Silvio and me to walk out onto the patio together. Mike raised an eyebrow at me. When I sat down, he whispered, "He may be rich, but keep in mind the turnover rate for his wives is high."

As his "whisper" is what most people call an "inside voice" I elbowed him in the ribs. "How much wine have you had?"

He responded, but in a much lower voice this time, "Leave me alone. Antonio's been trying to sell me part of his soccer team."

"Let me know when he gets to Paola. I like her. And I could use a new friend back home."

Silvio, meanwhile, had immediately gone over to his sister-in-law and thanked her for her hospitality.

Paola smiled at her ex-boyfriend. "We're just so glad you're out of that horrible place." Once again I thought of her connection to Royal Motors. Maybe Silvio was wrong about who was after him. Staying under Paola's roof would give her all the opportunity she needed for an "accidental" fall down the stairs, or faking another heart attack, or poisoning him....

Suddenly I had lost my appetite for lunch.

Sunny returned at this point, the aunts joined us, careful not to sit too close to Silvio, and we all sat down to eat. It was a fantastic meal of local meats and cheeses followed by a wide, flat fresh pasta in a rabbit-and-caramelized-onion ragù with porchetta, a rolled pork shoulder stuffed with garlic and herbs, as the third course. Afterwards, we were treated to café macchiatos and homemade biscotti.

I made sure to eat only what Paola did.

But it was hard to stay focused on the food and even harder to keep up with the conversation. I was still somewhat in shock from all that Silvio had said. I knew Sunny felt the same way. Not only was she uncharacteristically quiet, but whenever we caught each other's eyes we would start to exchange a look before one of us would get paranoid about who might see. I don't know what I found harder to believe: Silvio's story, or that I'd been right about it.

After the coffees, the aunts went to take their naps. Paola excused herself and said she and Antonio had to go pick up the boys, who had spent the day on a boat with friends. She still refused to drive and with Fabrizio gone, Antonio had to take her.

Silvio looked wary. "Be careful. In fact, why don't you let me call Enzo and he can get them? We're all having such a lovely time on the terrazza." He tried to make it sound casual, but I knew exactly why he was concerned. He believed someone was still after them.

"We'll be fine," protested Antonio. "And after such a meal the sea air will be good for me. Maybe I'll go for a swim while I'm there."

I saw a look of concern flash in Silvio's eyes. So much could happen to a person on a boat or in the water....

"We should be going, too." Mike stood up and said, "Thank you for an amazing meal!"

"The cook, she comes with the place..." Antonio made one last attempt to close the deal with The Husband.

We hugged Paola and they left. I knew The Husband would divorce me if we didn't get to enjoy at least part of the day at the hotel we were paying for, so we got up to leave, asking Sunny if she would take us to say goodbye to Nino on our way out.

Silvio walked the three of us to the foyer, which is where we ran into Enzo. I again wondered if he was the one to take our things and, if so, whether he had realized the stolen items had been repatriated. He wouldn't know it was us necessarily; the place was crawling with disreputable photags who could have taken the stuff... and one who had actually taken our picture and could have shown it to Enzo had he asked if any suspicious people entered the house while he was gone. Oh, well, we were leaving, now. This was Silvio's story to tell the Polizia, if it even was really his story.

It then occurred to me that validating the overactive imaginations of two writers would be a great thing for a murderer to do if he wanted to gain sympathy and throw suspicion off of himself. For all I knew, he made it all up as he went along. But no

215

sooner had I thought that than I felt bad for thinking it. Silvio's grief and confusion had seemed genuine.

On our way out we passed the cook, who was also leaving. I remembered that Paola had asked her to run some errands that afternoon, including picking up a new Epipen. Funny that she was so insistent about replacing the old one so quickly when she said Assunta never went outside. I reminded myself that I was out of the detective game as we continued along a path that led in back and to the right of the main house, where the old barn that had been converted to guest rooms and a kitchen stood.

Nino was on the sofa and fully recovered, judging by the way he complained about the lack of Wi-fi the minute we walked in.

"Oh, boo hoo!" Sunny burst out, her bedside manner clearly depleted. "Relax, we'll be back in Rome tomorrow."

"You're going back tomorrow?" I asked her, not really hiding my relief.

"Yes. I'd go back tonight but I think Nino needs one more day of rest, and frankly I think I had too much to drink at lunch. Although after that conversation I certainly needed it."

"What conversation?" our husbands asked at the same time.

"We'll tell you later," she and I answered in unison.

Mike turned his attention to Nino. "I'm sorry, to hear about your accident, man. What happened?"

Nino began in his beautifully accented English, "I don't remember much. I needed to use Enzo's phone because ours were not working, and so I went down to his room. He was not there, but his phone was on the desk and so I used it, and then ran into him on my way out. I explained to him what happened and told him it was an emergency; I didn't want him to think I was snoopy."

"What?!" Sunny looked at her husband incredulously. "You didn't want him to think you were a cartoon dog?"

"Take it easy on him, Sunny, he's had a head injury. He could have a brain bleed," Mike defended Nino.

"No, brain is not bleeding, I'm fine. I didn't want him to think I was snoopy."

"It's OK, Buddy." Mike patted Nino's hand. "You get some rest."

Sunny bent down over her husband. "Nino, how many fingers am I holding up?"

I looked from Sunny to my husband. "Snooping!" I said. "What the hell is wrong with you two? How much have you had to drink?"

Nino sighed and continued, "Enzo was very nice about it, though, even suggesting that I take Renato's motorino since it would be easier. The news vans were parked up and down the road leading to the villa and those roads are always so narrow. I got on the bike and next thing I knew I was in the hospital, with my beautiful wife yelling at me that I almost died." He smiled as he finished.

"Well, we're very glad you didn't. Who else is going to cook for us our last night?" I asked.

We hugged him goodbye and Sunny offered to walk us out, this time through what she called a shortcut across the lawn and back through the main house, although I suspect she was lingering, wanting to find some time to discuss Silvio's revelation. She got lucky: As we entered the main house, this time through the terrazza doors, Mike asked, "Where's there a bathroom I could use?" As she started to point towards the powder room he quickly added, "Preferably one that no one is going to have to go near for a while." Finally reunited with his beloved iPad, which he was subconsciously stroking fondly, I knew he was going to be a while. Sunny must have known it, too, because she led him up a staircase off the kitchen to the second floor and sent him down to the end of the hallway.

"It's Silvio Sr.'s old bathroom," she explained as he walked away. "They'll just think it's the ghost."

We both laughed although I did add, "Well, now we all know why he was so unhappy."

"Do you really think someone induced his heart attack?" Sunny wondered.

"I don't know. Do you?"

"If what Silvio said was true, it actually makes sense."

We were walking down the hallway to our favorite confessional, which unfortunately we could hear through the door was currently being occupied by Silvio and Enzo. We sat down at the bottom of the main staircase, suddenly too tired to find another room, not that the house was lacking in them.

"If there was just a way to find proof of who killed Elin," I said. "Who would have met her at the rest stop on the highway? Did she call someone? I wish we had her phone."

"They never found it," Sunny stated. "But someone had her phone in Rome that night, we know that."

The doors opened at the moment and Silvio and Enzo came out. Enzo immediately took out his telefonino and made a call as Silvio came over to us. "I wanted to thank you for your discretion at lunch today. So far, we are the only three who know, but I plan to tell the polizia later tonight, as soon as I tell Antonio, and my lawyer can get here."

Enzo finished his call and put his phone back in his shirt pocket, where he always kept it. And that's when it all came together. Right before his accident, Nino had used Enzo's phone. But Enzo always had his phone on him. So then whose phone did he use?

We needed proof of who killed Elin.

And I knew how to get it.

But what I didn't know was how to get the message to Sunny. It's not like I could just say in plain English—

On second thought, that's exactly what I could do.

"Sunny," I stared her in the eyes, so she knew what I was saying was important. "You have your phone, right?"

"Yeah, you need it?"

I looked at Silvio trying to implore him with my eyes to pay attention.

"I need you to call your friend." But I didn't want to say her name. Anyone could understand that. It would draw attention to what I was doing. "The one you met in yoga class."

She looked a little surprised, but picked up her phone, scrolled through contacts, and hit "Elin." Silvio saw what she was doing and looked at us both with a furrowed brow, puzzled.

Until the phone started to ring in Enzo's pants' pocket.

At first Enzo didn't understand what was happening. He was shaken by the phone ringing but hadn't been able to understand our exchange. However, when Silvio turned and looked at him with a mixture of sadness and fury, he began to get it. Silvio crossed to him, taking advantage of Enzo's confusion to reach into his pocket and pull out the phone.

Elin's phone. It had a custom case with a picture of the villa on it. Where she was happiest. This must have been the phone Nino had used, not even realizing it was Elin's. Men notice nothing.

Enzo started retreating back into the sitting room and Silvio started to quietly follow him. Only Enzo grabbed for one of the marble candle holders and immediately brought it down on Silvio's head.

That's when Sunny and I ran.

CHAPTER 36

Perhaps it would have been wiser to run outside, which is certainly a thought I had, but then I also remembered I had a husband in a haunted bathroom upstairs releasing an unearthly specter of his own and I should probably get him out, too. Also, he had the car keys.

Sunny and I fled up the stairs into the darkened hallway, kept that way, no doubt, as it was the aunts' naptime.

"Goddammit!" she cried.

"What is it?"

"I'm trying to call the police, only there's no cell service up here. I hate this fucking country. I'm moving my kids back to America as soon as I can escape here with my life."

We walked in the direction in which she had sent Mike not too long before, and I followed her through the door at the end of the hall, into the old man's bedroom. It clearly hadn't been touched since he died, which hopefully wasn't right here in this room; I had been touched by the cold hand of death enough for one vacation. Once inside, Sunny softly shut the door behind us. She motioned to the closed door to the right of the bed. I knocked on the door and called out in a whisper, "Mike?"

"I'm not finished," he responded snappily, put out to be interrupted during his "me time."

"You're finished now!" I hissed.

"I need another minute."

Sunny leaned into the door so he could hear her better. "Times up, Mike. Enzo is the killer and he just bludgeoned Silvio."

The toilet flushed, which I was torn about because while it was good manners to our hosts who had just served us that remarkable lunch, it would surely alert Enzo to our location. The door opened and Mike looked at us. "What the fuck?"

"My thoughts esattamente," Sunny answered him.

"We need to leave," Mike stated emphatically and began crossing to the door.

"I know," I agreed. "But Enzo is downstairs. We could be walking right into him."

Mike opened his mouth as if to argue, but no sound came out. Finally he just closed it again. I could see he was thinking. We were all thinking, and we were all coming to the same conclusion: We were fucked.

I was the first to admit it. "I don't know what to do."

"What if we just left?" Sunny threw out there. "Just went downstairs and tried to leave."

The three of us mulled over the various scenarios.

Mike asked the both of us, "Does Enzo have a gun?"

Sunny and I thought back to the scene a few minutes before. I spoke up first. "Not that I saw. But it's not like he would have showed it to us."

Sunny was weighing the possibilities. "We know he shot Elin with one. That has to be somewhere."

"Still," I said, "if he had one, why would he hit Silvio with a candle holder?"

The Husband just shook his head. "OK, we have to assume he has a gun then. He's already killed two people—"

Finally! The Husband admitted that Fabrizio's death wasn't an accident, although he still didn't know that Enzo had killed Silvio Sr., too.

"—There's no reason he won't try to kill us, too, if we run down there and into him."

"So we should stay put until we can figure out where he is."

"Yes. Although if we were just going to be stuck up here anyway, I really wish you hadn't made me finish up so quickly."

"Why? You want to die on the toilet like Fat Elvis?"

Sunny shushed us. "Everyone quiet. Let's see if we can hear him. The quicker we figure out where he is, the quicker we can figure out what to do."

We all held our breath for a minute and listened. There was a clock ticking. A faint whirring of a motor, maybe it was the air conditioner. After a minute we heard the sound of a car coming down the road. I went to the window to see if it was headed here, but no such luck; it didn't turn down the driveway. We continued to listen as the sound got further away. But we heard nothing from downstairs.

"We're sitting ducks up here," worried Sunny. "He could come up at any minute and attack us. And we still don't even know if he has a gun."

We needed to be able to defend ourselves. I looked at her. "We need to get to Paola's room. Where is it?"

Sunny motioned away from the room. "Down there." We had to go back the way we came towards the other end of the hall and past the staircase. Enzo could be upstairs already waiting for us in the hallway. Or he could hear us moving and run up the stairs to stop us. He also could have just decided that no good could come out of lingering here and he should just try to make his escape and leave. I was hoping for that.

Sunny peaked her head out into hallway and then looked back at us, nodding. We spent what felt like hours opening the door, careful not to pull it too quickly lest it squeak. Then the three of us stepped very silently into the hallway, grateful for the shabby runner which at least muffled our footsteps. Once again, we held our breath as we began our slow walk. Every time we passed a bedroom door, I was convinced it was going to pop open and Enzo was going to lunge at us like a murderous jack-in-the-box. Then I started thinking about what a creepy toy jack-in-the-boxes were anyway. What kind of thing is that to give a kid? Then I realized that I was totally getting distracted with unwanted thoughts and I really should mediate more to help free my mind, and then I thought that I was going to end up dead because I didn't meditate enough and that made me laugh, because of course that's how this was all going to end, and I might have cried, too, except that at that moment Sunny punched me in the arm. I looked up, taking in my surroundings, and saw that we were about to pass the staircase.

We approached, slower than even before, and very slightly started to bend our heads over the railing to see below, although to be honest, I didn't want to know. I was reluctant to even look, afraid of what I was going to see, and my heart was pounding, and my legs were twitching like someone with the DTs, which was maybe what I was after all the drinking I had been doing.

Mike looked first and I could feel him exhale in relief. I glanced down the stairs, but didn't see Enzo standing at the bottom, as I'd been certain I was going to. He wasn't there. But then where was he?

It occurred to me that Silvio was his meal ticket. If he died, Enzo would get nothing. All of his plans for nothing; it would all be

Antonio's. Maybe Enzo was downstairs trying to keep him alive right now, hoping the blow would cause him amnesia.

After that, we hurried as Sunny led us to Antonio and Paola's room. After a quick check to make sure we were alone, she once again softly closed the door behind us, this time locking it, too. I knew from my college days that type of lock could be easily opened with a credit card, or picked with a pin, or kicked down by an angry butler whose long con has just gone to shit. You'd think that Antonio, as a degenerate gambler who owed money to people who wanted to kill him, would have installed better security.

The master bedroom was in the back of the house with a balcony off their bedroom that overlooked the yard and vineyards. This meant it was also closer to the kitchen stairs, which worried me. Now, there were two ways for Enzo to come at us; but also maybe two ways for us to escape.

"What are we doing here?" The Husband asked me.

"This is where Paola keeps a gun. Remember? Just in case Antonio cheats on her."

"Oh Jesus Christ, you're not going to fire a gun," he droned. "You can't even kill a cricket."

"They're good luck," I insisted.

"Says who?" he wanted to know.

"I'm just going to start looking for a gun," Sunny interjected, cutting to the chase. She immediately went to Paola's closet, where clothes and shoe boxes started flying in her search.

I laid our situation out for him. "There's a killer downstairs. Sunny has no service and my phone with the Vice Questore's number in it is in the car and dead, not that I would probably have service here anyway. You have a better idea?"

"Turn my phone into a hotspot and email Patti?" he said triumphantly. "I have his email from when we sent him the crime scene photos the other night."

The Husband got to work immediately, which is good because if he had waited until after I was done arguing with him it would have wasted a lot of time.

"But that could take forever!" I contended. "Who knows how often he checks his email? And it's lunch time!"

Mike debated back, "He's in the middle of a murder investigation and his prime suspect just got released from jail. I'm going to guess he ate lunch at his desk today."

"I don't think Italians know what that means."

Regardless, he was now composing an email and in a moment I heard the telltale swoosh that meant it had gotten sent.

"Found it!" We both turned to where Sunny was holding a gun. "It was in the nightstand, next to the vibrator."

"Two ingredients for a happy marriage," I remarked, before asking, "Is it loaded?"

"I don't know, I'm a democrat." Still, Sunny fiddled with it, concluding that it had bullets and pocketing the box of extras that was also in Paola's nightstand of marital aids.

"Now what?" asked The Husband. "Do we wait up here for Enzo to come and kill us? Or do we try to leave so he can kill us on our way out?"

I thought for a moment. "What's our plan? What do we want?"

Mike responded quickly, "Get out of the house without him killing us and get in the car and go. Swing by the guest house for

Nino on our way out."

"What about the aunts?" I raised, concerned.

Whether out of genuine conviction or just self-preservation, Mike assured me, "They'll be fine. They're sound asleep. They have no idea what's happening. He's not going to come up here just to kill the aunts."

Sunny added, "And if he does, they've lived a long life."

"What if we fire the gun off the balcony? Maybe Enzo hears it, runs out back long enough to see what it was, and we run down the front stairs and make it outside to our car," I suggested.

"Or he hears gunshots out back and wants to avoid them all together and so he runs out front too. That's what I would do," The Husband determined.

"Well, maybe he doesn't have the fear of confrontation issues you have."

"Or the need for confrontation that you do."

"Kids," cautioned Sunny, "can we have this fight later when we're all hopefully still alive? I think it's as good an idea as any. We can watch over the balcony to see if he runs out back. If he doesn't, we know he's probably gone out front and we can go down the back stairs. And if he's waiting for us there, then fuck him, we have a gun."

"Fair enough," I agreed. The three of us walked out to the balcony. "Who should fire it?" I asked. "Has anyone fired a gun before?"

We just stared at each other. Finally, Mike spoke up. "I'll do it."

"You've fired a gun?" I asked my husband.

"No, but I've seen every *Breaking Bad*."

He grabbed the gun and pointed it out over the backyard.

"Careful of the kickback," I warned, which is something I've heard people say.

He winced and shut his eyes, which is probably the first thing they teach you not to do when deploying firearms. Crack. Crack. Crack. He shot the gun three times, trying to make enough noise so that Enzo both wouldn't fail to hear it and would also hopefully be curious. We stepped back into the room just far enough so that we could still look for him out of the window, but he couldn't see us. And then we waited. We heard footsteps down below, but we couldn't tell just where they were headed. For a third time we held our breath. Finally, we heard the terrazza door open and we watched as he ran down the steps and into the yard. Good news: He was outside the house. Bad news: He had a gun.

Now was the time. The three of us bolted out the door and into the hallway. When we reached the top of the steps, I thought I could hear the terrazza door open back up, but I wasn't sure. I reminded myself that he had that whole long hallway to come down first and I leaned into the railing so that I could start taking the stairs two at a time. I saw Sunny reach the front door and knew that Mike and I were right behind her. And that's when I did a faceplant into the hard foyer tile.

I could blame all the wine I had at lunch or the fact that I had chosen to wear heels, but it's not like when I made either one of those choices I had planned on fleeing a murderer with my day. Rather, I blame Antonio. The villa was falling into disrepair, no doubt because of his gambling debts. And the runner on the stairs was no exception. Threadbare in spots and coming loose in others, I landed on it wrong in my hurry, my heel catching on a loose thread as it skidded to the side, causing me to slide and lose my balance, which prevented me from saving myself from falling forward.

The wind had gotten knocked out of me and my knees didn't

feel so good either. And that's when Mike who had been right on my heels fell right on me, the gun flying out of his hand in the process. I noted later that he somehow managed to hold onto the iPad. From my vantage on the floor I could see into the living room where Enzo had pulled Silvio. He was still out cold. Or possibly dead. And now, so were we.

CHAPTER 37

I was happy that at least Sunny had made it out—until Enzo started barking at us in an Italian and I really needed a translator. It's pretty easy to understand someone when they're holding a gun on you, however. He motioned for us to get up and sit on the sofa in the living room. I wondered why he didn't just kill us right away, but I guess this wasn't what he had planned on doing with his day either, or he needed some time to rethink things.

We sat down on the couch and The Husband looked at me. "I remember saying I wanted to go to the beach today."

Enzo turned back to us with the gun. "State zitti!"

That one I knew. "He wants us to shut up."

He said it again, this time waving the gun, no doubt nervous about things being said around him in English after I tricked him previously in my clever—if poorly thought out—plan. I was really hoping Sunny had called the cops by now. And that it wasn't too late.

This is usually the part where the murderer confesses. Where they tell you they didn't want to hurt anybody, but no one would just mind their own business. Only with the language barrier, Enzo and we were denied that catharsis, and we'd just have to go to our deaths not knowing. I mean, I'll be damned if I was going to spend the last moments of my life trying to translate a language I wasn't going to have to know anymore.

Suddenly I was laughing.

"What's so funny," my husband asked me, ignoring our order to be quiet.

"The butler did it!" I snorted.

"I told you it was him!" The Husband announced triumphantly.

"You just didn't like the way he looked at you. It's not like you had any proof."

"Zitti!"

Enzo turned suddenly, pointing the gun at us, telling us once more to shut up.

We did so. But I began to think of how Antonio and Paola would be back soon, and this only made me laugh again. I turned to The Husband. "Do you think when Antonio and Paola pull into the driveway and see our car they'll be like, 'Are these fucking people ever going to leave?'"

He laughed. "No, Antonio will get excited. He'll think that we reconsidered and decided to buy the vineyard after all."

At the mention of Antonio's name, Enzo was becoming agitated again. Maybe he thought we were plotting something with him. Whatever it was, he started yelling at us loudly in Italian. I should have taken this more seriously, and not turned to Mike and said, "Well, at least the last thing you hear won't be me yelling at you," because this only pissed Enzo off more, and when I added, "But I see you'll be spending the last moments of our life checking your email,"—because he was!—Enzo fired two shots at the wall behind us just to make a point. Honestly, if he didn't do it, I would have done it myself, I was so irritated when I turned and saw The Husband with his nose in his fucking iPad. Nonetheless the gunshots quite frankly scared the shit out of us, but in retrospect I was glad that we had created the diversion because the noise covered the footsteps outside of the living room so that the next thing we heard was another gunshot, but this time it was coming from the doorway. And before we could see just who had fired it off, we saw where it had landed, somewhere in the middle of Enzo's chest. He went backwards into a ridiculously ornate credenza where he was either knocked unconscious or just killed instantly. We didn't waste time finding out.

Instead we ran for the door, where we saw Immacolata standing next to tiny Assunta, who had a gun in her hand. They were both in nightgowns.

Paola was right about one thing: The aunts did not like it when you interfered with their nap time.

CHAPTER 38

Now that the danger was over, the police came. Patti ran in, gun drawn.

"Where's the shooter?"

"Right here, having a glass of moscato," I answered, pointing to where Assunta and Immacolata were having an afternoon spritz. "If you want the murderer, he's over there and he probably needs a doctor. Or a coroner. Also, Silvio could use one, as well. Hopefully the former."

I probably should have checked on Silvio sooner, but after all the gunshots and the almost dying, my nerves were on edge and I'd readily accepted Imma's offer of a moscato instead.

Patti checked the pulse on both Silvio and Enzo. "They are still alive. Although this one," he nodded to Enzo, "has lost a lot of blood." He went to the front door and called for two medics to come in, giving them instructions in Italian. He then came over to us.

"Tell me what happened."

I took a sip of the moscato and began. "Well, last night we had this taxi driver, we were on the Argentario and we wanted to go to Stella d'Oro, have you been there? It was very good. Anyway, on the way there, Tommaso—"

"He doesn't need to hear all of this," The Husband groaned.

I gave him a look. "I solved a double homicide; he might be interested in how I did it."

"A double homicide?" The Vice Questore raised an eyebrow.

"Yes, clearly, Fabrizio. Enzo intended to take out Antonio's family, too. That's why he was so shocked to see Paola going to dinner that night. He figured someone was bound to kill Antonio; he could do it himself or just let any of the people after him take care of it for him. But if he died, Paola and the kids would inherit the money. He needed to make sure there were no heirs."

"Maybe you should start at the beginning," Patti suggested.

"You mean like when my friends were assholes to me, and I decided to come to Italy to mourn the loss of my life as I knew it?" I may have been in shock at this point.

"How about this morning?" Patti replied, pouring himself a glass of moscato.

I took him through seeing Silvio's arrest in the papers, and reading that Nino had been injured by a van, and our decision to come back.

"Wasn't really my decision," The Husband clarified. "I had wanted to go to the beach."

Patti smiled. "I will make a note of this."

I explained that Sunny had asked us to stop by the villa and that we had found our stolen stuff in Enzo's bedroom and then I told him all about my theory that Silvio wasn't really Silvio and how I know that seemed crazy, but I started wondering why kidnappers only ask for part of the money when you can have all of the money. I then remembered about the Epipen and without even realizing it blurted out, "Actually I solved a triple homicide."

Mike rolled his eyes, but Patti asked me to continue.

So I told him about the missing Epipen and how I thought it was used to induce Silvio Sr.'s heart attack, and how when I was explaining all of this, as well as the "Silvio not being the real

Silvio" theory to Sunny, Silvio was actually in the room with us and confirmed my theory! Both The Husband and the Vice Questore seemed genuinely surprised by this, and I wanted to ask them what it is about men that makes them always underestimate women, but by this point the wine was making me sleepy and I just wanted to get to the end.

"It was Nino's accident that helped me piece it all together. He had gone to Enzo's room to use the phone the day before. But Enzo always has his phone on him, which means that the phone Nino used wasn't his. It was Elin's. Then Enzo suggested he take the motorino because of all the news vans on the road, so he knew exactly what Nino would be driving and that he'd be vulnerable. Plus, one of the news vans was reported stolen—"

"Which was found out to be a mistake," Patti finished. "The crew had just looked for it in the wrong place."

"Yes, they didn't think to look for it in the place where Enzo had returned it to, after he tried to kill Nino. If you'll check their van, you'll probably also find evidence of a hit and run." I was getting at good this. But even as I was telling the story, a few details still didn't make sense. I knew they had the right guy, the phone and all the shooting confirmed that. But I still had questions. Nevertheless, I persisted in my account.

"I figured after such a close call, Enzo wouldn't take the chance of someone finding Elin's phone again, so he'd want to keep it on him. He could have tossed it, but evidence like that can come in handy later on if you need to frame someone else for the murder. After that, the biggest challenge was hoping one of us had enough of a signal to actually make the call to Elin's cell. Sunny did, fortunately, and so we called. And suddenly it rang in Enzo's pants pocket."

"That was your plan?! That was totally reckless," The Husband reproached me.

I narrowed my eyes at him. "Well, I would have consulted you, but you were in the toilet."

"What were you guys going to do after that?"

"We worked it out, obviously."

"I think I have everything I need." Patti tried to diffuse the situation and bring the conversation to a close. "I probably should not say this, Signora, but you did very well."

I turned to The Husband and smirked but then looked behind me to the wall where Enzo had fired the two bullets and I suddenly grew somber. "That was close. I really thought we were dead. If it wasn't for Assunta…"

Patti looked at me confused. "Didn't you get the email I sent your husband?"

"What email?" I looked to Mike, who was happily eating cookies off the plate Imma had offered him, and shot him a withering look.

Patti looked from Mike to me, no doubt wishing he had never asked the question. "I told him we were on our way. Then I sent him another email that we were outside and asked how many captors and who was armed."

I punched my husband in the arm. "Why didn't you tell me?!"

Through a mouthful of cookie, he said, "You were too busy yelling at me for being on the iPad."

"That would have been the time to tell me!"

"I couldn't exactly say that in front of Enzo, could I?"

"He doesn't speak English!"

The Husband looked sheepish at first but then shrugged. "I forgot."

Somewhere in there, Patti left.

CHAPTER 39

Silvio was the first one to be carried out to the ambulance. We followed as the medic wheeled him outside to where a collection of vehicles had amassed during our brief hostage situation. There were two ambulances, a number of police cars, and even the first of the news crews and paparazzi to arrive. Sunny had been waiting there this whole time, and when we walked out into the driveway, she ran up to us, makeup streaked down her face from tears.

"Oh, my God, thank God you're OK! I never would have forgiven myself for leaving!"

She threw her arms around me first, then Mike, then both of us together.

"No, no," we tried to assure her. "It's good that you did."

"That way you could call the cops and tell them what was going on."

"And make sure Nino was OK."

"He's fine," she said indifferently. "He's already talking about playing soccer tomorrow." She waved her hand in a vague direction and sure enough we saw Nino hobbling over to the ambulance and talking to the Mayor. He walked over to us a moment later and gave us the update.

"He's had a bad blow, and he's still unconscious. He needs stitches and to make sure there's no internal bleeding. But barring any complications, he should be OK."

I watched as they loaded Silvio into the back of the ambulance. And I thought sadly of how he was going to wake up in the hospital and there would be those first few blissful moments when he wouldn't know why he was there; he wouldn't remember what had happened to him. And he would think his life was still as it had been. I'd had many of those days in the last few months. He was going to think he was waking up from the nightmare only to realize he was waking into it.

They were about to drive away when a Mercedes came speeding down the long driveway and screeched to a halt in front of the house. Antonio jumped out of the car with the motor still running and ran right up to the ambulance, banging on the window, shouting, "Mio fratello! Mio fratello!"

My brother! My brother!

Only it wasn't his brother. Not really. And for the first time since I had learned the truth, I wondered what had happened to the real Silvio.

Paola turned off the car and emerged from it a moment later. Her boys were already running inside the house shouting gleefully about the "Polizia!" She shouted after them in either Albanian or Italian or both before coming to us.

"Thank you for calling us, Sunny! We were so worried! We were on the yacht having a drink when our friends said they had heard from someone at the dock that there was a shooting at our house. Can you imagine what we thought! I thought for sure poor Silvio was dead this time, and Antonio was so worried about who would do such a thing."

I bet he was.

The medic had opened the back of the ambulance so Antonio could see his brother for a moment, but I could see, by the way the Mayor was pleading with the younger brother, that they needed to go. Antonio nodded and touched Silvio one last time before stepping back and allowing them to close the doors. A moment later they were pulling out of the driveway, carrying Silvio away. Antonio's grief seemed real and I was reminded again how complicated people can be to understand.

The polizie had thinned out, too: Most of the cars were gone. Now that they had left, I saw one lone motorcycle parked in the driveway. Next to it was the lone photographer we had met earlier that day at the villa. I waved. It took him a second to remember me, but then he waved back.

The front door to the house opened again, and this time it was the stretcher carrying Enzo that came out. He had an oxygen mask over his face and a medic was monitoring his pulse. So, he was still alive. Antonio must have had this same thought because all of a sudden, he rushed past all of us and went straight for Enzo, yelling curses in Italian the whole time.

Nino ran towards Antonio, presumably to pull him back, but physically he wasn't at one hundred percent and couldn't keep up. In the meantime, one of the few polizia left tried to act as a barrier between the murderer and the angry brother. Eventually Patti came out of the house to find the source of the commotion and was able to help the polizia out. He had both his hands out and was saying something kind, yet cautionary, to Antonio, who didn't care and just kept shouting. By this time Antonio had stopped in front of Enzo anyway, so Nino had a chance to catch up. He put one arm on Antonio's shoulder and said something and whether it was because of this or if the rage had tired him out, Antonio appeared to stop talking. And that's when I noticed that Enzo had taken his mask off. It was his turn to speak. It didn't last very long before the medic managed to get the mask back on him and they continued transporting him to the vehicle. Once Patti and Nino were sure that Antonio wasn't going to run after them, they let him go and walked towards where we were standing with Paola and Sunny. We watched as they shut the ambulance doors and drove away. Antonio walked behind the ambulance for awhile down the driveway, no doubt looking for some outlet for the anger he still felt.

Patti stood with the five of us for a moment before sighing, "Well, the good news is that he pretty much just confessed."

"Nino, what happened?!" his wife wanted to know.

Nino did his signature eye roll to the Heavens. "Oh, dio mio, it was something! Antonio kept shouting, 'How could you?! How could you?! My father treated you like one of his own.' And finally, Enzo took off his mask." Nino was acting this out now, which I was enjoying. "And he said, 'One of you? Who would want to be one of you? You're lazy and ungrateful. No, we were never treated like one of you. We had to be better. We had to take care of all of your messes. Your fortune was made from the hard work of my family, not from the hard work of yours. You'd be nothing without us. Everything you have is mine!'"

No one said anything at first. Finally it was Mike who broke the silence by remarking, "Well, that's a little over the top."

We all laughed in spite of the situation, and whether because of the near-death experience or the shock, it felt really good. Even Antonio had walked off enough of his anger that he had joined our group again and asked what was so funny. Patti said his goodbyes just then, adding "I will call you if I need anything, but please do not call me." I couldn't tell what percentage of that was a joke, and at the moment I did not care. As he drove off, I turned to The Husband.

"Shall we get back to the Argentario? We have enough time for a nap before dinner, and by nap, I mean—"

Even though I think he knew what I meant, I never got a chance to finish the sentence because right then another bullet whizzed smack into the middle of the six of us.

CHAPTER 40

If you've ever seen the frenzy cats go into when the doorbell rings then you might have some idea of what the six of us were like when the shots rang out: Some of us hit the ground to hide; others looked around frenetically for the source of the noise; all of us screamed loudly. We were too far from the house and the closest thing to hide behind was the Mercedes which didn't feel very safe given that we didn't know where the shooter was and it was basically filled with several gallons of explosive, but I ran to it anyway.

"Mike?" I called out.

"I'm fine. Sunny and Nino?"

"OK," said Sunny's voice. "Sì," agreed Nino.

"I'm fine, too, Mike," I said pointedly. Before we could ask about the others, Paola's screams told us what we needed to know. She was kneeling over Antonio, a red stain spreading on the upper right half of his torso.

There goes my chance of ever sleeping with Antonio, I may have thought. But if I did, I'm sure it was the shock.

Nino took his t-shirt off and was holding it on Antonio's wound while Sunny was already on the phone calling for an ambulance. "If they have any available after this afternoon, they should give us a bulk discount."

Suddenly Paola cried out, "The boys! They're in the house!" and she started to run for the door. Nino pleaded with her to stop.

"Paola, you don't know who's in there!"

"Exactly!" she said, not stopping. I wanted to tell her they were in good hands with the aunts, but I knew that wouldn't stop her. It wouldn't have stopped me.

The shots seemed to stop. But there was no sign of the shooter and for a moment all was eerily quiet. Then we heard a low buzzing sound that grew louder very quickly as a motorcycle pulled around from the back of the house and started hauling ass down the driveway towards the main road.

It was the lone paparazzo from the villa that I waved at just a little while ago. I had waved at the hit man. Not my finest moment.

He sped further away from the villa, towards the exit, and it looked like he was about to make it onto the service road when a silver BMW pulled into the driveway, driving the wrong way around the circular path and skidding to a stop just in front of the hit man/photographer. He smacked right into the car, falling off the bike. As soon as he did that, the doors opened and a man and woman wearing well-tailored slacks and jackets got out. Both were armed and they quickly disarmed and cuffed the injured paparazzo.

"Better make that two ambulances," I called to Sunny.

"They are never coming here again. I swear I gave them the address and they laughed and hung up on me," she said.

The man placed the hit man in the car while the woman made a call and a moment later started walking down the driveway towards us. I really hoped she wasn't going to shoot us because I had had enough of this shit today. She finished up the call, placing the phone back in her pocket while pulling her black hair back into a ponytail. I thought to myself that if she was going to kill us, she wouldn't need to groom herself first. Only as she got closer, I became at first relieved, then alarmed again, because now I really had no fucking clue what was going on.

"Sorry I was so rude as to leave without saying 'goodbye'" she said in a much more polished British accent.

It was Aparna.

CHAPTER 41

Whatever brand of spy Aparna was, she had a strong medical training and helped to stabilize Antonio while we waited for the ambulance. Her colleague cleared the house to ensure the gunman was acting alone, although based on what they knew about him, they said, he always did. Still, the man went inside to check on everyone's safety and to tell Paola the ambulance was on its way.

Sunny wasted no time in finding a bottle of wine inside, and she, Nino, Mike, and I all sat on the front steps, waiting for the ambulance, as well as for an explanation. Fortunately, once the former showed up and Aparna felt Antonio was in competent hands, she was quickly forthcoming with the latter. As the ambulance with Antonio inside of it drove away, she came over to us on the steps.

"I'm not Antonio and Silvio's sister."

"I think we've figured that out by now, thanks," said The Husband.

"I'm with a special Interpol task force investigating an international gambling conspiracy that was trying to fix football games here in Italy."

"International?! Who in the rest of the world gives a shit about Italian football?" Sunny asked, rather bluntly.

"You'd be surprised. Some of the syndicates involved are from as far away as Singapore," she explained.

"Yes, Sunny, I told you it is only you Americans who don't care about football," Nino said, more than a little vindicated.

I looked back to Aparna. "And Antonio was reaching out to his old teammate Pietro Romano to help him fix games for his team?"

"Not exactly, but close. You've really done your legwork." Aparna seemed impressed, unlike that chauvinist Patti who always acted like I was a bother. "Pietro came across our radar for some other infractions."

"Drugs?"

Aparna nodded at me again. "Yes. We knew Antonio was up to no good, so we enlisted Pietro's help in our investigation. We thought the family connection would be a good thing, but it seems Pietro never got over Elin and he wanted to warn her about what was happening."

Sunny's eyes lit up. "That's why he was looking for her at the beach that day!"

"Yes, among other places. He didn't want to see her taken down with the rest of the family and it was clear he couldn't maintain his neutrality so a week or so before that we decided I would go undercover as the lost Corini sister in order to keep a better eye on things. There were plenty of stories about Silvio Sr's," here she paused, "...dalliances over the years, so it was an easy enough lie. We even had a lab standing by ready to fake the DNA results if need be, but Silvio never asked for a test." She shrugged here as if to acknowledge that it was strange, but that she herself couldn't be bogged down in figuring out how rich people's minds worked.

Sunny and I exchanged a look but said nothing about Silvio's reasons. Instead I asked, "Why was your story so all over the place? You were a nanny... you lived in Italy... you were kind of low rent sometimes..."

Aparna seemed a little put out by my assessment. "Yeah, well, it was a last-minute undercover operation. I was sort of winging it. And I'm a cop, not an actress."

"Right?" Sunny agreed. "I think it's always so weird when cops on detective shows seem to have improv training." Seeing that Aparna was softening back up she added, "Why did you leave?"

"It was too risky. I was afraid my cover was going to get blown. We didn't know who was committing the murders—if it was related to our investigation or not. We got lucky though. Seems the day I left, Antonio reached out to Pietro."

Because the day she left was the day I told Antonio that Pietro was in town.

"Now that Elin was dead, he didn't feel as conflicted and he agreed to help us. But it was clear from our sources that someone was after Antonio anyway. Hopefully now he'll give us the information that we need." She looked to the ambulance.

"If he survives," Mike said, which is just like him to be so negative when the rest of us are trying to be positive.

"He'll survive," Aparna said confidently. "The bullet avoided his heart and lungs."

Paola came downstairs at that point looking pale. Her shirt was still covered in her husband's blood.

"Sunny," she began, but seeing the wine, she quickly helped herself to a glass before continuing, "I do not want to leave the boys and I don't want them to see their father like this. Would you and Nino go to the hospital and check in on Antonio?"

Sunny immediately nodded, even though I knew that was the last place she wanted to be, especially after the day she'd had. She turned to Mike and me. "I hate to ask you this, but our car is still at the villa." She glanced to the Mercedes which had taken on some serious gunfire. "And I don't know if that's drivable. Would you drop us off at the hospital on your way back to your hotel?"

We immediately nodded. Because that's what friends do.

CHAPTER 42

Once again that day we were back at the hospital. Rather than just drop them off, Sunny had asked us to come in with them just for a minute, in case anyone had to rush back to the villa and get Paola. Also, I think part of us wanted to see everything through to the end. It felt weird to just be walking off into the Tuscan sunset, not knowing how everyone was.

We were told at the reception area that Antonio was stable, and we casually walked down the hallway towards his room with our thoughts turning to dinner that evening, as well as what we wanted to do our last night in Rome. We only had two more days on the Argentario before we would drive back to the Eternal City. And after that, it was home. I have to say the thought made me sadder than I had any right to feel after escaping death twice that day. It was a welcome break to be immersed in the problems of others all week. It was quite another thing to have to go home and actually solve mine. And a murder does have a solution; whether or not it's solved someone actually committed the crime, there is an answer. The rest of life's problems weren't so easy. I was beginning to feel like Dorothy when she says to the Wizard, "I don't think there's anything in that black bag for me." Only she had the solution with her all along. I wasn't so confident that I did.

We'd been told that Antonio was stable, but the scene when we got to his room was another story altogether. At least five medical personnel were frantically calling out to each other in Italian and running in and out of his room as we heard a cacophony of medical equipment beeping, whirring, and buzzing. Sunny tried to get answers but was shoved out of the way, and within a few minutes, Antonio was being wheeled down the hall, the whole pit crew following him.

It was time to get Paola.

Mike and Nino offered. Nino said he would stay with the boys if she wanted and Mike could take her back. I sat with Sunny in the meantime and we waited. She called ahead so Paola would be ready to go when they got there.

Sunny thought to check on Silvio while we waited, but when we found his room, we were told he was resting comfortably. We hoped that was actually the case. We didn't need any more surprises.

Mike returned with Paola who looked even more drawn and haggard, although she had managed to change her shirt. "I swear," she said, "if he lives, I will kill him myself for putting himself and all of us in so much danger!"

"You're going to need a new gun," I informed her. "We appropriated the other one."

"We left the vibrator, though," Sunny added putting her arm around her. Paola laughed weakly in spite of herself.
Finally, the doctor came out and walked over to all of us. She appeared to be in her fifties, which I only guessed because she had the most gorgeous silver hair underneath her surgical cap; her skin itself was flawless. As soon as she told us Antonio was OK, I was going to have to ask her what she did to look so great. I hoped she wasn't going to tell me she ran.

"I apologize. We thought we had stopped the bleeding. But he was shot through the liver, twice, and the damage was too severe. We need to helicopter him to Rome as soon as possible, for a liver transplant."

Paola started sobbing. The doctor tried to soothe her.

"Not to worry, Signora, he is very fortunate. His brother looks to be a match and can donate part of his."

Paola was relieved; she didn't know that Silvio wasn't Antonio's brother. But Sunny and I just exchanged looks.

Sunny looked at the doctor. "Are you sure?"

The doctor looked at her files and said to Sunny dismissively, "All of the preliminary tests show him to be an excellent candidate."

"Are you sure it's his <u>brother</u>?" I emphasized.

She looked confused and a little bit impatient as well. Here she had saved this man's life, and she was getting a serious of ridiculous questions from two American women who were no relation to the patient.

"At least twenty-seven DNA markers say he is," she said, before walking away down the hall.

CHAPTER 43

I still had questions: What were the kidnappers hoping to achieve when they sent back the wrong kid? Was that intentional? Did Enzo act alone? Why only start to kill off the Corinis three years ago? And if Silvio wasn't Silvio, then who was he? I didn't know what any of this meant, but for once in my life I decided I didn't care. Life was full of answers that you never get. We got the one we needed: Enzo was Elin's killer. And on a more personal note I had got an even more important one: Life was short. That's it. That's the only answer that matters to any of life's questions. Your days here are limited. I had three nights left on the Argentario and after that one in Rome, and I was going to make the most of all it. So, I bid our friends "Buona sera," and grabbed The Husband's hand so that we could enjoy the rest of our vacation.

Once we had reached the car, I looked at him and said, "Let's suck the marrow out of what's left of this trip!"

He kissed me. "No sleep till LA?" he asked.

"No sleep till LA!" I agreed. "Or at least the flight from Rome to LA."

We spent the next morning touring some old fort that was slightly boring, but that he took a million pictures of nonetheless, and I smiled the whole time. We then had another lunch of fresh seafood on the beach in Porto Ercole before heading back to the hotel and making the trek to our rocky umbrella in the cove below. We watched the sunset from our hotel on the edge of the Earth, enjoying the feeling that nothing could touch us.

We spent the next day trying to soak up all we could of the Italian waters, and so spent the majority of our day on our rocky perch, floating in the sea until we were so relaxed, I was sure we would drown. We finally left for a late lunch at the hotel bar, and then a wine tasting at a local winery the concierge had arranged. Tommaso drove, happy to get all of the money.

No one got murdered.

We left the hotel the next morning at a reasonable hour, wanting to get back in enough time to have a full day in Rome. I emailed Sunny with our ETA and she quickly emailed back saying that was fine and could we get there sooner as Jen was driving her crazy. It was the last few lines that I found surprising.

> Silvio is in the hospital in Rome, recovering from the transplant surgery. He'd like to see you before you go.

I read this aloud to The Husband. I could sense his reluctance; we had a full day of more eating and drinking and sucking of marrow planned. Mentally, I was preparing myself to not go. "What was the big deal?" I asked myself. "What would I lose by not going?" But I also knew that after everything else, it would nice to be able to get a sense of closure on one thing. Mike must have sensed this, too, because he just turned to me and said, "Thirty minutes. Then we go."

Silvio was in a private room that more closely resembled a hotel suite than a hospital. He was awake and fairly alert for someone who had just had part of his liver removed. I was encouraged by this, as I was going to need a liver transplant of my own after this trip. He told me it was the morphine, which was also encouraging.

"I do not want to take up any more of your vacation. I just wanted to thank you for saving me from prison, saving my life, and for finding out who killed my wife."

We nodded, solemnly. Smiling somehow seemed wrong.

Silvio went on. "I've taken the liberty of paying for your stay on the Argentario."

He was making it more difficult not to smile.

"That's really not necessary," Mike tried to insist.

"No, no, it's the least I can do. I feel it was due to me that you had to go elsewhere."

You, Enzo, Antonio, the paparazzi, an international gambling ring, and a Vice Questore who didn't like outside help, I thought to myself.

"Also, I would like you to come back next summer as my guests at the villa. You always have a place to stay with us."

I could no longer suppress a smile, and frankly now it just would have been rude not to. I added a slew of "Grazie mille"s to cover up all of The Husband's protests that it wasn't really necessary.

I could see Mike looking at his watch, no doubt wanting to get to lunch, but I had one last question.

"What happened?"

Admittedly it was a vague question, but I didn't know how else to ask.

"Enzo's father died when he was a teen. There was an accident at the vineyard, and he had a heart attack as a result. I think the boy always blamed us. He was the oldest and without his father, he and his mother were left with many young children to care for. In fact, he had a younger brother, about my age who they always said died of meningitis," he paused, trying to sound casual. "Or maybe he didn't…"

But he still had not come to terms with the implication, because he quickly rushed on. "Enzo became consumed with communism and revolution, as was the fashion. He went to meetings, met others who wanted revolution. It was they who must have helped him formulate the plan, however ill-advised it was. Maybe they didn't understand how finances worked or they thought I'd have clearer memories of my life before and would feel some loyalty and they'd be able to control me. He couldn't have done this on his own, initially, though I think probably anyone who was involved in the kidnapping has since died or been sent to prison or perhaps just become an elected official. The great thing about Italy is that you never know!" He laughed cynically.

"And the plan sort of worked for a long while," I admitted. "They made a lot of money."

"Yes," Silvio began before administering himself some more morphine, no doubt to get through the next part and say the truth out loud. "But an heir would have interfered with Enzo's plan."

Any heir other than Silvio, that is. Unless—

"That case you said you were working on right before the boating accident? The one up north?" I quickly asked.

I could see Silvio trying to remember and then slowly thinking through the details. "Ahhh… right. The corporation we were suing was family run, they controlled the stock. But an illegitimate daughter made a claim on it and was successful and suddenly the family who were still fighting us no longer had a majority."

"Because of the change in the law about illegitimate children."

"Sì," Silvio nodded distractedly, something else on his mind. "Enzo heard the details. He never cared much about my work before. But he seemed impressed that the law had changed. He even joked that for many families, the heirs would soon be the ones waiting on the help."

"And that's why the attempts on your brother's and father's life started," I concluded. But Silvio and Mike both look confused, so I went on. "If Enzo got rid of all the other heirs, the only one left is you. Then if he makes a claim to be an illegitimate son of your father and does a DNA test with you, thinking you really are his brother that he swapped out, you would match, and he has a claim against the estate. And he would finally get all the money."

"Except Silvio actually is a Corini," Mike interjected, looking to Silvio for back up. "Right? You and Antonio matched."

"It would appear so. But I don't know if Enzo knew that. Perhaps the wrong boy came out of that fire. Or perhaps Antonio and Enzo and I would all share some DNA anyway... If you've heard any stories of my father, you'd know that was a possibility."

"Whatever you do, don't do 23 and Me," advised my husband, always thinking of the bottom line. "Not with these inheritance laws."

But I couldn't quite let it go. "But what about the writing with the left hand?"

I could feel Mike rolling his eyes, wanting me to drop it so we could get out of there, but I just needed to know everything.

"An X-ray revealed that my wrist had been broken, probably during the kidnapping. I must have compensated by learning with my left."

The morphine was starting to take its effect on Silvio and his eyes were closing. The last thing he said before drifting off was, "They always told me they killed the real boy."

And in a sense, they had.

EPILOGUE

"Now that the hotel has been paid for, it's like we can take another trip!"

"We haven't even left this trip yet!"

"Who says we have to?"

"The bank that holds our mortgage."

I had to admit he had me there.

We were with Sunny and Nino, headed for our final dinner in Rome. Given the drama of the last week no one felt like cooking, so we were walking to the Monti district, stopping near the Coliseum to have one last drink from a rooftop bar overlooking it. I was channeling my inner Fellini and wearing dark sunglasses and a black cotton sleeveless dress with a tight bodice and full skirt for the occasion. While pumps would have been outstanding with the slightly-above-the-knee hem, I had paired it instead with ballet flats, having learned my lesson at Antonio's. The heels were killing me, almost quite literally.

"It's not like you have to go back. You still don't have a job, right?" inquired a flat, emotionless voice. Sage and Jen were still with us. It just seemed easier after the twenty-minute dissertation we got from Jen on how her child knew how to behave in a restaurant.

"Well, mine don't," Sunny had told her. "So I'm leaving them at home."

Life. It's not perfect. Even in Italy.

"No, Sage, I don't have a job. That happens to women in the work force sometimes. They get marginalized. Still. Ask your mom about it sometime. She can read you the studies."

This would have gone over most children's heads, but I knew for Sage, this was the stuff of nightmares.

No matter how in the moment you are and how much marrow you try to suck, there comes a point in any trip where part of you is already gone. It's not your fault: You've had to pack and check in for your flight and make sure it's on time and arrange the car that will pick you up to take you to the airport and also the one that will get you when you land in your final destination. It's the preparations that keep us tied to our lives. I was going back if for no other reason than I had a ticket that said I was. In this case I had no plan for what I was going to do when I got there, but I had a schedule that was telling me it was time to go home. I had to be grateful that, unlike Silvio for much of his life, at least I knew where that was.

According to the bank that held our mortgage, that home was in Los Angeles. But according to the man who held my heart, that home was wherever he was. Whenever we travel, The Husband unpacks all of his stuff, even if we're only staying for one night. I've always found that endearing, but I've never quite understood why. I find it funny that a man who is always so practical would compulsively do something so impractical, as if wherever he goes he has to make himself at home. But it was on this trip I realized that wherever he is, is home for me. And I was lucky that I had someone like Sunny who always provided us with a home in Italy whenever we needed to find our way back.

I raised my Prosecco to toast Sunny and Nino with some version of that, but I'm not sure I really got the point across as sucking the marrow all day meant pretty much drinking since noon, so I may have been a little tipsy and also inadvertently alternating between Italian and English. But it's not like this crowd needs a coherent invitation to tip a glass back and we clinked flutes with a chorus of "Saluti!" and "Cent'Anni!"

"So," Sunny then asked, "what do you guys want to do next time you're here?"

FEGATINI THAT
WON'T KILL JEN

During a certain trip to Tuscany a few years ago it suddenly seemed like fegatini, also known as chicken liver pâté, was everywhere. I was soon glad it was. Fegatini became my new favorite thing and I ate it every chance I got. On my last night in the country, I was out a restaurant with the real-life inspiration for "Sunny," telling her al about my newfound obsession with it. She then explained to me that she'd heard some supposed Chinese medicine trope where you're supposed to eat the parts of the animal your body needs help with. If you have a heart condition, eat heart. Brain problem, eat brains, etc. And there I was after a month in Italy, binge eating liver. Make of that what you will.

INGREDIENTS
5oz of chicken livers
1 onion, chopped
3-4 ounces prosciutto (optional)
White wine or chicken broth
2 sage leaves
salt & pepper to taste

Sauté onion and prosciutto in olive oil on low heat for about 20 minutes, until onion is soft and translucent. The recipe calls for 4oz of prosciutto, but I probably use less. Sometimes I throw in 1 or 2 slices of salami instead. I've also used pancetta. Basically, whatever pork is on hand that I can use to flavor the pâté.
After 20 minutes add the chicken livers and sage leaves. Cover and simmer until the chicken livers are cooked through. Add broth or wine as needed to keep the mixture from drying out.

Let cool. Then puree in a Cuisinart and add salt and pepper to taste. If after pureeing the mixture isn't thick enough, don't worry; it will thicken in refrigerator.

Fegatini can be served hot or cold on crackers or toasted bread and with a little balsamic vinegar on the side.

ACKNOWLEDGEMENTS

None of this would have been possible without the friendship of Kissy Dugan. Her generosity of spirit- and everything else- allowed us to experience an Italy that it always felt like we were coming home to and not just visiting. A debt of gratitude is also owed to Lene and Michele Gianni, who welcomed two American strangers into their home multiple times and showed us the magic of Capalbio, and Marco Lori who has treated us like old friends since the first time we met.

I will forever be humbled by the kindness and grace of Yvette Nicole Brown, Wendi McLendon-Covey, and Retta Sirleaf, three talents who believe in pulling others along with them and who always go out of their way to help all boats rise with theirs.

I am so thankful for the friendship and support of Dibs Baer, who introduced me to our fellow writer, Alison Gaylin. And I cannot thank Alison enough for responding to my combination of panic and fan-girling with kindness and a happiness to help.

When I first started this process, Maureen Driscoll and Christy Murphy patiently answered all of my questions and made me feel like I could do this. Likewise, Sarah McKinley-Oakes helped me to be less overwhelmed, diligently proof-reading, offering suggestions, enthusiasm and virtual hand-holding.

Much gratitude to my agent, Holly Root, who never gave up on this book, and to everyone who has read a draft: Tom, Robin, Kissy, Lene and especially Joanna, who read the last one when I didn't think I could read it one more time.

I am so grateful to everyone at WB TV: Susan, Clancy, Jennifer &

Ashley, who were early adapters to *Under the Tuscan Gun* and believed in Kat & Sunny long before anyone else.

I will never be able to understand my good fortune at not only having become friends with Tony Puryear, but having him offer to design the cover art for this book. I don't know how to begin to thank him for allowing me the pleasure of our collaborative phone calls and getting to marvel at the images he produced from them. And a very special thanks to Chris McGuire, who shot the original cover photo. He not only took such an incredible picture, but did so after getting up at six am to drive me to the train station. Thank you for the ride, the photo and for being my favorite traveling companion and loving Italy almost as much as I do.

Speaking of photos, thanks go out to Justine Ungaro who took the world's best author photo, Gary Kordan who helped set the stage, and David Marvel who made me look as good as the cake!

Lastly, it was several years ago that Robin Jones commented on a picture of myself and my husband in Italy and said, "You two are one high society murder away from being Nick & Nora Charles." I realized that we were only one novel away and that I should write it. Thank you, Robin. Here it is.

ABOUT THE AUTHOR

Tess Rafferty

Tess Rafferty has written on many televi-
sion programs including Martha and
Snoop's Potluck Party Challenge, @Mid-
night, The Comedy Central Roast of Ros-
eanne and The Soup. She has also written
and developed both half-hour and hour
long shows for numerous companies including Warner Brothers. The creator of
2017's Take Back the Workplace March Against Sexual Harass-
ment, Tess is a featured blogger for Dame and Ms. Magazine, and
also writes the cooking/political blog, Recipes for Resistance.
Her essay, "The Revolution Will Be Catered" was featured in
Rage Baking: A Collection of Recipes and Conversations for Our
Time. As an author, Tess made her debut with her memoir Recipes for Disaster. Under the Tuscan Gun is her first novel. You
can follow her on twitter at @TessRafferty or read more about
her Italian travels at TessRafferty.com.

BOOKS BY THIS AUTHOR

Recipes For Disaster

Made in the USA
Las Vegas, NV
17 December 2021

38168401R00163